CAN AN OLD VETERAN L...
LOVE AND PAIN HE LE... ...HIND?

SHADOWS
OF
SAIGON

MARK R. ANDERSON

 OLD STONE PRESS

SHADOWS OF SAIGON
By Mark R. Anderson

© 2021, Mark R. Anderson
All rights reserved.

Disclaimer

*This book is a work of fiction. All dialogue, events, and characters with the
exception of some military historical figures and actual operations during
the Vietnam war, are products of the author's imagination, and any
resemblance to real persons living or dead, events, or activities is
coincidental.*

*This does not constitute an official release of U.S. Government information. All
statements of fact, opinion, or analysis expressed are those of the author and do
not reflect the official positions or views of the U.S. Government. Nothing in the
contents should be construed as asserting or implying U.S. Government
authentication of information or endorsement of the author's views. This
material has been reviewed solely for classification.*

For information about special discounts for bulk purchases or autographed
copies of this book, please contact John H. Clark, publisher, Old Stone Press
at john@oldstonepress.com.

Library of Congress Control Number: 2020922783

ISBN: 978-1-938462-52-8 (print)
ISBN: 978-1-938462-53-5 (eBook)

Published by Old Stone Press
an imprint of J. H. Clark & Associates, Inc.
Louisville, Kentucky 40207 USA
www.oldstonepress.com

This is a fictional story about an American patriot, Grady Cordeaux. Grady reveals his life's journey to us, retrospectively, through his relationship with a decades-long friend, R.C. Carter.

His story, set in the turbulent Vietnam War era and beyond, is one that many Americans can relate to; that is, a rural upbringing, a loving family, high school sweetheart, and finding his post-high school dreams suddenly diverted and out of his control.
While describing Grady's army duties, relationships, and heroism in combat, the author gives us an unusual but insightful accounting of the Vietnam War from the perspective of a junior non-commissioned officer. Those young men and women came home with mixed emotions; just happy to be alive, dejected, rejected, physically maimed, mentally broken, appreciated, and proud. Those experiences shaped a generation of Americans for better or worse.

Shadows of Saigon, by this gifted new novelist Mark Anderson, artfully builds on itself page-by-page. You will find yourself playing mind games predicting where Grady's life is headed only to be surprised, elated, and sometimes disappointed all in the same spellbinding chapter. You will find it difficult to put this book down. ~

Marvin Covault, Lt. Gen. US Army, retired. Vietnam 1967/68 and 1971

Part 1: Cardiac Arrest

The Awakening

The patient was slowly gaining consciousness. He squeezed his eyes to break the crust that formed between his lids after several days cementing them closed, while trying desperately to make sense of the sounds echoing around him. Eventually, he recognized voices, and then sentences.

A nurse quietly said to the doctor, "The patient is coming out of sedation."

Grady, still struggling, wondered who was talking? What were they saying? He tried speaking, but nothing came out of his mouth. He felt a sensation from long past of heat rising in his chest, as if hot blood was being squeezed upward causing heart palpitations and profuse sweating. He remembered the panic attacks from years before and struggled harder to re-enter the world of the conscious.

The beeping of the heart monitor grew faster and louder. Nothing made sense right now! He kept wondering over and over why can't I wake up? Who are these people? Throbbing in his head and the weight on his chest was unbearable. His mind was racing, and he wanted answers but was unable to speak. He was trapped inside his body! Was this his hell? The panic and frustration were insufferable. The more he struggled, the heavier the pressure in his chest. Shock-like exhaustion overtook him, and he collapsed back into unconsciousness.

"Mr. Cordeaux? Mr. Cordeaux? If you can hear me, squeeze my hand," asked a voice. Grady applied all the pressure he could to the gentle grip on his hand.

The ICU nurse barked out, "Page Dr. Sayeed and let him know Mr. Cordeaux is becoming responsive, STAT!"

Grady was cognizant enough to detect urgency in her voice. "I must have dozed off," he murmured.

In reality, he had succumbed to the anxiety-induced strain on his heart during his initial awakening and fell back into a deep state of unconsciousness for two more days.

Dr. Sayeed was making his rounds at the right time. "Good morning, Mr. Cordeaux. Do you know where you are?"

Grady barely cracked opened his eyes to see a man in a white jacket standing at his bedside. He winced, allowing his eyes to adjust to the sunlight. The eyelid crust from two days of sleep made it difficult to fully open them anyway.

Grady responded, "Yep. Judging by your jacket and these tubes in my arms and nose, I'm guessing I'm in the hospital. But how the hell did I get here?" After a week of being unconscious his throat was expectedly dry and his voice raspy. All Grady remembered was being at RC's farm until waking up today feeling like someone was sitting on his chest.

Dr. Sayeed assured him, "You must be quite confused. However, you need to relax and let us help you. I'm Dr. Sayeed. You have been unconscious in Alexandria Hospital for six days. You suffered a heart attack and were rushed here by EMTs. You are here, largely in part because of the actions of Mr. Carter. He performed CPR on you until the EMTs arrived. Do you know Mr. Carter?"

Grady started to chuckle until the chest pain stopped him. "I've known that old fart forever." RC Carter was Grady's best friend. They got together as often as time would allow to target shoot, go fishing, or talk about whatever was in the news or at the barbershop.

Honestly, Grady was surprised RC knew CPR. "Wait a minute! Did he put his mouth on me? That old redneck has been trying to kiss me for years."

Dr. Ali Sayeed, the Chief Cardiologist at Alexandria Regional Hospital Center, showed a hint of a smile despite his "all business" demeanor. Grady's humor was a good sign. Sayeed smiled, but Grady sensed concern behind the doctor's smile too. Sayeed responded, "Well Mr. Cordeaux, I do not know about trying to kiss you, but I do know that Mr. Carter's chest compressions kept you alive." Dr. Sayeed, a Pakistani was also glad that Grady did not appear to lack confidence in him. Although Sayeed was a highly respected cardiologist in his own country and in the U.S., he was accustomed to unenlightened people questioning his credentials because of his ethnicity. Most Americans did not understand that for him to get to his education level in Pakistan meant he was in the top one-half of one percent among millions of students.

Something Dr. Sayeed said earlier suddenly registered in Grady's mind causing him to blurt out, "Hold on! Did you say six days? I've been in here for six days? Who is looking after Boone? Where is my wallet? I need my wallet! I have to go home and let Boone out. That dog is all I got, Doc!"

His patient's sudden agitation alarmed Dr. Sayeed. He tried to calm Grady, assuring him that friends were taking care of his dog. "Your wallet is right here in the drawer with your personal belongings." The agitation was not good for a man in Grady's condition, but Sayeed also began to wonder about his patient's brain functions. He did not know anything about Grady, but it seemed odd that a man in Grady's condition would gain consciousness and worry first about his dog and his wallet. These were not the first things his patients usually asked about when they gained consciousness.

What Sayeed did not know about Grady was that his dog, Boone was one of the only things Grady had let into his heart, and that in his wallet he carried a reminder of the most precious thing he ever knew, the reason he should go on living. Sayeed told Grady, "Let's not worry too much about other things. You need rest more than anything right now, okay? We will talk some more tomorrow."

In a hushed voice so as not to alarm his patient, Dr. Sayeed instructed the ICU nurse that he wanted an EKG every 12 hours, unless there was a dramatic change, then they should call him. They were to maintain sedation levels and IV drip, rerun cardiac workups and enzymes every six hours times three.

Sayeed turned back to his patient, "Mr. Cordeaux, I will stop in later and we will chat." Sayeed quietly asked the nurse if the next of kin had been contacted. "I need to find out about his family history, especially any congenital heart defects."

She answered, "Doctor, according to Mr. Carter, the patient has no family."

He asked her if Grady had an advance directive. She told him the only things they knew so far was that he was a farmer, an armored car driver, and a Purple Heart recipient. Sayeed understood the Purple Heart to mean that Grady had been a wounded combat veteran, which could have implications about his current condition.

Sayeed instructed the nurse, "If Administration sends someone up for insurance information, Mr. Cordeaux is not to be disturbed until I give the authorization. They can speak to me if there is a problem." He warned that Grady would not survive another myocardial infarction, and said he would notify Dallas Cardiac Center about the case. As Dr. Sayeed was leaving, he asked the nurse to have Administration check the nearest VA hospital for Mr. Cordeaux's records.

RC

RC Carter called the hospital every day to ask about his friend's condition. He had to lie and tell them he was Grady's brother to get any information from them, since they talked only to family. The most they would say was that Grady's condition was stable, and that RC should speak to Dr. Sayeed. Six days later, RC came to the Intensive Care Unit (ICU) and waited for Grady to wake up. RC watched Grady stir for an hour before opening his eyes. The first sign of improvement was when Grady recognized RC and broke into his one-of-a-kind grin. Grady did this thing with his mouth when he was up to no good. He pursed his lips in such a way, which skewed more to one side, and had one dimple that formed a very unique smile. RC called it Grady's "shit-eating" grin. When that grin showed up, mischief was about to happen. On any other day, it signaled Grady was feeling full of himself. This time, though, it was merely something about which to be hopeful.

After smiling, Grady tried to talk. Six days had turned his voice to a whisper. "I open my eyes and your old, ugly mug is the first thing I see? Are you trying to repulse me to death?" RC chuckled.

Troy "RC" Carter was Grady's best and only friend. He was a 72-year-old Louisiana farmer and banker who looked more like a cowboy straight out of Tombstone, Arizona in 1880. He was 6'1" and lean with silver hair, a weathered ruddy face, and eyes squinted from too much time in the sun. He wore a suit at the Credit Union where he worked, but the rest of his time was spent in a pair of duck denim jeans, work boots, and a flannel shirt. The rough look of his face, the steel in his eyes, and his deep voice were enough to dissuade anybody from trying to tangle with him. It was a good thing too because what people did not know was this old farmer had the toughness to back up his look, despite his age. RC was physically imposing for sure, but his disposition was mostly gentle and easy-going. He was typically friendly and engaging. He had strong opinions, born out of ugly life experiences, but in later years, he did not begrudge other people from having opposing opinions. However, the few things he would not tolerate were bad-mouthing his country, or spouting off about politics when the speaker had no qualifications to do so. One of his frequent sayings was, "If you want to complain about the very country, one of the few on the planet, that allows you the freedom to complain, you better know the facts." Having served his country with distinction in Vietnam, he especially had little tolerance for people who criticized the country, or demanded their rights but never did anything to earn those rights.

RC tried to stay informed about current events by scanning several major newspapers each morning. He read with a critical eye, how different newspapers would report the same story differently by using misleading titles, and provocative words to lead the reader. In Vietnam, he had firsthand knowledge that the media slanted stories. He participated in operations and battles where the media omitted facts or misled the readership about what actually happened. He knew politicians and military leadership were lying to the American people about how the war was going and it disgusted him. The American public did not know or think about the American soldiers fighting under rules of engagement that the enemy did not follow. We had to fight a conventional war against an insurgent enemy. US troops could have used the same guerilla tactics the enemy used to greater effect, but the leadership would not allow it, and the American public would have been mortified. People back home also had no clue how the troops dealt with harsh daily life in the bush. Eventually, America turned her back on the men who answered their nation's call to duty.

RC served two tours in Vietnam as an Army Ranger. When his 2nd tour was over, he came home to his parents' farm, where he grew up, just outside of Fort Polk, Louisiana. During his time "in the Nam" he learned far too much about life and himself. He arrived in Vietnam a young man, but he came home an old one. Time in "the bush" under constant threat of death did that to men. It aged them like few other things could. He remembered seasoned soldiers talking about the 1000-yard stare. It was the look a soldier had on his face after being in battle and witnessing the horror. If you could climb into the beam of that 1000-yard stare you would know that horror that comes from seeing what bullets and explosives do to human flesh. You would be paralyzed by how humans are capable of inflicting unimaginable suffering, pain, and death on one another. The stare was the vacuum left in a man's brain as a result of exceeding its capacity to witness evil.

RC came home from war to find cowards and leftists protesting in the streets, hiding under the umbrella of civil disobedience. The "peace-loving" protesters called it a revolution. There were a lot of people shouting about peace, but they were not shouting it to the Chinese or the Soviets supporting the North Vietnamese communists. He saw a generation of Americans abandoning their values, and he hated them.

When he came back from the war, one of the things that bothered him most struck him like an epiphany. He learned in Nam that men in a firefight do not care about skin color. Black men were fighting and dying for America as much as or more than white men. RC grew up knowing a different way in the deep South, but in Vietnam he came to know and respect those men. When he came home, he saw black Americans taking to the streets to be treated as equals. It disgusted him that they felt the need to march for respect. They had his complete respect, but they were not getting it from the Americans that stayed home during the war, the America that forgot about them.

RC did not want to be part of a country where his brothers in arms had to beg for anything, when they gave everything for their country.

RC grew up and learned a lot of things by going to war, but much of it was not good. It took years for him to deal with his anger and disillusionment with Americans after he came home. He became a belligerent bar-fighting drunk the first few years, and almost landed in prison, except for the Veteran's Administration's intervention and AA meetings. They helped him find peace. However, he never healed enough to let people get close to him, until they earned his trust.

RC's tours in Vietnam and disillusionment upon returning home were not the only wounds on the Carters' farm. His parents suffered terribly during the war. The Carters worked hard and raised two boys in a spiritual, loving household. Farm work was hard, and Mr. Carter was tough on his boys growing up. Like most farm boys they got their share of a backhand across the back of their heads, or a horse rein across their backside. But, with lots of mother's love and attention to balance out the discipline two boys grew into men and made their parents proud. They both did well in school, had excellent work ethics, and were ready to face the world when they came of age. RC heard the call and volunteered for Vietnam. Jimmy, the younger son, worked on an oil rig in the Gulf of Mexico. Working on a rig was a coveted job for young men because of the pay scale. It was risky work with one month at a time of isolation at sea, but it paid more money than most young men could handle. Jimmy was very lucky to have landed one of those jobs.

When the boys left the nest, the Carters only worried about the son that went off to war. Each night they hesitantly watched the nightly news for grisly details and body counts coming out of Vietnam. For two years, they lived in constant fear of the mail, or sight of a courier coming to the door delivering a letter from the Secretary of Defense. Then, one night the Carters got a call that changed them forever. All the worry about RC stunned them with guilt when they learned that Jimmy was killed in an accident on an oil rig.

Mr. Carter needed his boys to help run the farm, and he never wanted them to go away but he understood the call to arms, having served in WWII. He had to let RC go. He also knew that Jimmy needed to go out on his own and find his way to become a man. He always hoped the boys would sow their wild oats and come back to the farm. Over time, the constant worry about RC in combat was hard on Mr. Carter, but ultimately, the death of Jimmy took what was left of the old man. RC never again saw the father he remembered before going to Vietnam. Instead, he came home to find a broken old man, who aged twenty years in four, ambling about the farm, without purpose or reason, unable to keep it going.

Mr. Carter suffered a stroke and passed away a few years after RC returned home. The death left RC to care for his mother and the farm, but, as painful as it was, that responsibility was the "rock bottom" RC needed to get on with life.

After much counseling, AA meetings, and time, he pulled himself together and reconnected with a girl he knew in high school, Suzie Jamison.

One of the things RC figured out about life while humping through the bush in Nam, was that life was too precious and you should never let good things slip away. After his emotional recovery when he could appreciate life again, he remembered Suzie from high school. He called some of his old friends to see if she still lived in the area. They reconnected and within a year he knew she was the one. Six months later they married.

Suzie was one of the best things to happen to RC. She may not have been the prom queen, but he remembered how kind and funny she was in school. Suzie was not one of the popular girls in high school, being more concerned about her studies than her make-up and clothes, but she was attractive, especially to RC. She was a softball player and he liked how she filled out her uniform like a woman. RC's experiences overseas taught him to look deeper to find the truly important things in life. He realized that physical beauty was fleeting, but a beautiful heart was everlasting. Suzie was beautiful and had a curvy figure he appreciated, but when RC got to know Suzie's heart, she was the most beautiful woman he had ever seen. The fact that she was an amazing cook sealed the deal. It made him want to be a better man for her. She always felt his devotion and adoration. In return, she loved him back deeply and took good care of him over the years. With her love and partnership over time, he bettered himself by using his G.I. bill to get a business degree from LSU and make the farm profitable again. It eventually became self-sustaining with the help of a farmhand, and RC took on a second job at the Southern Finance Credit Union at Fort Polk, becoming Senior Manager. Most of his accomplishments were done so Suzie would be proud and glad she married him.

After RC and Grady met and eventually became friends, Grady joked that if you looked up "redneck" in a dictionary, you would see a picture of RC. Truthfully though, he knew RC was much more than just a hard working farmer and businessman. On more than one occasion, Grady would have a laugh when RC struck up a conversation with a stranger and talk so far over the stranger's head he could only nod just to pretend to stay in the conversation. RC was a deep thinker, a voracious reader, and could recall facts, figures and dates quicker than any man Grady knew. He was versatile too. He could be in a tuxedo discussing tax reform at a National Banker's dinner as easily as he could be in coveralls repairing his tractor. RC was not a book to be judged by its cover. However, Grady also knew RC's flaws. Earning RC's trust was a herculean feat rarely accomplished by anyone lacking a long-term relationship. Once in a while, something as innocuous as a helicopter flying overhead would wake up demons from Vietnam in RC's head making him moody and unpredictable for a day. He chewed tobacco on the farm which stained his teeth and repulsed city folks if they saw him. Although RC joined AA after Vietnam, later in life he was able to drink alcohol in moderation and small doses. Grady understood the mental discipline this took, but he always kept a watchful eye on his friend anyway. As long as they were friends, RC never crossed that line.

A Bond Is Forged

Grady first met RC in a gun store near Fort Polk, Louisiana in 1979. He remembered a store advertisement for a Colt 1911 at a great price. It was the same gun the Army issued to him in Vietnam, and he loved that handgun. When he came into the gun shop, another customer was looking at the 1911 also. The salesman and the customer were discussing the design, the trigger weight, and the grip. It was the kind of conversation that only gun enthusiasts would appreciate and understand. As Grady listened in on the conversation, the salesman asked if he wanted to take a look. Grady nodded, asking if it was the Army issue in Nam. RC went through the safety procedures and handed the firearm to Grady, saying he had one in Nam just like it too.

RC said, "IV Corp, 67."

Grady replied, "Delta gunboat, 70, Da Nang and Saigon, 71." They shook hands.

"RC Carter."

"Grady Cordeaux. Good to meet ya. You know your firearms."

The two men talked for a while about guns, eventually moving into hunting, fishing, Vietnam, and farming. When there was nothing more to say they shook hands again and went their separate ways. In the span of a year, they ran into each other a few times in Pineville and Ft. Polk, exchanging more war stories and shooting tips. Early on, even though they seemed very like-minded, neither man was willing to share anything more than the most obvious, impersonal information. Over time though, trust and respect were earned and a friendship began to take root.

In time, their common interests and beliefs made them best friends. Grady was one of the few people who knew that "RC" was a nickname bestowed on him in Vietnam by his army buddies. It turns out that liquor was hard to come by at some of the remote hilltop camps in Vietnam, but RC was always able to get rum. He liked his rum and coke, or RC, so the moniker stuck. A lot of guys earned nicknames over there; it grew out of closeness and camaraderie. Grady became "lover boy" because of all the love letters he received in country. Of course, on payday or during R&R (Rest & Relaxation) every G.I. in Nam was a lover boy at one time or another. When he first learned about Grady's nickname, RC wondered if there was more to it. Over the years and a few too many drinks later, he learned the truth about Grady's deepest secret.

People keep secrets buried for any number of reasons. They can be too personal, too revealing of weakness, too bizarre or too painful. RC never pried into Grady's secret because he understood the need to suppress horror and misery. He understood there were things seen and done in Vietnam, and certainly other wars, that men would never want to think about again. It was understood between brothers-in-arms they held on to things they wish could have been left behind. They were the kind of things no one should ever experience, the kind of things that can never be unseen. Some men handled it, or pretended to, but few ever let it go completely. RC never pried, but he expected that at some point Grady would reveal his deepest truth.

From the time they met in '79, the two men became the best of friends and part of each other's lives. Grady watched RC's kids grow up, move out, and marry. He spent holidays with them, shared milestone events, joys and sometimes heartaches. They always knew they could call on each other for any favor big or small. Conversely, RC and Suzie watched Grady spend his life in search of something impossible to find, missing out on the life right in front of him. Grady laughed, cried, ate, drank, and even prayed with the Carters, living vicariously through them, but Suzie sensed Grady had a hole in him that would never be filled.

The first few years after meeting Grady and sensing his emptiness, Suzie tried to play matchmaker. She would arrange for friends to join them at Sunday picnics after church. Grady stopped complaining after the first few times, because he did not really mind the company. Suzie would be giddy when Grady showed polite interest in someone she invited, but time after time it never took. It was always the same story. The women would be charmed and excited by Grady, but eventually grow frustrated because no matter how hard they tried they could not ignite his spark. On occasion, a relationship would turn into something deeper and more intimate, but even those ended when the women realized Grady had no long-term intentions. After several failed attempts, Suzie stopped trying to fix him up, and resolved to let him be content in his hollow loneliness. Some years later, when she learned Grady's secret, she wished she did not know because one small piece of her heart would forever feel his unbearable sorrow. For the many years that followed, Suzie loved Grady as much as her husband did. He was part of their family.

Recovering in ICU

A few days in the hospital, and many tests later, Grady felt strong enough to complain. He gladly let the nurses and doctors know what he thought about the poking and prodding. Every hospital employee that entered his room heard Grady cursing and complaining. He tried to convince the doctors that his collapse was brought on by working too hard and not getting enough sleep. However, the louder he protested, the more it fell on deaf ears.

He was becoming frustrated. While his bad bedside manner was annoying, it also indicated his strength was returning. However, his lack of strength was merely a symptom. As much as Grady tried to convince everyone he was well, deep down, he knew this time he could not slap mud in the wound and ignore the pain.

Dr. Sayeed, during daily rounds, listened to Grady's heart and asked questions. "Can you sit up by yourself?" Grady would try, with the nurse's help. "Had you ever felt out of breath before your heart attack?" Sayeed asked.

Grady was becoming agitated. "What the hell is going on, Doc? Why does it still feel like someone is sitting on my chest?"

Sayeed answered that he would not know until the tests were completed. RC listened in from the corner of the room, pretending to be oblivious. As a rule, hospitals made RC uncomfortable, but he was especially anxious this time thinking about his friend's mortality.

Quiet Men

RC and Grady knew each other forty years. Forty years of friendship, laughter, working on projects, and relaxing together was enough time for even the most introverted and unemotional men to learn each other's strengths and vulnerabilities. Psychologists say that a person's behavior and personality are the result of nature and nurture, genetics and life experiences. Grady's and RC's personalities, like many children raised on rural farms were initially forged from hard, demanding childhoods. Naturally, the brain's processing of five sensory inputs every second of every day ultimately makes each human unique. Grady and RC were individually unique, but also similarly nurtured at young ages by hard discipline and firm hands of fathers teaching them how to work the land. Their fathers received the same kind of cold, harsh training from their fathers before them. It was all they knew.

Grady and RC were discouraged from expressing emotions because their fathers believed it signaled fear and weakness, and was not something men did. It had no place on a farm. Farm work was too hard for softness and sentiment. There were chores that had to be done regardless of feelings. Animals were to be used or harvested. The work was physically demanding regardless of aches and pains. Debate and discussions were not needed, nor was playtime. Typically, farms were too far apart for children to play with neighbors. Siblings played together but only when all chores were completed. By the time a child turned five, he or she was expected to help with light chores and housework. When they were older, they worked outside. Most 12-year-olds on Louisiana farms were driving tractors and riding horses. Out of necessity, rural children learned discipline, responsibility, self-reliance, and solitude.

Grady was an only child and the responsibilities laid on him were more demanding. By the time Grady was helping with outside chores, his mother, Gloria worried that her husband, Tom was too heavy-handed on their son. On the rare occasions when he got too physical in disciplining young Grady, she would gently say something to him, even though a wife in the 1950's rarely questioned her husband. He would tell her he got much worse from his father. Most of the time she accepted Tom slapping the back of Grady's head, or taking his belt to the boy, partly because she wondered if her son might need that strict discipline. Once in a while though, Tom Cordeaux's frustrations were taken out on his son.

Gloria also worried because she secretly suffered from depression and anxiety. It was not something she talked about or sought to relieve with medical care; it just was. Her illness emerged during Grady's toddler years. People knew very little about mental illness in the mid 1950's and were afraid because of the unknown causes and stigmas attached to it. When Gloria could not "snap out of it," as her husband demanded, she decided to ignore it and not disappoint her husband. She did not have other women to talk to, nor would she ever reveal such a thing. She considered it her privacy to be kept private.

However troublesome, Gloria did not fear her son developing anxiety. Instead, she worried about him being like her brother. Gloria's brother, John, was quick-tempered through his teen years and short adult life. He was never diagnosed, although she suspected it was a mental illness that drove him to aggression and sudden anger. John's anger often got him in trouble. It was his anger that got him into the bar fight which ended his life before his 25th birthday. Gloria prayed every Sunday at church that her husband's firm hand would be balanced by her nurturing, and the combination would keep Grady safe. Some days she worried about the kind of man Grady would be.

Their rural farm upbringing shaped Grady and RC into the men they became, but while they were still teenagers, they also experienced the trauma of war, which changed them forever. It changed them in so many ways. They did not have many friends, like most children raised on farms in rural America because of the distance between neighbors, so they learned to be self-reliant and comfortable being alone. Then too, in Vietnam, they learned that a friend might be the next one you piece together in a body bag to send home. Those experiences welded shut for years their ability to have friends, and care, because caring for fragile things in wartime usually meant suffering the loss.

In Vietnam, they learned other lessons as well. They witnessed the evil and horror humans are capable of inflicting upon one another. Then they had to reconcile within themselves that they too were guilty of inflicting the same evil on the enemy. The right and wrong of it was lost in the gunfire. Existing 365 days surrounded and haunted by that kind of evil made it nearly impossible to ever see goodness in another human. They learned in Vietnam that kindness and trust get you killed. When something as innocent as a mother and a child in a village was trying to kill you, the GIs lost their ability to feel anything. It took a long time for soldiers to find the parts of their humanity they lost in the war; some never did.

Sometimes a soldier's only humanity was with other soldiers. They had gone through hell and come out the other side. Their experiences in Vietnam bound them together. They were part of a brotherhood that had seen and done horrific things. While they each carried burdens, it helped to know that others carried burdens too.

Over the years, the intensity of Grady's and RC's horrifying memories in Vietnam lessened. Occasionally though, the repetitive chop, chop, chop of a UH-1 Huey flying overhead from Fort Polk, or the thunderous boom of an artillery gun during a military training exercise at the Fort dredged up those gut-wrenching feelings, especially for RC. When Suzie would ask him to talk with her and let her ease his burden, he would withdraw from life for a few hours. Like many veterans, RC kept those memories private to spare Suzie from having his same nightmares. For their loved ones to feel safe and for them to feel human again, war-hardened veterans learned to be quiet men.

Despite his quiet nature, RC felt that the hospital room was too quiet when Grady slept. The silence gave RC too much time to think about his friend. He thought about the tough old farmer in the bed bearing scars of physical and emotional wounds from over forty years ago. He cursed fate for being so cruel by allowing Grady to survive

Vietnam, only to take away the thing he held most dear, make him be alone the rest of his life, and then take him down by a failing heart.

RC thought too about Grady's deepest wound, his secret. It was the all-consuming thing that kept Grady from ever knowing happiness. RC wondered if that was what finally broke him. He knew about Grady's lifelong search for resolution. He knew about the letters, the phone calls, the trips and the dead ends. He knew Grady tried every avenue to reach back. RC always told Grady he understood, but truthfully, only Grady could know the depth of his own torment and loss.

Knowing that everyone has secrets, RC came to accept there were things about Grady Cordeaux that even a best friend would never fully know. But the secret that defined Grady was what troubled RC now because it might be the thing that takes down his best friend. He wanted to do everything he could to keep his buddy around for a few more harvests. In the deafening quiet of the night, RC thought about their friendship and asked himself when did he get this old?

He eventually left the hospital that night and headed home, needing to hold Suzie. He cussed himself for being so emotional. When he came into the house, she had dinner waiting. Suzie Carter worked a full-time job, and now that her kids were grown, she did not have dinner on the table every night waiting for her husband. She was an independent, strong woman and RC loved that about her. Tonight however, she understood the sorrow her husband must be feeling, and she wanted to support him as much as he would allow.

She asked about Grady's condition and was genuinely concerned. But more than that, she wanted her husband to talk about how he felt. She knew if he did not, he would bottle it up inside and it would eat away at him. RC was getting to an age where illnesses did not need much of a reason to invade his weathered body, and the stress from a friend dying could be a reason. RC was the closest thing Grady had to next of kin. He even gave RC medical Power-of-Attorney some time back and listed him as beneficiary. Suzie worried that the legal responsibilities would be a burden her husband could not handle emotionally. She loved Grady like a brother, but she worried about her husband even more.

Diagnosis

Dr. Sayeed came into Grady's room and heard, "So, Doc, you've done all the tests and poked me enough to know what is wrong with me. How about you level with me for a change?"

Sayeed replied while looking over Grady's chart. "Mr. Cordeaux, I have not kept anything from you. I do not speculate on my patients' conditions. We start by examining you, reviewing your symptoms, and your history. Next, we start ruling out possible causes until we pinpoint one. However, you are correct; we have poked you enough. It would help if we knew your family medical history, but since you do not know very much, I have to make some assumptions about your condition.

"I believe you suffer from a congenital heart defect. I am leaning toward a heart disease called Eisenmenger Syndrome. In laymen's terms, you have a hole in your heart. It is almost a certainty you have had this since birth. In rare cases the symptoms do not present until later in life. In your case, it is rare for it to go undiagnosed until now, but you could have been living with the symptoms for many years and ignored them. I asked you before about feeling out of breath. This disease results in the heart's inability to circulate enough oxygenated blood through your circulatory system. The symptoms would present as weakness, fatigue, shortness of breath, swollen ankles, and headaches. Often, a telltale symptom is cyanosis, or the bluing of certain body parts like your lips, skin, or fingernails."

Grady did not say anything when Dr. Sayeed mentioned the symptoms. He hoped RC was not paying attention. RC was paying attention and knew Grady had many of the symptoms described. He could not remember how many times he said something to Grady about his blue fingernails, but Grady discounted it. He considered himself too tough to go to the doctor for blue fingernails.

Convincing Grady

After Dr. Sayeed finished explaining his diagnosis, he discussed a treatment plan. "Mr. Cordeaux, I am relatively confident in my diagnosis, but there are a few more tests needed to determine the severity of your condition. I would like to send you to Dallas for those tests. Dallas has one of the best cardiac centers in the southwest, with doctors who specialize in rare cardiac conditions."

After hearing Sayeed's recommendation, Grady sat up as straight as he could. "Listen, Doc, I appreciate everything you've done for me, I really do, but I am fine and I damn sure ain't going to Dallas to hear more doctors tell me what you just told me. You're a cardiac doctor, right? Just sew up the hole, give me some antibiotics, and get me back on my feet."

Dr. Sayeed slowly removed his glasses and pointed them assertively, "Mr. Cordeaux, perhaps we have not been clear. I am trying to be optimistic, but your condition has not shown any signs of improvement since you were wheeled in on a gurney. You have not had any exertion for more than a week, but you still feel the same heaviness in your chest as your first day. Your condition is not improving and will not improve unless we let specialists help you. There are doctors in Dallas that are highly specialized in these cases. Do you understand? You may try to walk out of this hospital, but you would not be able to get as far as the elevator. We require your signature and complete cooperation to transport you to Dallas. The nurse will attend to you. Do we understand one another?"

Sayeed walked out of the room. Grady was exhausted. He looked across to RC, and softly said, "I am not going to Dallas."

RC tried to hide his smirk. He had never seen another man talk to Grady that way and get away with it. Grady was helpless for once in his life, and it was funny for a second until RC remembered the seriousness of his condition. He told Grady it might be time for a road trip. Grady gave that one-of-a-kind tilted mouth, dimpled smile, shook his head, and drifted off to sleep.

Before Sayeed ever mentioned Dallas, RC knew Grady would be hardheaded about going to yet another hospital. He knew because Grady was not one to seek help and go to one hospital, let alone two. Both men had the immortal mentality that if they made it through hell and back in Nam, it was ridiculous to complain about a papercut back in civilization.

"What is happening? Why can't I keep my eyes open?" Grady mumbled to himself.

Coming out of his stupor, Grady slowly focused on RC moving closer to the bed. "How ya doin, redneck? Bout time you came back to us. You've been tapped out almost two days."

Grady squinted in disbelief. "Bullshit!" he protested. "I just dozed off for a power nap!" RC informed him he had been power napping for two days. "No shit?" Grady asked, "You got my dog?" Then he looked over at the nightstand for his wallet.

RC replied, "Yep, I got ya covered, but listen up. I got something real important to talk to you about." Grady tried to focus. RC had a particular look on his face when he was serious. It was the same look he used when teaching his grandchildren about important things like gun safety or working on the farm. Grady thought whatever he was about to hear was serious.

RC asked, "Remember a few years back when Suzie and I had our wills done?" Grady nodded. "Well remember we got talking about someone having a limited power of attorney for you in case you were incapacitated, and because you ain't got no one that can speak for you?"

"Yeah," Grady answered with a questioning inflection. He wondered where RC was going with this.

RC continued, "Well, it's a damn good thing we did that because I am here now to help you."

"Help me with what?" Grady asked.

"Help you shit in your mess kit, dumbass! What do you think I'm helping you with? I'm helping you get well. See, the doctors around here feel like your condition is not improving. Apparently, your heart is weaker than it should be. You haven't been able to lift your head or keep your eyes open for more than a few minutes in the last week. I gotta be honest, they are telling me that things ain't so good right now. They need to get you to a hospital equipped to deal with your specific diagnosis."

"Goddamnit, RC! What in the hell did you do? I'm going to be fine! I just need a little time. Why don't you go home and take care of that wife of yours before someone else does?" Grady was becoming agitated.

The heart monitor beeped faster when he snapped at RC. Grady tried to conceal the pain in his chest, but RC could see it in his face. RC wanted him to calm down, but Grady needed to know RC had authorized the transfer to Dallas.

RC tried changing the subject. "Hey, you wanna know the best part? Someone in here got Tricare to pick up the bill after Medicare pays its share. Whoever did it must be a slick son-of-a-gun to be able to wrangle that deal, and look, Suzie and I will be along to look in on you up there. It's only a five-hour drive, and when you get back on your feet, I'll teach you how to catch them big ol' good 'uns on the Cane river."

"The hell you say!" Grady responded less agitated. "I catch more and bigger bass every time we go." RC heard the resignation in Grady's voice, and was glad. It was the right thing to do and Grady needed to get out of his own stubborn way,

The two men had reached an unspoken agreement. Dr. Sayeed came in during his rounds. He glanced at RC for acknowledgment that Grady was on board with the transfer plan.

RC asked, "Okay, sport?"

Grady looked at Dr. Sayeed, softly cursing, "Jesus, I'm fine, but if going to Dallas will get you people off my back, I'll go. I don't want to get anyone's panties in a bunch."

Sayeed did not understand the panties analogy, but he was satisfied that his patient agreed to go to Dallas.

They all looked at each other until Grady broke the silence, "Okay, Doc, what happens next?"

Dr. Sayeed explained that tomorrow morning the ICU staff would administer a sedative to help him sleep during the trip. Hopefully, he would experience a very restful sleep for the duration of the five-hour ambulance ride, and then wake up in Dallas Cardiac Center.

"Tomorrow morning? What the hell is the rush?" Grady asked.

"Mr. Cordeaux, your condition and lack of improvement thus far has convinced us you need treatment as soon as possible. I do not want to alarm you unnecessarily, but your condition is very serious. Your heart has suffered major damage, it has a small perforation between chambers, and my diagnosis of Eisenmenger syndrome, which could be confirmed and treated in Dallas, is very serious, indeed. Frankly, we are surprised you survived such a strain on your heart. There is one consideration on our side."

"What's that, Doc?" Grady asked.

"In my consultations with the Dallas Cardiac Center, I've learned that one of the world's leading experts in congenital heart defects and pulmonary hypertension, from London, is teaching there for another few weeks. He will most likely take the opportunity to review your case. You might be used as a teaching case, but you will be getting the best expertise in the world."

RC piped in, "If Grady's condition is so serious, why isn't he being taken by helicopter?"

"Yes, this of course would be our first preference. However, Mr. Cordeaux's condition does not meet a certain threshold to justify the air transport. We also would be concerned about increased air pressures and turbulence. He will be very comfortable during the ambulance ride. We will see to it."

All night Grady lay in his bed staring at the ceiling. Reality had just kicked him in the balls and, for the first time since his heart attack, he began to ponder the possibility of dying. He wondered if anyone was ever truly ready.

In Nam, he remembered feeling invincible. He saw men die right next to him, but no one ever thought he would be next. Maybe soldiers thought about it in the deepest recesses of their minds, but rarely did it hold anyone back. The drill instructors in basic training drilled it into them that if you let those thoughts about dying get into your head you might as well jump on a grenade. Their belief in immortality, combined with intense training, are what pushed them onward. It was nature's way in war.

However, the officers and senior enlisted were older and wiser. They had been through more of the war, and had time to accumulate things to lose. Those were the real tough guys; the ones who knew they could lose everything they loved. Those tough sons-of-bitches still went in, leading their men; they were the battle-hardened heroes.

Grady never criticized his superiors in Vietnam because they had enough experience to fully understand the dangers, and yet they charged in anyway. Sure, every unit had an asshole or two, especially the green lieutenants that were rotated every six months and made mistakes. Those greenhorns tried to lead men who had far more experience in combat, but even those guys eventually left it up to the sergeants. A good lieutenant always had a great sergeant with him.

Grady remembered the time in Vietnam when he began to feel vulnerable. It was when he had something to lose.

"Grady? Psst! Hey? Did you understand all that?" asked RC.

In a split-second Grady was back from the Nam and in his room, "Huh? Oh, yeah, I heard what the Doc said. I was just thinking about that ambulance ride, that's all."

RC and Suzie would go to Grady's house, pack some things, take care of Boone, and get whatever else Grady might need.

Grady looked at RC as if he was looking right through him, "Yeah, yeah. Hey RC, thanks man, thanks for everything."

"Alright asshole," RC shot back, "we're not doing this, we're not saying our good-byes. You are going to be fine. We've been through tougher shit than this."

Grady's tired eyes looked up. "I know. All I'm saying is you been like a brother to me for a long time. I don't know if I ever told you, ya' know. I…"

RC cut him off. "If you pull a ring out from under those sheets I'm going to say yes, so you better mean it. What is this shit anyway? We're brothers, right?" Grady nodded. "Okay, we don't need to say nothing. I'll always have your back."

Before Grady dozed off, he said softly, "Hey RC, where is my wallet? Is she…?" He was out.

RC never heard Grady give up before. This was not good! He needed his mental toughness now more than ever. The thought of Grady giving up the fight made RC sick to his stomach. He felt his heart palpitate and sweat bead up on his skin. Grady had described his panic attacks to RC before. This was the first time RC experienced one.

RC caught up with Dr. Sayeed in the hospital and let him know that Grady was saying good-bye. Sayeed gently shook his head in disappointment.

He told RC that when they prep Grady in the morning for the ambulance ride and give him a sedative Sayeed would convey optimism to Grady about being treated by experts in Dallas. Sayeed did not mean to alarm Grady, but it was his responsibility to make his patients aware of the realities of their condition.

He assured RC, "I will work on my optimism tomorrow."

Sayeed redirected the conversation. "Mr. Carter, you understand that your friend is in critical condition, yes? The sedatives will keep him calm during the transport, but you too should understand the reality. His heart is very weak. We expect he will endure the treatment protocol prescribed in Dallas. However, he has suffered damage to an already weak heart. If the treatment is successful, Mr. Cordeaux will need a great deal of time convalescing. If the treatment is not successful, we have to be prepared. Do you understand what I am telling you?"

RC's contemplation

RC knew what Dr. Sayeed was telling him. At that moment he wished Suzie was there. It was a 45-minute drive back to the farm and he did not feel like being alone. He drove into the night realizing that the conversation between him and Grady could have been the last, and he cussed as moisture filled his eyes, wiping it away with his sleeve. *Fucking pussy!* He thought. Emotions were difficult and awkward for

RC. They were buried deep, but every now and then they would bubble up.

RC had shed tears at his daughters' weddings. He hated being emotional, but no one could ever question his love for his two little girls. They were his angels and all their lives they made him proud. He thought of them and their lives right now. Both girls were college graduates, married to good men, had children, and were happy. One lived in Shreveport, the other in Baton Rouge so RC and Suzie got to see them often.

It was just RC and Suzie at their empty nest ranch, but they loved their simple life. They saw their grandchildren often, the farm was productive, his bank job was going well, and they could afford to travel just about anywhere.

Suzie loved to travel. Usually, once a year they would take off to an exotic place, or tour the U.S. RC recalled his favorite trip when they packed up the girls and headed out west. Jolene was 14, and Emily was 11. They rented a camper in Denver and stayed at campgrounds in Colorado, South Dakota, and Wyoming. They were in Cheyenne during Frontier Days, toured Mt. Rushmore, Devil's Tower, Yellowstone, Jackson, the Grand Tetons, and several National Parks. For two weeks they experienced the wide, open prairie. The best part, which RC will never forget, was the closeness he felt being with his family.

These memories cheered him up until he pulled off the paved road to his farm. It was late, but he had to take Suzie to Grady's place, another 30 minutes to Pineville, to get some of Grady's things. It was going to be a long night.

After just a few hours of sleep, RC and Suzie pulled up to the hospital. The sunlight peeked over the horizon. This time of morning was RC's and Grady's favorite. It was when the turkey and deer began to stir and the woods came alive. Every hunter knew the feeling of serenity and exhilaration.

RC and Suzie walked in just as a team of nurses and technicians were moving Grady out of the ICU. They explained to him what was about to happen and that he would have a very restful journey. Grady grabbed the nurse's arm and asked him to hold on for just a minute before pushing the IV sedation.

He looked around for RC and Suzie. "We're right here pal, we will tag along in the truck and see that you get there in one piece."

Grady needed to tell them something; it kept him awake all night.

RC said, "We can talk in Dallas."

"No! I need to tell you now!"

RC leaned in. "Okay, pal, I'm here. What's up?"

Grady spoke as loudly as he could but it was little more than gasps, "Listen RC, I asked you to answer for me in case I couldn't, right?"

"Yeah, yeah, I got your back, no worries, we're good, but let's not worry about that right now, nothing's going to happen, okay?" RC whispered.

"I know you don't like talking about this stuff, but we have to; you are my beneficiary. If something happens, I want you to take care of my place, okay?" RC nodded.

The anesthetist moved into position beside Grady and began the flow of the sedatives. "Alright, Mr. Cordeaux, I need you to count backward from 100."

Grady began, "100, 99, 98, 9……….." He was out.

They wheeled Grady into the ambulance. RC and Suzie let the driver know they would be following along. The ambulance driver pulled away from the hospital to the highway. The drive was going to be interminable for RC and Suzie, as neither could take their minds off Grady's condition. They scanned the radio for a distraction, but it did not help. RC's thoughts took him back to Nam, to the ICU, and to his farm where they would target shoot. Suzie dwelled on how this might affect her husband.

Part 2: The Long Ride

Football Season

The announcer's voice blared over the loudspeaker. "The Lions are deep into Rebel territory, the referee signals first and ten on the 19."

Grady was playing his last high school football game. He and the rest of the Pineville Rebels were pumped up on adrenalin. The Ouachita Lions were threatening to score for the win with two minutes left. It would be only the second loss this season for the Pineville Rebels, but they did not want their winning season to end with a loss and jeopardize the championship. Grady was defensive captain. He called the defense's formation. The stands were packed with Pineville's faithful. Everyone listened for the announcer.

"The Rebels' defense is set. The Lions come to the line. Roberts comes under center. He calls the cadence. Roberts moves back into the pocket! There's the snap, the backfield rolls to the right. Roberts in the pocket. Johnson and Williams are double covered in the end zone. The Rebels blitz! Someone has a hand on Roberts. He fumbles! The Rebs are indicating they have the ball! Let's wait for the referee's call. Yes! Yes! The Rebels have recovered the fumble on their 24-yard line with less than two minutes left! And what a sack for number 53, Grady Cordeaux!"

As each team changed players, the announcer once again came on the microphone. "Again, middle linebacker, Grady Cordeaux, who has had a very impressive senior year, caused the fumble. It will be the 26th sack for Cordeaux and, as we are hearing now, a new school record. The Rebels' offense takes the field, the last time for some of these young men. The coach is signaling all his seniors on offense in to play this last series of downs. Meanwhile, on the sidelines, the team is jumping on Cordeaux. What a career this young man might have in store for him. The Rebels only have to hold the ball for one set of downs, and they will have another great winning season for Coach Cramer and his Pineville Rebels of Rapides Parish. Jamison takes a knee, letting the clock run out. That's it!! The Pineville Rebels are the 1970 Central Louisiana champions!"

After taking off his uniform for the last time, showering, and getting dressed, Grady slowly walked out of the locker room basking in the glory of his last high school football game at Pineville. He and the rest of the team were ready for Friday night celebrating. The coaches stopped a few players, who played exceptionally well, to talk about scouts and college offers to come. It was a night for the record books!

Grady felt like a victorious gladiator as he made his way through the crowd giving high fives, handshakes, and taking pats from parents and students. Grady's mother and father were there, as usual. His dad hugged him and told him how proud he was of his son.

Tom Cordeaux was a tall, husky built, hardworking farmer outside of Pineville. He was in his mid-50's, but the sun, the land, and the work had aged him beyond his years. His 6-foot, thick frame, slightly bent with bulging lumbar discs, walked with the weight of 40 years of good and bad harvests on his shoulders. His face and neck were weathered and wrinkled from the sun, and his teeth were stained from tobacco chew. His eyes gleamed with the wisdom that comes from hardship and regret. Sometimes he secretly wondered if he would do things differently given the chance, but not tonight. On this night Tom knew how his son was feeling as he remembered his own glory days at Natchitoches. He remembered what he did the night after the last football game of his senior year. It may have been a different time, but he knew Grady would want to go out with his friends and release all his energy.

With his hint of a Cajun accent, Tom advised his son, "Now, keep your head about you tonight boy. Go out and have you a good time but come home safe and no trouble! Ya hear wha' I'm telling you?"

"Yes, sir," Grady answered obediently. Grady loved and respected his parents. They did the very best they could for Grady, and he knew it. He never wanted to shame them. He also knew how strict his father could be. Tom had not had to physically discipline Grady in a long time, but Grady knew his father's strength and he was always afraid of what his pa might be capable of if he ever got uncontrollably angry.

"Grady," his dad called back to him, "you be careful with that pretty little girl too, son. Don't be getting into any trouble either." He winked. Grady knew what his dad meant.

Gabriella

Grady was on top of the world, especially when he saw Gabby in her cheerleading uniform waiting for him at his truck. In their senior year, Grady and Gabby became "the couple."

The two met in their junior year, not long after she arrived at Pineville High. The Montoyas moved to Pineville from California. Her father was in the military which relocated him every three years. Military kids were accustomed to moving, but for Gabby, this time was the worst. She was in her junior year of high school, the most influential years for a teenager. Compounding the difficulty, Pineville was the kind of place where people lived all their lives, many never leaving Louisiana. The community was close knit, strangers were suspect and Gabby was the "new girl."

She was Hispanic and very pretty with almond-shaped brown eyes, a smooth complexion, a cute rounded nose, plump lips, shoulder-length thick brunette hair, slightly darker skin, and 20 pounds heavier than she wanted to be. Her mother always scoffed at her daughter when she complained about weight, but for a 16-year old girl being tossed into the passive aggressive girl world of high school, 20 pounds might as well be 100. Another faux pas was her wardrobe. Her clothes were more suited to the California climate and style than central Louisiana. Being a pretty girl offset a multitude of sins, but weight and bad fashion were a major handicap to breaking into the social order.

The high school social hierarchy and romantic pairings were firmly established by junior year. However, Gabby was studious, shy, and an outsider so not an immediate threat to the social order. She did not get invited into the "it" cliques. Her shyness allowed her to forgo the catty girl process of trying to find a place in the pecking order. She devoted a lot of time to studying. She needed excellent grades to get an academic scholarship to college, since her parents could not afford a good school.

Grady was a popular, but atypical jock. He was an outstanding athlete but also a good student. He was an obedient, devoted son who helped his father on their farm, a churchgoer, and kind-hearted. He was sturdy and strong like his father, but he had his mother's kind and gentle disposition, most of the time. Grady was easy-going usually preferring to suppress and bottle up the small things that annoyed him. He considered himself in control, not worrying about the little problems. He was taller than the average high school junior at 6'1" with a muscular physique. Working on a farm all his life made him strong and quick; weightlifting for football made him muscular. He was a handsome boy with thick shoulder length brown hair, bright blue eyes, a unique bright smile, a tanned complexion, and a thick moustache. Not very many boys in high school had full facial hair, but Grady and some of his teammates matured quickly, and the girls took notice. Many girls in school wanted to date him. Grady wanted to date, but he was so shy he used his chores and studies as excuses to avoid spending too much time with anyone steady.

By his junior year Grady was mentally and emotionally maturing. He began dreaming about college, travel, and what he might want to do with his life. His dreams were limited because of his limited experiences. He lived in the same house in the same town where he was born. All he knew was raising cattle and crops, hunting and fishing, and playing sports in Central Louisiana.

A month after Gabby's arrival at Pineville, Grady noticed her around school, keeping to herself. He thought she was cute and liked that she was smart too. True to his friendly nature he found an opportunity to strike up a conversation with her one day in the courtyard. She already knew about Grady and was excited that he would come talk to her, but she was surprised and charmed to find him so shy and awkward. He was nothing like the boys she knew in California who were very bold for their age. She liked that he was caring enough to go out of his comfort zone to make her feel welcomed. At first, she wondered if he was merely being friendly or if he was attracted to her. Neither his shyness, nor the conversation revealed anything about his intentions. With no indications, she assumed he was just being friendly. Their friendship developed over a few weeks, and Grady began including her in his circle of friends. As the school year moved into spring, Gabby found herself on the fringes of the "cool" clique.

Grady's friendship with Gabby remained constant through their junior year. The more they talked, the more she confided in him about personal things. She told him about her dad being in the military, and that while he was in Vietnam she cried herself to sleep many nights wondering if he would ever come home. She shared with him her feelings about how her friends in California were Hispanic, but to people in Pineville she was a foreigner. She also shared with him that school and grades were very important because she had to get a scholarship to be able to go to college.

Grady told her things too about growing up on a farm and working every morning, and about his goal of getting into college on a football scholarship. He told her he didn't know what he wanted in life, but it probably was not the same thing his dad wanted for him. It was never spoken, but he felt like he was supposed to carry on with the farm after his parents were gone. Once in a while he and Gabby talked about what guys and girls wanted from each other, but they always kept it generic to not cross the "friends" line. Gabby never sensed that Grady wanted more from her than friendship, and for now she was happy to be part of his group.

Grady's friends were the popular kids. They were a mixed bag of teammates, girlfriends, and cheerleaders. Their commonalities were sports, farming, or popularity. Most of the girls in the group were the "pretty girls" who wore the latest, most expensive fashion trends, with hair and make-up to match. Some were from well-to-do southern families. A few of the boys were from wealthy families, but the football players usually came from farms where the physical demands turned them into athletic machines. Around school they were likely to be dressed in jeans and tee shirts, cowboy clothes, or farm clothes. The hippie fashions of bell-bottom jeans and flower shirts had not taken hold in Louisiana like they had in much of the country.

Occasionally, some of Grady's friends wondered why he was friends with Gabby. She was not from central Louisiana, she did not wear the right clothes, her family did not have money, she did not look like them, she was not sexy, and she was not a cheerleader. Even though their opinions were irrelevant to him, Grady told them she was groovy, smart, and aware of real-world issues. He liked that she talked with him about important things. She believed that even though 1970 was the beginning of a new decade and men had walked on the moon, it seemed like the world was going back to the dark ages. She introduced Grady to racial and social issues flaring up around the country. She even confided about how her family felt confused because they were something other than black or white. By the time their junior year ended, everyone liked Gabby, and she liked the attention.

The hot Louisiana summers demanded a lot from farmers. The Cordeauxs were up before sunrise and exhausted by suppertime. There was little time for Grady to vacation, go to the lake, or hang out with friends. Gabby and her family vacationed with friends in California for most of July, so she did not see Grady during the summer.

Before anyone realized, summer vacation was over, and it was back to school for their senior year. On the first day back, Grady did a double take when he spotted Gabby in the hallway. She had changed! Her black, silky hair had gotten long, hanging down to the middle of her back. Her jeans and tight top revealed a slimmer, sexier figure. She wore her make-up differently which made her look more exotic. She was not wearing designer clothes, but Gabriella Montoya was suddenly getting noticed. Her friends saw the change over the summer, but so did many other boys outside of her clique.

Although Gabby was still laser-focused on her studies, she decided to try out in mid-August for the cheerleading squad. By first day of school, the cheerleading roster had been posted. After school, all the girls rushed to the coach's office to see if they made the squad. Gabby squealed when she saw her name on the list. It was a *Who's Who* of the "pretty" and "popular" girls. She knew the selection had less to do with athleticism and more with popularity, but who was she to argue the coach's decision. She glowed in the affirmation of knowing she was deep into the cool clique her senior year. As her popularity grew, Grady began to see her in a different way.

They were good friends, but the way she looked made Grady feel like he needed an excuse to get her attention this year. Little did he know her feelings for him were changing too.

Fortunately for Grady, football provided him the excuse he needed to spend time with Gabby. The football coach told Grady he needed to improve his math skills to get a football scholarship. One afternoon, he was poring over a math book in the library and angrily scribbling out of frustration. A voice over his shoulder whispered in his ear that he needed to do the multiplication first. He looked up and Gabby's deep brown eyes were a few inches from his face. "You know how to do this?" he asked.

"I'm okay, I guess. I do know that you should multiply the numbers inside the parentheses first," she replied.

"What about the numbers and the letters?" he asked.

"Well, if you multiply 2 by X you get 2X, and the same with 2Y. You probably know the rest."

She was being kind not to embarrass Grady, but he was too smitten at that moment to notice. After an awkward silence she asked about his summer.

"Worked on the farm," he replied.

She said, "I miss talking with you—over the summer, I mean. Is everything alright?"

Unsure how to respond, he quickly changed the subject. "We will have to figure out our class schedules, so we'll know where we intersect between classes—I mean cross paths. You made cheerleader, right?"

She was surprised. "Yeah, I wanted to do something other than homework this year."

"Yeah, that's cool!" he said. "You're good!"

It took a few seconds for her to figure out what he meant. "Oh, so you've seen me cheer?" she asked coyly.

Grady thought to himself, *this is not last year's Gabby.*

"I can help you with math, if you want?" Gabby wanted an excuse to spend time with him also.

He immediately accepted the offer. "I come to the library most afternoons, or we could study at my house." The moment the words came out of his mouth, he regretted them. He was shy and nervous, and that comment seemed too aggressive.

With a tiny smile she said, "Well, Mr. football captain, let's see how it goes in the library before we decide you need extra-curricular activity at home, okay, Tiger?" She backed him down a bit but left a little room for the possibility. In truth, she liked the idea.

He had gone too far, so he played if off like he meant it in a purely academic way. "I really need help with math to get into college, so any help would be groovy."

She could tell that he picked up on her sense of respectability. He got it! "Okay, we can start tomorrow."

Grady blurted out, "That's great!"

Immediately, "Shhhh!" echoed from the library desk.

The couple giggled under their breath. *Game on!* he thought.

The fall arrived, and the rainy season with it, easing the sweltering Louisiana heat. Farm chores were at their peak. The Cordeaux farm was preparing for the harvest and fixing the livestock stalls for winter. Grady helped when he could, but homework and football took up a lot of his time.

He and Gabby were together every day in school, and as much as they could be on weekends. They were growing closer each day. Most Saturday nights they would go out, despite his exhaustion from farm work. When he took her home after their dates, they would stop along the way and kiss. She enjoyed kissing him, and he liked it even more, but over time she wanted more. He was gentle, respectful, and shy, and she liked that about Grady, up to a point. She liked that he was always a gentleman and never pushed her to go beyond her comfort level during their make out sessions. She also liked that no one teased her in school or made inappropriate comments. It let her know he was not bragging to his buddies. He could keep secrets and respected her.

Now that she had a lot of friends, she was invited to parties. The beer and pot at the parties surprised her because she assumed athletes were more conscientious of their health and bodies. She knew about the drinking and drugs in California high schools, but not here. Surfers and hippies got high, not cowboys and debutantes. Most of the girls did not overindulge, but the guys drank too much and were obnoxious.

When the guys drank, they lost their inhibitions. She was constantly approached by drunk boys asking her out or to dance with her. This kind of attention was new to Gabby, and while she pretended to be annoyed, she secretly felt good about being sought out. Her cheerleading teammates laughed at the boys and told them to get lost.

By mid-October it was generally known she and Grady were a couple. When Grady would see guys flirting with his girlfriend, he got angry. He did not know how many times it happened when he was not around, but he wanted Gabby to be more annoyed than she seemed. This was especially true after football games. Grady was kind most of the time. He was the kind of person that dogs and little children liked. However, when he put on his football gear and walked out onto the field, he was a beast. The team went through rituals in the locker room yelling and hitting each other to raise their levels of aggression and adrenaline. Grady was a standout linebacker because he had the intensity of a wild animal. His adrenaline surges were great for his football prowess, but when the games were over it was difficult to turn it off.

He was falling for Gabby, and he loved the feeling he had when he was with her. It was new for him and nothing in the world was as intoxicating as when they were making out and becoming more intimate each time. He had never been this emotionally attached to a girl before and he did not want to lose the euphoria it brought. So, when he saw another bull in his pasture trying to steal away his girl, the football-induced adrenaline in his bloodstream made him furious. The challenger was not respecting him. He began telling classmates that any challenger better back off or get a beat-down. He also began to fight with Gabby over her lack of rebuffing their advances. Over time, his jealous temper was taking a toll. Grady did not know he might have been genetically predisposed to angry outbursts.

Gabby did not like this side of Grady. When he saw her with other guys, he accused her of encouraging the flirtation. They argued more and more about his jealousy. She felt trapped and angry. "Am I supposed to tell every guy to not talk to me because I'm your girlfriend? It's not fair, Grady. I'm not doing anything wrong! This is who I am, and who I was before we were together! I'm not a rude person. It doesn't mean I want to make out with every guy I talk to! You can't tell me who I can talk to." Gabby would never admit it, but her new popularity and sex appeal made her feel good to be wanted.

After fighting, she would cry and Grady would feel like a jerk. He knew he was wrong, but he could not ignore his fears. He tried explaining that she made him feel better than he had ever felt before, and he loved the attention she gave him. He did not want to lose that intense feeling to another dude more interesting or exciting. They always made up after the fights, but the shiny luster on her perfect guy tarnished a little each time. When she thought about her future, Grady's jealousy did not fit into it.

The Bonfire

One Friday night in November, the Boosters club sponsored the annual bonfire and pep rally. Grady and Gabby arrived happy and hopeful about the upcoming holidays, especially the winter formal. Grady made it official and asked her to be his date. She accepted and was giddy about it. It was her first high school formal. Her parents had not allowed her to go to school dances before this year.

At the bonfire, the couple walked around greeting all their friends. Grady spotted Junior Caville's truck, where they usually hid the beer keg. He asked Gabby if she wanted anything to drink. She asked for a soda and said she was going to find her best friend Melissa.

He said he would come find her. After chugging a few beers, Grady knew he had taken too long and Gabby probably was annoyed so he went into the crowd to find her. When he finally spotted her on the outer edge of the gathering she was talking with a guy.

Unbeknownst to Grady, Gabby was making small talk with Melissa's cousin, Todd, from out of town. Todd's family was visiting, and Melissa invited him to the bonfire thinking he might like to meet her friends. He was a tall, thin good-looking guy with curly blond hair. His jeans, loafers, and button-down shirt under a sweater were dressier than most of the local kids so he stood out. Todd was being very polite, but awkwardly trying to make conversation until Melissa returned.

When Gabby found Melissa in the crowd, they squealed as if they had not seen each other in years. Melissa introduced Gabby to Todd before she began dishing the latest gossip. "Chad is trying to get with Rita tonight!" and "Do you believe what Carrie Anne is wearing, with her boobs hanging out?" Moments later, another cheerleader, Judith, came running over to them. She interrupted, asking Melissa to go to the porta potty with her. Todd felt embarrassed and tried to be invisible.

"C'mon, Gabby, let's go," Melissa said.

"No, Grady is coming to find me anytime now. I'll wait here."

The two girls walked away leaving Gabby standing with Todd. She politely began making small talk. Grady spied her and approached with a beer in one hand and a coke in the other. Her face lit up until she saw the look in Grady's eyes.

Grady was a solid, athletic farm boy; Todd was a tall and slender suburban kid. Grady's beer buzz clouded his judgment and anger rose in him like lava in a volcano.

He got close to Todd's face and stammered, "What the fuck do you think you're doing, preppie?"

Todd was caught completely off guard. He didn't know why this drunken farm boy was in his face. "Do I know you?" Todd asked, trying to act unafraid.

"No, but you seem to want to know my girlfriend!" Grady slurred.

Gabby locked eyes with Grady. She was completely embarrassed and demanded he take her home right now! Grady looked at her and, although tipsy, he recognized the look of desperation in her eyes. He paused for a moment, gained his composure, and much to everyone's surprise, turned to walk away.

Gabby felt immense relief and reached for Grady's hand. Unfortunately, one of those moments happened that cause a lifetime of regret. Todd chose to get in the last word.

"I was here with my cousin, asshole, is that okay with you?"

Gabby squeezed her eyes in anguish knowing the fuse had just been lit. In the blink of an eye, Grady dropped his beer, turned, and sent his fist up between Todd's jawbone and throat. Todd dropped like a sack of rocks, spewing blood out of his mouth. The lightning uppercut knocked Todd's jaws together with such force that his front teeth went flying. The instant swelling knot in his windpipe nearly cut off his breathing.

He tried to yell but the only thing that came out was gurgling through the blood and the damaged windpipe. The bloody mess that was Todd's mouth made onlookers start screaming and crying. The guys standing nearby just looked in disbelief. A few of Grady's football buddies pulled him away.

"Man, you gotta split right now before the cops come."

In less than a few minutes Grady began gaining control of his adrenaline and what had just transpired. He could hear people talking, but in slow motion.

"Yeah, yeah, right," he said. "Where's Gabby?"

"I think she split," a teammate answered. "You need to go now, dude!" They rushed him to his truck.

"I can't leave Gabby!" he yelled.

"Don't worry man, someone will get her home, okay, now go!"

Grady fumbled for his keys and found the ignition. The truck tires chewed up grass and stones as he peeled out off the field, racing to the highway. He was able to stay between the lines on the road, but his awareness of other traffic and road conditions was absent. His mind was in a state of confusion.

When he got home, he stumbled into his room, without waking his parents. He showered, hoping to sober up. *I have to call Gabby!* he thought. He went to the kitchen, reached for the phone on the wall, and began pushing buttons. Just as he was about to push the last number, he realized it was after midnight, and the Montoyas would not appreciate a phone call that late. He hung up immediately and went back to his room.

He thought about going to her house and throwing pebbles at her bedroom window until he got her attention. His buzz was fading, leaving him agitated. He hated not knowing what to do, and kept saying to himself, "What a stupid, stupid thing you did! Why, why did you hit him? Dumbass!"

He was feeling remorseful about hurting Todd. It happened so fast. He did not know that one punch would do so much damage. Grady wished with all his heart he could go back and undo it. The anxiety and remorse were grinding in his brain, churning into deep sadness. He realized too that his jealousy, quick temper, and lack of trust put him on thin ice with Gabby. This was bad, but he did not know how bad it was about to become. He lay on his bed furious with himself, until he finally stopped the bed from spinning and fell asleep.

The pounding on the door woke Grady. He heard his dad stomping down the stairs muttering, "There had better be a dang good reason for someone pounding on my door at 2 a.m." Tom Cordeaux opened the door to two Pineville sheriffs and a lighted squad car in his driveway. "What's happened, Sheriff, is someone hurt?"

"Mr. Cordeaux, is your son, Grady, home? We'd like to ask him a few questions."

Tom said, "He better be up in his room at this hour, Sheriff. What's this all about?"

"Sir, if we could just talk to the boy?"

Grady could hear the sheriffs at the door. A panic attack hit him hard. He could feel it rising, and his chest was going to explode. *Oh shit, oh shit!* He thought to himself over and over again. He put on shorts and sheepishly crept down the stairs.

Tom Cordeaux was a fair man and a loving father, but the look in his eyes was like none Grady had ever seen before. "Boy, do you know why the sheriff is in my door at this hour?" Mr. Cordeaux used a tone Grady had never heard.

"Yes, sir," Grady answered, "I kinda got in a fight tonight, sir."

The sheriff interrupted, "Son, were you at the bonfire tonight?"

"Yes, sir," Grady said quietly."

"Did you assault a boy while you were there?"

"No, sir, it was just a little fight, that's all."

"A little fight? Well, son, your little fight put a young man in the hospital, and he has to have his jaw wired shut!" the sheriff shot back harshly. "Grady, turn around and put your hands behind your back!" He slapped handcuffs on Grady and read him his rights.

Tom Cordeaux, in a state of bewilderment, tried to reason with the sheriff. "Sheriff, you take boys in for getting in a little scuffle these days? What the hell is this?"

"Mr. Cordeaux," the sheriff answered. "It wasn't a scuffle; it was an assault. It was unprovoked, and your son caused a young man to lose his permanent front teeth for the rest of his life. Now we all know that Grady is a football star and the town is proud of him, but he is 18-years old and will be charged as an adult. The victim's parents are pressing charges. We have to take Grady in. You can see him tomorrow, and possibly bring him home if the judge posts bail."

The sheriff walked Grady over to the squad car, pushed his head down, placing him in the back seat. Tom, and now Gloria Cordeaux, stood there in disbelief. This was the first time the police had ever come to the Cordeaux farm. Gloria put on a pot of coffee and the two stayed up the rest of the morning. The incident reminded her of similar times with her brother.

By morning, the news of Grady's arrest had spread all around Pineville. As soon as the jail opened, the Cordeauxs drove there and sat in a small room waiting to see their son. The sheriff got Grady out of the holding cell to meet with his parents.

Tom looked at his son for several minutes before speaking. "Boy, I have been disappointed with you a time or two and angry every now and again, but this is the first time in my life I have ever been ashamed of you!" Tom Cordeaux's voice quivered. "What are your mother and I going to do? We got no money for lawyers! You're 18 now! They want to lock you up! What the hell happened last night? You never lied to me so don't start now, I want to know everything," his dad demanded. Grady's mother just sat there with tears in her eyes and fear in her heart.

"Pa, I was with Gabby last night at this bonfire. I left her for a minute and when I came back some guy was trying to pick her up. I lost it!"

His dad asked, "What do you mean trying to pick her up?

"You know how it is dad." Grady said. "A guy sees a pretty girl and he wants to be with her."

"Were they kissing?" Tom asked.

"No, sir."

"Was he touching her?"

"No, sir."

"Was she touching him?"

"No, sir."

"Well then, what in this world gave you the idea he wanted her? Don't you trust Gabby enough to handle things?"

Grady didn't have an answer. "Pa, it's different these days. He wanted to have sex with my girl!"

"Son, you better listen good. Gabby may be your girlfriend, but she is not your property. And you need to start having trust or you will be alone the rest of your life. Gabby is a nice-looking gal, and guys are going to talk to her; you can't stop it. The only thing that might stop another man is a wedding ring, and even that ain't enough sometimes. A woman will set a man straight if she wants to. You got no right making decisions for her, and I don't ever want to hear about you starting a fight. If you get hit first, I expect you to defend yourself, but you better never start one. Do you hear what I'm telling you?"

"Yes, sir," Grady answered. He expected his father to be much angrier, but the fact that he was not angrier scared Grady even more, because it meant his pa was more afraid than angry.

Tom continued, "I suspect you probably lost that girl. If we can figure a way to get you out of this mess, that's just one problem you will have to deal with. Son, your Ma and I are going to try to get you out of here, alright?"

"Yes, sir." Grady's eyes filled with tears, "Pa, I'm sorry I shamed you. I will work hard from now on, I promise." He hugged his parents as the tears rolled down his face. Their 18-year old son looked more like a boy at that moment.

His mother held onto her son when the sheriff pulled him away to go back into the holding cell. Through her tears she told him she loved him. "We'll do whatever we have to do, son," she said softly.

Coach's Deal

The Cordeauxs walked to their car outside the Sheriff's Department. Coach Cramer was coming up the sidewalk toward them. Tom shook hands with the coach. "I guess bad news travels fast, don't it?"

Coach Cramer answered, "We heard about it this morning. Tom, I try to stick by my boys whenever I can, but I do not condone what Grady did. I am terribly disappointed in him, and he could end up paying dearly for his lack of self-control. But I might have a little good news for you. It's a small world, and Mr. Jackson, our defensive coach knows the Seviers up in Deridder."

Tom interrupted, "That's all well and good coach, but who are the Seviers, and what does this have to do with Grady?"

"Well, sir, Todd Sevier is the boy that Grady beat up last night. Coach Jackson called the Seviers and talked to them about Grady. He explained that Grady is a decent boy from a good family, a farming family. He explained that the boy must have had something wrong with him last night, like a prescription imbalance, associated with his anxiety. He asked if they would reconsider pressing charges.

"Todd's parents are good Baptist folk, and they believe in Christian forgiveness. After a long discussion and a few phone calls from other people testifying on Grady's behalf, they agreed that they would not press charges. They demand, however, that Grady pay for the boy's hospital bills, which could be substantial."

Tom Cordeaux didn't know what to say. He was grateful that his son was not going to have a police record, but he did not want his boy to go unpunished. "Thank you, coach, thank you, beau coup! We deeply appreciate you speaking on our behalf."

"Like I said, I try to look out for my boys. I still will have a 'Come-to-Jesus' meeting with Grady, for sure."

"Yes sir, I hope you do!" Tom Cordeaux said.

Coach Cramer suggested they stick around a little while, "so when the call comes in to drop the charges, Grady can get a ride home."

Within an hour, the Sheriff's Office processed Grady and released him to his parents. The ride back to the Cordeaux farm was one of the longest and quietest rides of Grady's young life. Neither of his parents said a word. Grady knew there were no words that would lessen their disappointment. He was old enough to be a man, but at this moment he felt like a child.

As they got closer to the farm everything seemed to be moving in slow motion. The car pulled up to the house. The Cordeauxs went inside with purposeful steps. His father changed into his work clothes, and his mother made lunch. No words were spoken.

The silence was so intentional Grady could almost see it hanging in the air. He went to his room and lay on the bed all day trying to stop his head from spinning out of control. All the thoughts racing around in his head gave him a pounding headache. Panic and depression fell on him like 400 pounds on the bench press.

He wanted to run somewhere, anywhere but there was nowhere to go. This was a living hell. His mind was spinning out of control. *Why did I do it? Why didn't I just walk away? I didn't have to be jealous of that guy. Gabby had no interest in him. Did she like the attention? Was she trying to sample what else was out there? No! Stop thinking! You are over-analyzing everything like you always do. Let it go! Why was she talking to him? No, no, no, no! Why were the charges dropped? I mean that's what they said in the sheriff's office, right? Maybe the guy is okay? I guess I can go to school on Monday. The fight wasn't during school or on school property. I'm not expelled. I'm sure I'll be able to go to school, right?* Panic overtook him and the minutes turned to hours.

Grady squinted from the morning sun through his window landing on his face. *What time is it,* he wondered? He looked over at the alarm clock. It was 9:30 Sunday morning. His dad did not come and get him to feed the cows. *Oh man, he must be so pissed! Wait! Did they go to church without me?* He walked out of his room in the same clothes he wore in jail. He fell asleep yesterday in those clothes and slept through the night. *I must've been exhausted,* he thought.

He crept down the stairs. The creaking wood sounded his approach but it did not matter. When he came into the kitchen no one was there, the breakfast dishes were done. His mother did not leave breakfast on the table. It was at that moment that Grady truly felt the weight of his mother's disappointment. She had never left without making a plate for him.

His dad always woke him on weekends to help with the chores. It was their special time together. Many times, he went to church with them after breakfast but not today. This morning everything had changed. He felt ashamed, but more than anything, he felt alone.

He poured himself a cup of leftover coffee from the pot and reached for the phone. He was afraid of the response he might get, but he still had to try to talk to Gabby. He dialed her number.

It rang a few times and then he heard a woman's voice with a thick accent. "Hello?"

Grady hesitated, but then asked, "Is Gabriella there?"

Mrs. Montoya hesitated, "Just a moment, please." Grady could faintly hear a discussion in the background. Mrs. Montoya came back on the phone, "Gabriella is not available now, okay?"

Grady expected she would not want to talk to him. "Ma'am, would you please ask her to call Grady? I really need to talk to her."

Mrs. Montoya hung up the phone without acknowledging his request. His heart sank, and that flushed feeling of panic rose within him. The depressed boy, who only a few weeks ago was a big man on campus, went to his room and cried into his pillow. He kept thinking over and over how things went so wrong in the blink of an eye. He felt like his life was over.

The sound of movement in the house awoke Grady from his midday nap. He could hear his parents down the hall, changing out of their church clothes. There was no conversation, only the sound of clothes hangers and closet doors. It was a pattern that developed over twenty years. They would go to the kitchen, Pa would look through the Sunday paper, and Ma would fix lunch and then start getting things ready for supper.

They would sit for a while until Pa decided to tend to a few farm chores. They weren't dyed-in-the-wool Baptists, but they tried to observe Sunday as a day of rest. Sometimes a neighbor would come for visit, but not today. Grady knew that today was going to be a day of little conversation with long blocks of silence. They rarely gave him the silent treatment, but words would not help, not today.

His father may have been a simple farmer, but he was intelligent. His thoughts and feeling ran deep. Grady's mother was the same. She wore more of her feelings on her sleeve than her husband, but she also carried a very worldly wisdom within. He respected his parents immensely, not because he had to, but because he came to know and trust their wisdom. Their advice and warnings bore true more times than he could count.

He did not know if they were aware, but their disappointment was the worst punishment they could hand down. It wore on Grady like heavy chains around his neck. It made him exhausted and unable to think clearly. All he wanted to do was climb back in his bed and hide under the covers. Sleep was a sanctuary from the anxiety.

World in Chaos

By mid-afternoon Grady emerged from his room and came down to the kitchen. He was like a stranger trying to go unnoticed. Without looking up, his mother felt his presence when he entered the kitchen. The sandwich on the plate was the only thing on the table. Perhaps she did not mean it this way, but the single sandwich on an otherwise empty plate was yet another stinging reminder of his exile. He sat and ate in silence, all the while wanting to tell his parents how he regretted his actions the other night, but it was too soon.

Not only was the incident too fresh, but also a part of him doubted his parents could fully understand what it was like to walk in his shoes during these crazy times. The world was in chaos! Communism and democracy were drawing lines in the sand, protests about war and civil rights were happening all over America, hippies gathered in Woodstock, San Francisco, and Washington D.C., young men were being sent to Vietnam, and the Beatles split up after their best albums. Everything was messed up. The only good things that happened were Americans going to the moon and 18-year-olds getting the vote.

He also believed his parents did not know anything about being young and in love. Grady suddenly caught himself. Was he in love with Gabby? He had not thought about it until just that moment. She was his first serious girlfriend. He had dated a few girls before and fantasized about having sex, but he was inexperienced and he worried about getting a girl pregnant. His sexual exploits so far were heavy kissing, getting to second base, and Playboy magazines. His feelings for Gabby were different than just wanting sex though, and they were growing more intense each day. He wondered if she felt it too, or if she still felt that way at all. *Gabby? Oh shit, I should call Gabby*, Grady thought. He went down to the kitchen to make a call. "Hello, is Gabriella there?"

One of her sisters answered the phone. "She is not available."

Grady winced. The answer was too rehearsed. Gabby must have told her sister to say she was not available. "Okay, would you please tell her that Grady called?"

The young voice said, "I think she knows, goodbye." The phone went silent.

He felt nauseated and went back into his room for the remainder of the day dwelling on her rejection. "Please, Lord, please don't let her break up with me," he prayed silently. "Please!" His night was torturous, seemingly lasting forever until he finally fell asleep.

"Grady, let's go." Tom Cordeaux shook his son.

It was time to feed the cows. Grady woke up bewildered. His father was talking to him. Even if it was to do the chores, it felt good. It was Monday and he would see Gabby in school. Grady threw on jeans and a sweatshirt to feed the cows and clean up the barn. After chores, he showered, dressed for school, ate some cereal, and jumped in his truck.

His mother still did not speak to him this morning. It made him sad, but he knew it would take time and small steps. It would get better each day, or so he hoped.

Mr. Kenner

Students were looking and pointing at Grady as soon as he pulled into the high school parking lot. He jumped out of the truck and walked into the building trying to ignore everyone. It was more of the same inside. He got to his locker and he could feel people staring at him, and whispering. Obviously, what happened at the bonfire had spread around town. Everyone was wondering if he got expelled, or if he was going to jail.

A couple of his football buddies walked up behind him. "Hey, dude, we didn't know if you were coming in today. I bet your dad was pissed. Word is out on you, brother. What does Gabby think of all this?"

"Guys, peace! It's cool, relax," Grady said.

He went to his locker waiting for Gabby. They always walked to class together. The bell rang and no Gabby. This was one of the signs he hoped not to see. Gabby's no-show meant either she was not in school, or more likely she did not want to see him. He felt a lump in his throat. The school day was just getting started and it had already turned to shit. He held on to hope, but going to his hardest class, math, with a heavy heart was not helpful.

Grady was having difficulty paying attention to whatever Mr. Kenner was teaching. It did not help matters that Kenner kept looking at Grady during the period. They did not like each other. Mr. Kenner was a small man with a few long hairs combed over his bald head, beady eyes covered by round wire-rimmed glasses, a skinny face and bad teeth. He wore bow ties and plaid shirts. Grady pictured Kenner as the guy in high school 30 years ago who did not get the girl, and likely spent his time in the chess or audio/visual clubs. He definitely did not play sports, and he probably got bullied a lot.

Several times a year Kenner made comments in class about high school athletics doing nothing to expand the mind, and how athletes were not very bright. He never attended sporting events and he did not like athletes, especially those who had poor math skills.

He already had warned Grady several times to drop football and concentrate on math or he would fail. Grady tried hard, but football practice and other homework left little time for extra math homework. In the fall, Grady told Kenner he got a tutor. Kenner asked if his tutor was a girl. When Grady answered yes, Kenner just shook his head.

The bell rang and the students started exiting Kenner's classroom. Mr. Kenner called to Grady, "Mr. Cordeaux, would you stay behind for a moment, please?"

Grady stopped in his tracks, knowing it could not be good. "Yeah?"

Kenner looked at him with a hint of glee in his eyes. "You are barely passing my class, Mr. Cordeaux. I do not see any improvement despite being tutored. Now I hear you assaulted a young man and put him in the hospital. This just reinforces my beliefs. In a few weeks the semester will be over, and I will issue mid-year grades. Yours will not be good. I cannot imagine how your grade in my class, or this most recent unfortunate event, will help your chances of getting into college," he said with sneering satisfaction. "I just thought you should know. Good day."

Grady felt like punching the little geek in his mouth. Kenner loved seeing jocks fail. Grady was everything Kenner could never be, and Kenner despised Grady for it. Now that he had the power, Kenner was going to ruin him.

"What a dick!" Grady muttered aloud as he stormed out of Kenner's classroom. The day was going badly. He needed Gabby.

The anxiety demons teased Grady in the morning, but he was relieved too that the rest of his classes were easier. He loved his next class, philosophy. His teacher, Mrs. Thibodeux, appreciated Grady's participation. He often brought alternative, highly developed opinions into class discussions. His ability to articulate his thoughts was more developed than that of his classmates. One day they were discussing the anti-war protests and John Lennon's "Give Peace a Chance" media event. Most students agreed with Lennon's mantra and supported his ideas. Grady sat quietly listening to the discussion.

Mrs. Thibodeux noticed Grady's expression and asked if he had an opinion. He sat up, paused to gather his thoughts, and asked if Lennon should really be saying, "Give Freedom a Chance."

Grady explained. "If we backed out of the war, the U.S. will be at peace, and the protesters will be satisfied, but South Vietnam will not have peace. The North will force their will upon the South. The only way South Vietnam will not be at war is if they capitulate and submit to communist rule, but that is not synonymous with peace. Plus, they give up freedom. True peace can only happen if North Vietnam stops the invasion and allows the South to be free. So, shouldn't we be asking the communists in the North to give freedom a chance?"

The other students stared at him saying, "Man, you don't get it!"

Mrs. Thibodeux sat silently. She was impressed with Grady's argument, despite her liberal leanings. She asked the class to consider

Grady's point because "it will be the focus discussion next week." The bell rang. Grady packed up and headed into the hallways to find Gabby.

Shot Down

As he spotted her, she tried to disappear into the crowd.

He caught up to her and said, "Hey!"

"Oh, hi," she responded coldly.

"Look Gabby, you dodged my phone calls this weekend and you've avoided me all morning. Can we talk? Please!"

She snapped back, "Talk about what? How you almost killed a guy for standing next to me? How you don't trust me? How insecure you are? Which one Grady? Which one do you want to talk about?" Her voice was rising with each word and students were listening. "Look, I have a lot to think about and it is better if you are not around. Please leave me alone in school. Okay? At least give me that much respect!"

She brushed past him headed down the hall. Grady felt Gabby's verbal axe sticking out of his skull. He tried to act like it did not bother him. He had never seen her like this, a mean, vengeful Gabby. She cut open his soul and didn't even blink. She was a different person.

Grady picked up the tattered remnants of his dignity and headed down the hall. He skipped the next period and went to the cafeteria to lick his wounds in solitude. Other students were in the cafeteria, but they left him alone. He sat quietly in the back of the room, unsure what to do. The fear of Gabby breaking up with him felt like a raging hailstorm in his head. He was having a terrible panic attack, but he knew why.

He also thought her timing was terrible. The holidays were approaching, and he wanted to be with her, especially over the Christmas break. He imagined a picture-perfect Christmas together, holding each other close by a fire in the cool Louisiana night air.

A loud opening of the cafeteria doorway snapped Grady back to reality. A reality where Gabby hated him. The thought brought tears to his eyes. What could he say to her? He would tell her he was sorry. He would tell her he was not himself that night. He would tell her how much he loved her, and he would never mistrust her again. How could he tell her these things if she wouldn't talk to him? He might never get the chance if she cut him loose. "Love sucks!" he muttered to himself.

Just then he heard, "Hey dude, what's up?" Two of his teammates, Mongo and Joe, saw him. "Are you waiting for somebody?" they asked.

"No, it's cool," Grady said. "Sit and eat, I'm hungry." His thoughts about Gabby were gone for the moment. He was with his bros.

The Word Is Out

Mongo and Joe started talking at the same time. "Hey man, we just heard what happened. You and Gabby break up? That is not cool, not cool at all, man. Foxy chicks are messed up! I always say don't be with a cheerleader. They are full of themselves."

They were trying to cheer him up. It wasn't working, even though Grady tried to act cool and play it off. Grady told them, "No guys, it's not like that. She's just a little pissed at me about the other night at the bonfire."

"Oh dude, that's right! We forgot. What happened man? We heard you went to jail."

"You are a hardened criminal now bro, you are in the system!"

Grady quickly tried to clear up the story. "No guys, c'mon, peace out, it's cool. I went to the sheriffs to answer some questions. The charges were dropped because it was just a fight, and that's all."

Mongo and Joe looked at each other. "A fight? A fight? No bro, you laid that dude out with one punch, it wasn't no fight. That was the baddest thing I've ever seen."

"Everybody here, and in Ouachita knows about it. Word got out man. You got a rep."

Grady looked at them in shock. This was the last thing he wanted. He acted badly and was ashamed, so he would rather not have everybody remind him. "People are making too much of it. I wish it would just go away." Grady walked out.

He was worried that if football scouts heard about the fight it would threaten his chances for a scholarship. This was bad! The rest of the day he lumbered around as if in shackles. Students kept asking him about Friday night, and if Gabby broke up with him.

He was suddenly even more popular, but in a notorious way. His body language signaled he did not want to talk about either thing. He acted like it was no big deal. People did not know he was merely going through the motions. Anxiety and depression were hitting him hard, so hard he was barely listening to anything anybody was saying. His expression was unemotional, but inside he was in a downward spiral of doom.

He watched the second hand on the clock tick away until the bell rang. Finally, he darted past his friends to his truck and drove straight home. "Jesus Christ!" he yelled to himself, banging his palm into the steering wheel. He was so glad Monday was over. Hopefully Tuesday would not be as bad. When he arrived home, he went to his room and threw himself on the bed. Anxiety always exhausted him. Sleep was his body's coping mechanism. He slept through to morning.

The remaining school week dragged on, every day an emotional challenge for Grady. Fortunately, the students' interest in him waned by mid-week, thanks to the next item of gossip. He felt relieved to not be the center of attention anymore.

Gabby's knack for avoiding him was hurtful. She did not show up at their usual meeting places, nor did he see her in the halls. She did not phone him, and he thought it best not to phone her. He hoped she did not tell her parents about what happened.

It hurt most when she stopped tutoring him. She knew Grady enjoyed their study time. Instead, she sent an underclassman to go in her place. Grady accepted the underclassman's help, but he was embarrassed, and he knew Gabby chose a younger boy to further punish and embarrass Grady.

Grady withdrew from social interaction and chose to spend more time helping his father around the farm. He was waiting for time to heal the wounds. The Cordeauxs believed in forgiveness, and Mrs. Cordeaux slowly eased back into her routine, including talking to her son without disappointment in her voice.

In a forgiving gesture, she made Grady's favorite meal. During dinner conversation and with mother's insight, she asked Grady, "Shouldn't you be getting things together for the winter formal? You better eat more of that jambalaya. I made that special for you and your pa."

"Yes ma'am," Grady answered.

His mother looked at him, "Yes to which one? Yes, you are preparing for the winter formal, or yes, you will eat more jambalaya?"

Grady reached over and spooned out another helping of jambalaya. He heaped the spicy rice, sausage, and okra onto his plate and gave his mother a big grin. He figured that was his answer. He loved his mother's cooking, especially Cajun.

Tom Cordeaux was busy eating, and unintentionally hearing the conversation. "Well, son, are you taking that little gal to the dance? How come you haven't said too much about her lately? Everything okay?"

"Yes, sir, everything's fine," Grady answered, avoiding eye contact. "We've been so busy studying for finals that I haven't had much time for anything else. In fact, I've been thinking I might not even go to the dance. It seems like a lot of work, especially with the Christmas break coming up and all. Gabby probably feels the same way. I think we've just grown out of it, ya know?"

Try as Grady might to convince them, the Cordeauxs knew that all was not well. Until recently, he phoned Gabby several times a week. He took her on dates and drove her around in his truck. They made plans for the near future. Suddenly, he wasn't sure if he was going to the winter formal? Everything was not fine. Tom and Gloria were certain, however, that Grady did not want his parents involved in his romance life. They let it go, hoping their son would work things out on his own, or learn from his mistakes

Call Me

Grady had low expectations and low morale at the start of the next school week. So, he was pleasantly surprised when he saw Gabby twice in the hallway. The first time he saw her, she smiled; the second time, she asked him to call her. He was excited that she talked to him. His world order was not yet restored, but this was a good start. Maybe she did care after all. Maybe she missed him? Maybe this was going to be a better week!

As Grady drove home from football practice, he felt better. He turned onto the long gravel drive to the farm, and then stopped at the mailbox and picked up the mail like he did every day. Rarely was there any mail for him, so without looking he tossed it onto the truck seat, and then brought it in and laid it on the kitchen counter before rooting through the fridge. He grabbed a snack and changed his clothes to help his dad. The days were getting shorter and Tom Cordeaux was working faster to get things done before sundown. Both men finished up in the barn, cleaned up and came in for supper.

After supper, Tom flipped through the mail. It was the same routine every night, rifling through the mail saying to himself, "junk, junk, trash, bill, junk, and bill." Suddenly, his cadence stopped. The abrupt silence got Grady's and his mother's attentions. Tom stared at an official-looking letter. His eyes rose up to meet his wife's curious look. Trying to not raise concern, he said, "Son, this one is for you."

Grady was surprised because he rarely got mail, and certainly nothing so official looking. He saw on the envelope it was from the United States Selective Service Board. Grady opened it and carefully read the letter. His parents watched him as his eyes moved intently across the page. They also noticed the angst that came over his face.

"What is it, son?" his mother asked.

"I'm not sure," he replied, handing the letter off to his dad. "Pa, does this say I am getting fined and could go to jail for not turning in my draft registration card?"

Tom took the letter. "Let me see, son." He read it and paused, "Grady? Didn't you mail your draft registration card when you turned eighteen?"

Grady looked to the ceiling trying to remember. "I thought I did, right after I signed it." His voice dropped off as he recalled his motions. "I had it in my truck and was going to drop it off in the mailbox."

His father said sternly, "You had thirty days after your birthday to register." Then looking at the letter, he read, "If you do not register within thirty days after your eighteenth birthday you may be charged with a felony."

Gloria Cordeaux yelled out, "Lord, have mercy! Your birthday was almost two months ago. Son, you better find that card! Or you go get another one before the Army comes looking for you!"

Grady jumped up from the table, fumbled through a drawer for a flashlight, and dashed out to his truck. He looked through his schoolwork and papers in the front seat. He rifled through all the newspapers and burger wrappers on the floorboard. He slid the bench seat forward. There it was! His draft registration card had fallen down under the seat on the passenger side. He grabbed the dog-eared card and ran inside. "I found it under my seat! I'm going to the post office to mail it."

Tom nodded, since there was nothing more to say. He figured this kind of oversight happened a lot, and the U.S. Government would not go after every young man whose registration came in two weeks late, especially with so many deliberate draft dodgers out there. It could've easily been lost in the mail.

It Sinks In

Grady returned from the post office feeling exhausted and nervous. He asked his parents if they thought he was in trouble.

Without looking away from the TV to intentionally convey a sense of calm, his father said, "They probably get late registrations all the time. It is why they send out those form-letter reminders."

His dad's response eased Grady. Seeking calm, he joined his parents in front of the TV. He did not watch very often because of chores and homework, but tonight he needed to be close to his parents to calm his nerves.

They turned on the TV as the evening news was almost over. The somber looking anchorman came on and announced, "As we end tonight's broadcast, we bring you the current body count of American G.I.s, South Vietnamese, North Vietnamese, Viet Cong, and civilian casualties for the first two weeks of December. It looks as though President Nixon and American troops in Southeast Asia will not be getting peace on earth this Christmas season. From this station and all our affiliates, good night."

The rest of the evening was blurry. Grady had it stuck in his head that he had just registered for the draft, the same draft that sent young men to Vietnam! At least ten guys from Pineville had been drafted in the last few years. Some of those guys came home in body bags. All the bodies that the newsman spoke about would not be home for Christmas ever again. The weight of his draft registration was coming down on Grady like a thick, black fog. His mother and father felt it too. A sobering quiet hung in the air at the Cordeaux house.

Gabby's Doubt

The next day, a group of girls at Gabby's locker were talking about what everyone was wearing to the winter formal. Pineville High School girls dressed for every event as if it was a debutante ball. Gabby said she did not know if she was going, but she already had her dress just in case. She was angry at Grady for not calling last night. One of the girls spotted Grady walking toward them. Everyone turned to look and the conversation stopped. It was awkward. The girls quickly dispersed, including Gabby.

Grady caught up to her. "Hey, I thought yesterday you were talking to me again?"

"I was," she replied. "But that was before you decided not to call. Grady, I have been going over and over in my mind why I liked you so much. You were so confident and cool around school when we met. It was okay, but it didn't win me over. Then I got to know you a little better and you seemed like you were capable of emotion; a guy who cared about others. I don't know who you were at the bonfire. You became a jealous asshole, who could explode at any time. You almost killed someone for no reason. I've been wondering when you will hit me?"

Grady butted in, "I would never, ever hurt you, I swear!"

She continued. "Of course, you say that now, but you became Mr. Hyde that night. I asked you to call because I was ready to listen to what you have to say. But you didn't call. Is this a game you are playing with me? I don't know Grady; I just don't know."

Gabby's eyes welled up with tears. Grady wanted to comfort her, but he was afraid to touch her and feel the hurt of her pulling away.

He surprised himself by grabbing her hands. "Gabby, please believe me when I tell you I will never be that guy you saw the other night. I don't know what happened. I love you so much and I just got crazy thinking about someone taking you away from me."

"The past week had been a nightmare for me. I haven't dated many girls and I don't know how to handle jealousy, but I will try so much harder if I you let me." He stopped for a moment wanting to say more, but her eyes took on a new look.

Finally, in a whisper she asked, "You love me?" It came out of his mouth before he realized it. He stammered, "Yeah, I mean, I think of you every second, and I'm not okay unless I can talk to you. When

I'm anxious you calm me. I want to be with you and hold you, kiss you, and." He stopped before he said too much.

Her tears stopped and a shy, adoring smile formed on her perfect lips. "If you feel that way, then why didn't you call me last night?"

The bell rang and they were late for class. Grady told her he would meet her in study hall and tell her about last night.

Study Hall

They met in study hall. Grady wanted to hug her and feel that everything would be okay, but Gabby just wanted to hear what he had to say. She spent the last two classes wondering if he realized what she didn't say this morning. She did not know if she loved him. She cared for him very much, but her long-term goal to do her very best in school surpassed everything. She had to get a scholarship. While most students were in study hall for actual studying, Grady and Gabby were there to talk.

"So, why didn't you call me last night?" she asked right away.

"Yeah, there was a couple of things that threw me off track last night, and still have me rattled," he answered. "I have been really down in the dumps since last week. Then, seeing you yesterday gave me hope. When I got home, I did my chores, sat down for dinner, and I was going to call you right after. I was even going over in my head what I wanted to say."

She thought it was cute that he had a script in his mind.

Grady continued, "After supper, my dad was going through the mail and handed me a letter from the draft board." He looked at her with dread. "Gabby, I missed my draft registration! Right after my birthday I had the card in my truck and was going to mail it. I don't remember what happened, but it fell under the seat and I forgot. Now they are telling me I could be fined or go to jail for not registering. I trashed my truck looking for the letter. When I found it, I flew down to the post office to get it in the mail."

He told her how relieved he felt about getting it in the mail, until he got home. "After getting home and relaxing it hit me—I just registered for the Vietnam draft! If I don't get into college, I could be shipped off to Vietnam next summer! We watched the body counts on the news and it messed up my head. I could be one of those bodies! Don't you get it? I'm one of those guys from small town America that gets drafted into the Army and gets killed in Vietnam. I'm really scared Gabby!"

They sat in silence holding hands, and then Gabby spoke. "Look, let's worry about getting you through math so you can get your football scholarship, and all this worrying will be for nothing." She liked that her big, strong boyfriend was feeling vulnerable and insecure. It made her feel needed.

She then said, "I think we should also think about what time you are going to pick me up for the winter formal. I might have a little surprise for you afterward." Gabby not only had forgiven him, she was flirting too, and his fears disappeared. She reached across in front of him to turn his math book page and brushed her boobs across his cheek. Then, she dropped a pencil and bent over so he could get a good view of her perfect butt.

Learning math right now was useless. Her teasing was sending his mind in a very different direction. As study hall ended, Gabby looked at him and whispered in his ear, "Don't make any plans after the dance." He stared at her as she walked off into the mass of students in the hallway. She knew he was watching.

Anticipation

The weekend could not come fast enough. Grady was as happy as a pig in a trough thinking about the dance. Tom and Gloria saw a huge difference in his demeanor and assumed he had stopped worrying about the draft notice. It was good to see him light-hearted again. He was his easy going, witty self. On Thursday night he went to the mall to get a tux for the formal. His mother asked if he wanted her to go along.

"No!" he blurted out in a respectful way. "I think I can handle getting a suit by myself."

Gloria was not surprised, but she had to ask. Pineville, nearby Parish Seat Alexandria, and even the entire Rapides Parish were very small when it came to gossip and rumors. Word would get out quickly if Grady Cordeaux still needed his mother to help buy his clothes.

He parked at Alexandria mall and went into Wellers department store. Wellers was one of the most upscale stores in Alexandria, and Grady knew one of the guys who worked in the men's department.

Maurice Tilden was from Pineville High class of 1968. Grady had met him before and talked about the football program. "Mo" had been one of the best receivers in the school's history. He never made it to college because of his grades. He tried to join the military, but had a heart defect. So, he got a job at Wellers and made the most of a knack for fitting his customers with the right suits. Grady thought Mo was an okay dude.

Mo saw Grady coming into his department. "Hello, my brother, what can I do for you?" He grabbed Grady's hand and they did the latest handshake. "Now, what can I do for you, my man?"

Grady asked what kind of tux a guy should wear for one of those "special" nights.

Mo thought for a moment and told Grady he had something that would make him as hip as a brother can be. He said, "The foxes will be lining up to get down with my man. You will be the baddest cat in the place!"

Grady was not as confident about all that; he just wanted to look good for Gabby.

Mo asked him what color his foxy lady was wearing. Grady shrugged his shoulders, so, Mo pulled out the finest ruffled shirt, plum tuxedo with a plum bowtie, and shiny patent leather shoes. "This is too hip. Can you dig it?" Mo said.

He reminded Grady to get his lady a corsage and bring her to the dance in a style ride. "You dig?"

Grady said, "All I got is my truck."

Maurice drew back a little. "Say what? Well you better get your ride clean and mean if you want to make the scene. You dig where the brother is coming from?"

"Yeah, I got it, Mo. Thanks."

Mo rang up the rental, saying, "It's cool, super fly, and don't forget to cover up, if you know what I mean?"

Grady walked out with his tuxedo over his shoulder. He was pretty sure he knew what Mo meant. On the way home, he stopped at a drugstore to pick up condoms. Up to now he had only tried on condoms; he had never had a reason to use one. He was sexually inexperienced, but he was hoping things might change Saturday night if he got Gabby's drift. It would be okay if she was not ready, but he would be.

Saturday finally arrived. Grady did his chores with so much vigor he finished early. Winter was a little easier because the winter crop and livestock did not need as much tending as the rest of the year. Still, he fed and tended the livestock. When everything was done, he cleaned his truck, especially the back seat. Afterwards he ran in the house to get ready. He was picking up Gabby at 6:30 for dinner, and then going to the dance. His parents were excited for their son, watching him take interest in high school rituals.

The Winter Formal

Grady came down the stairs in his plum-colored tuxedo and his mother gushed about how handsome he looked.

"Tom, grab the Polaroid," she said. As his dad looked for the camera, Grady pleaded with his mom not to make a fuss.

"It is only a dance," he insisted.

Gloria ignored his protests and hugged her son. They took several pictures, each one taking precious minutes to be spit out of the camera, waved vigorously in the air, and watched come to life. Grady looked awkward in the photos. After enough pictures, he kissed his mom and darted out the door.

"Be careful, son!" Tom warned. "Have a good time, but let's not have any drinking or repeats." He winked at Grady. The man-to-man exchange was clear.

"No sir!" Grady assured. He hustled to his truck. Mother came out on the porch holding up a corsage in a clear plastic box. "Shit!" Grady cursed as he threw the truck in park, ran to the porch, grabbed the corsage, kissed his mother again, and was gone.

When he finally arrived at Gabby's house a few minutes late, he leapt out of the truck, nervously smoothed out his tux, and rang the doorbell.

Gabby's little sister opened the door yelling back into the house, "Gabby, your hunk is here." She walked away leaving Grady standing in the doorway.

He could hear an annoyed exchange between Gabby and her sister in the back bedroom. Mr. Montoya came into the living room and greeted his daughter's date. He made small talk with Grady about school and the football season. It was awkward, but Grady was polite and confident as he could be.

Mr. Montoya was not a tall man, but he cast a strikingly solid figure with wide shoulders, thick chest, and a firm handshake. He was a senior enlisted man in the Army and the look on his face, even at home, looked like he did not tolerate bullshit from anyone. His hair was thick, slightly graying and crew cut to precision. His face relaxed in a permanent scowl, like he was constantly disappointed. He wore a short sleeve shirt revealing large bicep muscles and thick forearms of a man who lifted weights. His deep voice was friendly, but his thick brows and focused eyes were intentionally intimidating. Montoya wanted Grady to know that each line on his weathered face came from a life spent protecting his family. The message was clear.

A few months earlier, Gabby had tried to explain to Grady her father's rank. Grady remembered that Mr. Montoya was an E9, the big dog in the enlisted ranks. Mr. Montoya earned a college degree while he was in the Army, which qualified him to become an officer, but he decided to stay enlisted because he loved the work. He also served a few unaccompanied tours overseas. Gabby did not like to talk about those times he was away.

After what seemed like an eternity, Gabby finally appeared in the living room. She was as beautiful as Grady had ever seen! Her long, silk dress accentuated her curves. Grady tried to avert his eyes from the low-cut front. He was certain Mr. Montoya would put him in a chokehold for ogling his daughter. Mr. Montoya seemed a little taken aback at how grown-up his daughter looked. Mrs. Montoya came out of the back room with a camera as Grady was giving Gabby a corsage. Gabby's mother helped pin it on, which provided Grady much needed relief from her father's watchful eyes. The couple posed together for pictures and said their goodbyes.

Grady prayed no one noticed the firmness in his pants pocket. Gabby felt it when he stood behind her pressed together for the photos. She smiled. Ever the gentleman, Grady opened the truck door for his date. Mr. Montoya announced loudly he would be waiting up when she got home. It was a warning meant for Grady. He heard it loud and clear. Off they went.

"Oh wow! That was awkward!" he blurted.

Gabby asked what he and her father talked about. Grady didn't remember anything Mr. Montoya said to him, or what he said back. He was too stunned by how foxy she looked, how perfect her make-up was, and how mature she seemed tonight. He was nervous too. Gabby told him he looked handsome. She asked if he was tense from meeting her father.

"I'm groovy!" Grady answered. "You look so beautiful."

She blushed. She was happy that her effort to look extra special was noticed.

On the way to the Bay View Yacht club for dinner, Grady fumbled through his 8-tracks to find the right music. He thought James Taylor would be a nice touch for his special girl. Gabby sat next to him on the bench seat holding his arm, feeling like a princess. She glanced out the passenger side window and saw her friends in the car next to them at the light. It was then, out of the corner of her eye, she noticed a blanket in the back seat. Her perfectly glossed lips made a gentle smile at the thought of what that blanket might be used for tonight.

The couple arrived at the restaurant. Grady jumped out and opened her door. They walked in and were greeted by the hostess.

Grady said, "A reservation for two under Cordeaux."

"Right this way," the hostess replied.

On the way to their table, several high school friends shouted out, "Grads! Grady dude! Bro!" Gabby smiled at their friends.

All the girls tried to outspend each other on hair, make-up, manicures and dresses. Their hair and make-up were perfect, and their dresses cost small fortunes. It didn't matter if a girl came from a low-income family or old southern money; each one looked amazing.

During dinner, many of the girls went around to other tables talking about what each was wearing, and gossiping. The guys paid little attention to the Pineville High school fashion show. Grady and Gabby finished their meal and chatted with friends. None of her friends knew about Gabby's plans after the dance, and neither she nor Grady brought it up. Truthfully, Grady wondered if he mistook her signals. It didn't matter. He was with the most beautiful girl in school, and that was enough for him.

The two arrived at the dance fashionably late. It was an unspoken rule that only underclassmen, bookworms, and dance committee members arrived on time. The theme of the dance was "We've Only Just Begun." It was cliché, but it fit. A DJ was playing dance tunes as couples mingled with their friends and girls showed off their dresses.

Grady got punch for Gabby and himself, while she gossiped with her friend, Lenora. He returned with the drinks and one of Gabby's favorite songs started playing.

She looked at Grady and squealed, "You know I love this song."

She grabbed his hand and led him to the dance floor. They put their arms around each other and moved slowly to the music. For a few minutes it felt like no one else was in the room. She buried her head in his chest; he buried his face in her hair. She smelled delicious. He loved her so much right now. She could feel his heart beating.

She looked up and they kissed, then she whispered his name and put her face back on his chest. It was perfect.

For a few hours, Grady and Gabby forgot their problems. Everyone was dancing, talking, and laughing. They wanted to remember this night forever.

After a while, Gabby invited Trisha and Vinnie to join them. Trisha was a good friend and an honor student. Everyone assumed she would be the class valedictorian. Vinnie was the state champion wrestler in his weight class as a junior, and was setting new school records as a senior. He was a military brat, like Gabby, and a math genius.

Grady and Vinnie knew each other, but not enough to be friends. In their junior year, Grady tried convincing Vinnie to play football, but Vinnie was committed to wrestling. He was a quiet, pensive type, despite garnering a lot of attention from girls because of his muscular build, long dark hair, blue eyes, and full moustache. Lots of girls liked Vinnie, but he was too focused on wrestling and his studies to be serious about girls right now.

The couples shared stories, laughed together, and danced. Grady noticed Gabby was very friendly with Vinnie, but everyone was friendly and having so much fun he convinced himself it did not mean anything. Besides, Trisha was very foxy herself, and Vinnie was lucky to be her date.

Gabby's Surprise

Gabby kept her eyes on the time during the dance. A slow song came on and she led Grady to the dance floor. They held each other tightly knowing the evening was ticking away. Neither wanted it to end.

They looked into each other's eyes and Grady asked about the surprise she had for him tonight. Was it how beautiful she looked, or how good she felt in his arms? She smiled.

The song ended and she whispered to him. "Why don't we say our good-byes and go someplace quiet?"

Grady's heart jumped into his throat. All he could do was nod and try to keep cool. Gabby excused herself to the ladies' room, and when she returned, the two slyly made their way to the truck. They listened to the radio without conversation on their way to a quiet place to park. Grady thought for a moment and then drove toward his farm, pulling onto a dirt road a quarter mile before the turn to the farmhouse. The dirt road led to a field overlooking a pond at the back of the farm. No one would know they were there. He turned the engine off, but kept the radio on, and put his arm around Gabby. They kissed.

Aware of the time, Gabby asked why he had a blanket in the back seat. He knew he was caught, but mumbled something about having it for emergencies.

She smiled. "Is this an emergency?"

Grady shrugged, not knowing what to say. He did not dare tell her his expectations, for fear of being rejected or being too assuming. Gabby was in the mood. She did not have time for shyness, and he was not getting rejected.

Grady was confused when she got out of the truck, until she opened the back door and climbed in the back seat. She gave him a look and he knew what to do. Without hesitation, he got in the back seat where she unbuttoned his shirt. They resumed kissing. She whispered in his ear to look in her purse. He reached over the front seat, opened her purse, and saw a pair of lace panties. He wondered why she had panties in her purse.

She rolled her eyes, pulled him close and whispered, "I took them off in the ladies' room at school."

Grady's heart beat faster and beads of sweat broke out on his forehead. This was not a panic attack; it was something very different. He was nervous, but in a good way.

Gabby unzipped her dress and pulled it off. She unhooked her bra and pulled Grady toward her. He began caressing and kissing her. She wrapped her legs around his waist and pulled him onto her. He slowly pulled away.

"What are you doing?" she gasped.

"I want to see all of you," he said.

He fumbled with his belt and pants. Naked, he moved his body against hers. She could tell it was his first time.

"What's wrong?" she asked. "Don't you want to make love to me?"

Grady wanted her more than anything, but he was too nervous. His body was not responding the way it should. She kissed him deeply and told him it was okay to be nervous. She loved him so much and wanted him to make love to her. She pulled his hips against hers. It was all he needed.

The two began moving as one. They were clutching each other intensely and passionately. It did not take long for Grady to feel the rush of desire. Gabby knew enough to push him away just in time. They fell into each other, glistening from sweat, kissing in their intense afterglow. Grady's hormones were rushing intensely through his brain and he felt total love for her. Nothing could ever be as perfect as this. As their passions waned, they heard the time on the radio. It was getting late, and for Grady, it was the first time, as a man, to say goodnight.

Scholarships

Grady jumped out of bed Monday morning like it was the first day of school. Tom noticed his son doing the early morning chores with unexplained enthusiasm. He wondered what happened Saturday night, but he did not want to ask. He only hoped that his son had sense enough to stay out of trouble.

Grady was excited to go to school. His dad asked if there was something special going on this week.

"You mean other than the last week before Christmas break?" he replied.

It was a good enough answer for Tom.

It was also the time when athletes began hearing from scouts about scholarship offers, and seniors who had applied for early decision were getting responses from colleges of choice. Grady would hear something soon. He had been unofficially approached last year by LSU, Georgia, Texas A&M, Vanderbilt, and a few smaller schools. The Cordeauxs were confident Grady would get a football scholarship, even if it came from a lesser school. Grady needed it since the Cordeauxs did not have enough money to pay for tuition. Tom Cordeaux might have wanted his son to run the farm, but many farmers had college degrees in agriculture and did very well. He wanted the best for his son and a college education would open doors for Grady if he decided against farming.

Grady arrived at school and raced to his locker to see Gabby. He felt like hugging her, kissing her, and telling her how much he loved Saturday night. He did not see her on Sunday, choosing instead to give her alone time for church and family. She showed up at his locker with a look that told him everything he needed to know. It assured him that the other night was real, and that she loved him. They kissed briefly and then continued through their weekly schedules as if nothing had changed. The difference was now they shared a deeply private secret.

The Math Mid-Term

Grady had worked diligently all semester to bring up his math grade. His mid-term exam was first thing Friday morning, and then he had a few easy classes until winter break. He went into the exam feeling confident. Gabby wanted him to get a football scholarship, maybe even at Mississippi.

After math class, she waited at their usual spot. He arrived and she asked, "Well, how did you do?"

He had a disappointed look on his face.

"Oh no!" she winced. "What did we not cover?"

His expression slowly turned into his big crazy smirk with the dimpled side.

"Grady Cordeaux!" she yelled. "How could you give me a heart attack like that?"

He answered, "I was far out and groovy, baby. I think I am a math machine."

"Oh, honey, I'm so happy for you! Now there is nothing keeping you from going to college."

He hugged her and whispered, "I love you for helping me with this."

He told her the only thing that bothered him was what Mr. Kenner said when he turned in his exam. Grady laid his exam on the pile and smiled sarcastically at Kenner.

Kenner said, "It takes more than a passing grade, Mr. Cordeaux. It takes character."

He was not threatening, but he was not fatherly either. Grady did not know how to interpret it, but it appeared to be the only dark spot on an otherwise promising holiday.

Winter Break

The last bell signaled the beginning of winter break. Underclassmen ran to the buses, seniors headed to their vehicles in the parking lot. Most students still had Christmas shopping to do, or they wanted to hang out at the mall. Grady and Gabby jumped in his truck and headed for downtown Alexandria. Many of their friends were going to the mall, too.

The storefronts were dressed up in holiday decorations. Grady and Gabby walked through the mall looking at clothes, shoes, make-up, and records. Grady asked what she would like for Christmas. She just smiled and told him he did not have to get her anything. She knew his job on the farm was not a paying job, other than allowance. He was not like some other students who worked in the mall over the holidays for minimum wage. Grady earned less than that, and she did not want him spending his hard-earned money on her. She did not work, either.

He insisted that she give him ideas because he wanted to give her something special. As they walked through the stores, she spotted a beautiful scarf on a mannequin.

"I think this is really pretty!" she said.

"C'mon, Gabby! Don't be a square, I'm not going to give you a scarf, or a knit cap, or a toothbrush for Christmas. Never mind, I will figure something out."

He already knew he wanted to give her a ring, but he needed her ring size. He would ask one of her sisters. They continued shopping, passing jewelry stores, but Gabby showed no interest.

They went to the food court to meet their friends. Everyone sat around, talking about Christmas, describing family holiday rituals, sharing junk food, and spending good time together. Grady and Gabby sat next to each other in a booth. For a moment during the conversations, they looked at each other, and the rest of the world melted away. Separately and together in that moment they shared a feeling of love for each other, their families, and their friends. Their futures were unwritten and uncertain, but today was a day to appreciate.

After a while it was getting late and the gang decided to disperse. Grady drove Gabby home and said good night. There was no sorrow nor anxiety to deal with tonight. For the first time, it felt like Christmas.

On his drive home, he reflected on the events of the past two months. He had deep remorse about a few things, but also had profound satisfaction too. He had suffered a few weeks of getting through edgy tension one minute at a time, but time helped smooth it out. He wished he could hold on to this euphoric feeling. He wished it would vanquish that ever-present nagging that some thing or event might send him down the dark, lonely road of depression. He was beginning to understand that the darkness was always lurking just under a thin veneer.

He got home and his mother was decorating the Christmas tree. It was late, but she wanted to finish before bed. The Cordeaux house was looking like Christmas. She asked Grady about his night, and if the tree looked alright. The tree looked beautiful. Once again she had outdone herself. Grady appreciated the things his mother did to make their home a warm, inviting place. He said good night and started up to his room. Halfway up the stairs he stopped, looked down at his mother, and asked her if she had any idea about girls' ring sizes. It took a few seconds for his question to register in her mind.

She looked up. "Grady, why are you asking about ring sizes? Is there something we should know?" Her tone conveyed concern.

He looked at her and laughed. "No, ma! There is no ulterior motive or life-altering reason. Geez, you think I'm ready to get married? I want to buy Gabby a ring for Christmas, just a steady ring, not an engagement ring. Don't you know me at all? Geez!" He mocked her all the way up to his room.

The next morning, Grady and his father came in from the barn to the smell of sausage, eggs, biscuits, gravy, and coffee. The smell of a country breakfast, and the oak logs burning in the fireplace, put everyone in good spirits. It was the holidays.

They sat down to breakfast and Gloria asked Grady about his plans for the day. Before he could answer he needed to know if there were any more chores. Tom was scanning the newspaper, and without looking up, the farmer in him reminded them there was always something that needed doing. He stopped, and then added there was nothing that could not wait.

Grady told his mother he was going shopping. She winked at him and said he should be looking for a size seven. She did not know Gabby's ring size, but she did know that high school girls likely had a size seven ring finger. It was a good size to start and if it needed adjustment the jeweler could do it after Christmas. Grady did not say anything after that, hoping his dad was not paying attention.

After breakfast, Grady cleaned up and headed out. On his way out the door his mother warned him to be careful to get the right ring, and not one that conveys the wrong message. Grady was not worried, but he assured her everything would be groovy.

Gabby's Gift

The mall was so crowded it was difficult to find a parking spot. It was a beautiful day, despite the low temperature, and throngs of people rushed out to do their last-minute Christmas shopping. Grady had already bought presents for his parents, so today was all about Gabby. He was looking for a ring but did not know what kind. After the third jewelry store, he began to understand his mother's concern. He learned from jewelers that rings with fake gems were worn as accessories, rings with real gems were worn at formal events, birthstones meant more when given as a gift, and diamonds were the most expensive. Considerations like color, clarity, carat, silver, gold, or platinum were very confusing, to say the least.

By the fourth store, Grady decided maybe he should tell the salesperson why he wanted a ring. He would also give Gabby's birth month, her ring size, and how much he had to spend, hoping a good salesperson would make the right selection for him. Finally, after looking at 15 rings he decided on the perfect one. It was an aquamarine stone surrounded by small diamonds on a gold band. He wanted the ring to say, "I love you, and be true to me." He spent more money on it than he should have, but Gabby would not wear something cheap. The store clerk gift-wrapped it, and Grady walked out feeling accomplished.

His friends were at the food court. "Hey, Grady man, peace! What are you up to?" They called him to join them. "What's in the little bag, dude?" One of the guys asked.

Grady sheepishly replied, "Oh, nothing, you know, just doing a little last-minute shopping."

Jonesey asked, "Hey, Grady, you know Vinnie?"

Grady nodded. "Vinnie Carmone? Yeah, I know him, he's a good guy."

Jonesey replied, "Yeah, he's groovy, but he's also a monster on the mats, you dig. Well, we hear that they already told him he's got a full ride to Mississippi State. I also heard that a couple of the guys on the football team got calls from scouts, too. You heard from anybody yet?"

Grady smiled, and acted like he was not surprised. "Guys, the scouts can say all they want, but it doesn't matter until spring when they make offers and accept letters of intent, so relax!" He pretended to be unaffected by what he had just heard, although it troubled him that no school had contacted him yet.

The guys figured if anyone would know how it worked, it would be Grady, so they dropped it. Grady hung out with the group for an hour until it was time to get home for supper. He also had plans to be with Gabby tonight. He said his goodbyes and rushed home so he could get ready for his foxy lady. His expectations were high.

All dressed and groomed, he picked up Gabby, asking her what she wanted to do tonight. He already had something in mind but did not want her to think sex was the only thing on his mind. He did not know if girls thought about sex as much as guys did. Still, he was certain Gabby would not jump in the back seat right away. She was too classy even if she thought about it. He respected her, and his love for her was not just about sex. He took pleasure in getting to know more about her each time they were together, and he liked being with her, especially if it led to sex.

Gabby thought about what she wanted to do, and then she smiled, "Why don't you get some beer and we can go to our parking spot."

Grady stomped on the accelerator. He quickly bought a six-pack and headed to the pond on the back of the Cordeaux farm. He was pleasantly surprised this was her choice. He also realized he truly did not know anything about women. For now, though, doubt and gamesmanship were gone. They got in the back seat.

Christmas Eve

Grady and Gabby made plans to be together Christmas Eve to exchange gifts. When Grady picked her up, Mr. Montoya reminded his daughter to be home early to go to midnight Mass. Grady was a Baptist and did not know much about Catholic services, but he figured it meant a lot to the Montoyas. Gabby looked gorgeous. She looked good all the time to Grady, but when she was dressed up, she was sexy, elegant and mature. Gabby appreciated him dressing up too. He wore slacks, a pressed button-down shirt, and a blazer.

Alone in the truck, they chatted about Christmas plans, and family gift expectations. Neither one said anything about gifts for each other. This was their first gift-giving event and the stakes were high. Gabby smiled when they pulled in to Tunk's Steak and Seafood House. It was a local favorite restaurant overlooking a lake on the outskirts of Alexandria. The maître d' sat them at a table overlooking the lake. The moon's reflection lit the surface of the water and outlined the cypress trees in the water. A winter chill was in the air. It was perfect.

The couple looked over the menu and ordered their food. Gabby continued talking about the upcoming holiday family events, family gatherings, and past Christmases. Grady did not have much to contribute to the conversation as an only child with few relatives. However, he envied and enjoyed Gabby's stories about large family holiday traditions.

After dinner they sat nervously enjoying each other's company, holding hands across the table. Grady signaled for the check. He had been nervous the whole evening but figured it was time to give Gabby her gift. As he reached into his pocket he said, "Oh, and I have a little something I want to give you for Christmas."

Before he could retrieve it, she stopped him. "Grady, why don't we do this in private. We can go somewhere."

He thought about it for a moment, and agreed, but reminded her they did not have a lot of time.

She smiled at him saying, "I don't mean at your farm pond, superman. That's not the kind of gift I have for you. I mean, I do, but not tonight, not in these clothes. I just want to be alone with you."

Grady thought it was a good idea. He paid the bill and they left to find a private place to park. They came upon a parking lot near a lighted neighborhood playground. He turned off the truck. She moved next to him to kiss him and cuddle in his arms. They gently separated after a few minutes of kissing.

Gabby reached into her purse and pulled out a small, beautifully wrapped box. She handed it to Grady. "I didn't know what to get you, but I thought you might like this."

He assured her, as he unwrapped the box, it would be perfect no matter what, because it was from her. He recognized the box and looked at her with awe when he saw the beautiful pocketknife inside. He pulled it from the perfectly fitted case and saw his name engraved on the gold-plated side. The other side read, "Yours eternally, Gabby." He examined it for a few minutes telling her he would keep it with him forever and think of her always. "Thank you so much." He leaned over and kissed her.

He reached into his pocket and pulled out a small, silver wrapped box.

Gabby drew a sudden breath, "Oh Grady!" She knew it was jewelry, most likely a ring, but she felt sudden panic. Many thoughts raced through her mind about the future, her college plans.

Grady was confused by her reaction. "Open it," he insisted.

She nervously unwrapped the box and lifted the lid. "Oh, Grady! It's so beautiful!" Her eyes teared up. She put the ring on and it fit perfectly. "It's my birthstone. It's so beautiful! Darling, I love it! Thank you so much."

Grady smiled, but lots of doubts were banging around in his head.

"Gabby," he said softly, clearing his throat. "I wanted to get you something that would be special, something you could look at and think of me. I know our lives could be heading in different directions soon, but I hope that our love can keep us together, even if we are apart. I want you to be mine. I'm not saying we should get married or anything like that, not now, but maybe one day."

She moved her face close to his and looked into his eyes. "Honey, we have a lot of life ahead of us. No one knows what tomorrow will bring, so let's enjoy what we have today and not worry about tomorrow. I love you, and I love this ring. It looks expensive!"

The only thing he heard was "I love you" and it was enough for now. He drove her home and walked her to the door. They kissed, wished each other a merry Christmas and said goodnight. On the drive home, Grady thought about her reaction before opening the ring, then he replayed in his mind what she said. He could not remember her exact words, but something bothered him. He wanted to believe she loved him as much as he loved her, but it did not seem so. He rationalized away his doubt because he wanted it to not be so, and because he had so little experience in relationships. Still, it left him unsatisfied.

His mother and father were sitting in the family room when he walked in. He joined them for Christmas treats and eggnog. It was a quiet Christmas Eve at the Cordeaux farm.

Winter Break on the Farm

The holiday break was exactly what Grady needed to reflect deeply on the life-changing events he had experienced the past few months. Engulfed in the holiday spirit and warmed by the simplicity of the farm, the Cordeauxs enjoyed the holidays by visiting friends and neighbors, savoring holiday feasts, relaxing by the hearth, and going to church. Scheduled time off, however, was only for organized institutions; few things on a farm ever took a break. The Cordeaux farm grew winter wheat for their livestock. The wheat required little maintenance, but the livestock was a full-time job, especially in the foulest winter weather. If foul weather hit, goats instinctively went into the deepest, thickest brush to birth their kids. The cows grazed in the fields closest to the barn so they were much easier to care for, but still needed to be milked daily. Winter was also a time to do maintenance on equipment and machinery.

Tom enjoyed having Grady at home to help with the farm. The two men worked together usually without much talk. After so many years, both men knew what needed to be done and how to do it. This time, however, Tom looked at his son by his side and wondered if it was the last year they would ever work closely together. He wondered how Grady would do in college, living on his own, being on the college football team where football is the priority, and would he ever return to Pineville? Grady, at 18-years-old, was legally a man, but Tom had seen how life on the farm turned Grady into a man long before his eighteenth birthday. His son knew real responsibility before he was a teenager. Grady was driving a five-ton tractor years before ever driving a car, he could birth or butcher livestock before other kids reached puberty, and he knew when to harvest crops before his peers could mow the lawn. Tom thought back on how hard he had been on Grady teaching him to be a man. Tom understood that his son was going to make mistakes, but he believed he taught Grady to learn from those mistakes. Tom was a man of few words, but he loved his boy, and he was damn proud of the man Grady had become.

An Intimate Party

Gloria Cordeaux answered the phone as she was preparing lunch for her men. Gabby was calling. Gloria cheerfully greeted Gabby, asked her about her Christmas, and said she would tell Grady when he came in. Shortly after, Tom and Grady came in from the barn to take a lunch break, and Gloria passed on the message to her son. Grady tried to hide his feelings so as not to draw too much attention, but the growing smile on his face was enough to catch even his father's eye. He waited after lunch for his parents to leave the kitchen before returning her call. Gabby answered and his heartbeat quickened. They exchanged greetings, and Gabby got right to the point. She wanted Grady to pick her up at the mall and take her to Lisa Graves' New Year's Eve party. Grady agreed without hesitation.

At the end of the day, the two men headed up to the house for supper. Grady ate quickly, got cleaned up and asked his folks if it was okay if he went to a New Year's Eve party. His dad said they did not mind, but he advised his son not to drive if he would be drinking. He would prefer Grady sleep it off at the party rather than getting a DUI or causing an accident. Tom also reminded him there would be plenty of police on the roads, and to be careful. Tom finished by saying, "Call us and let us know you are okay." Grady nodded.

Grady arrived at the mall excited and found Gabby with friends in the food court. She looked good in her jeans and tight sweater, but it was not what he thought she would wear to a New Year's Eve party. The group got up just after Grady arrived. He did not know they were waiting on him. The other girls went to their cars, Grady and Gabby went to his truck. He told Gabby he did not know where Lisa lived, so she directed him to the Grantville neighborhood, which was one of the wealthier neighborhoods in Pineville.

On the ride over, Gabby's unusual quiet aroused Grady's suspicions. He asked what was going on? Smiling, she confessed that it was not exactly a party. Lisa and she had talked earlier in the week and planned a sleepover on New Year's Eve. Lisa's parents were going out of town and they thought it was a great idea for Lisa to have her girlfriends over on New Year's Eve to keep her company. Gabby stopped talking. Grady liked the idea of a small get-together, but he was still confused. Still smiling like the cat that ate the canary, Gabby then confessed that the girlfriends conspired to invite their boyfriends. Lisa invited Bo, Trisha invited Vinnie, and Gabby invited him. He listened intently to her plan, and his heartbeat started pounding out loud. He did not believe what he was hearing!

Gabby jumped out of the truck in front of Lisa's house and instructed Grady to park down the street, out of sight, and then come around to the back of the house. He looked at her quizzically.

She explained, "We don't want any of Lisa's neighbors to get suspicious, so we can't have a bunch of pick-ups in front of the house while her parents are gone!"

Ahh, he got it! As he looked for a hiding place to park down the road, he wondered who he just dropped off and what had she done with Gabby. She looked and felt like Gabby, but the girl in his truck was a first-class conspirator. He was learning things about Gabby Montoya every day. This was a new side of her, and he liked it.

Everyone had arrived. It did not take long for the guys to find the beer, while the girls were making mixed drinks in the kitchen. Lisa turned on the record player. All three couples, with drinks in hand, made their way into the living room and danced. The lights were low, and the music was slow. Grady was nervous, partly because Gabby had lied to her parents, but also because he was unsure how to proceed. He knew what he wanted to do, but not in front of two other couples.

The plan became clear when Lisa and Bo quietly snuck off to her bedroom. Eventually, Trisha and Vinnie went into the den, and Gabby led Grady into an empty bedroom.

Once in the bedroom, she locked the door and pushed Grady backwards onto the bed. She crawled on top of him and started kissing. Grady responded immediately. His heart was pounding. After he was completely aroused, she got up and told him she would be back in three minutes. With a sly grin, she pointed to the door, saying there was a bathroom down the hall and he might want to get ready for bed. Before she closed the door to her bathroom, Grady was up and scrambling down the hall. He already showered before going out tonight, but he washed his face and finger-brushed his teeth. Next, he found a phone in another bedroom and called his dad to let him know he was staying the night.

His father heard something in his son's voice. He asked Grady why he was talking so quietly, and if everything was really okay.

"You asked me to call so you wouldn't worry. I'm calling. Everything is cool and I'm just playing it safe."

"Alright son, thanks for calling." Tom was not completely satisfied, but he felt like his son was safe. Tom figured out what might be happening, but he was not about to reveal his son's intentions to Gloria. He told her Grady was safe.

Grady came back to the bedroom to find Gabby lying on the bed in lingerie. The room was dimly lit but it was enough for Grady to see all of her. It was the sexiest thing he had ever seen. His nerves were on high alert with anticipation. He ripped off his clothes and lay next to her. While they were kissing, she reached over and turned on the radio. Much to Grady's amazement, she stood up on the bed and began dancing in a way he had never seen before. Her moves were making him more excited than ever.

She asked, "Do you like it?"

He could not speak, so he nodded. She slowly moved onto him, and for the next hour, led Grady through lovemaking like he never imagined. She did things he liked, and she told him what she liked. School was in session. Afterward, they fell asleep in each other's arms.

Lisa shook Gabby awake the next morning before daylight, whispering that the guys had to go. It was not quite 6 a.m. and chilly outside when all three guys slipped out the back in the darkness. Grady made sure Gabby had a ride home before he left. Lisa would take her home later. Her parents would see that she had been with Lisa.

All the way home Grady wondered if last night was a dream. It was so awesome. He spent the night with his girlfriend! Still in the afterglow, he could not stop thinking about it. He wondered if Gabby's pleasure has equaled his own.

All through the morning he could not get last night out of his mind. The more he analyzed it, the more he questioned things. It was his curse. He mostly wondered how she seemed to have so much experience. He was a virgin, but he did not know if she was, and he did not want to ask. Did she read books, did her friends tell her things, or did she have experience? Doubts kept running through his mind and it began to cast a shadow on last night. He tried to wipe it out of his mind. The smell of freshly brewed coffee at home took his mind off his doubts for a few moments. His dad was already done with the livestock for the morning, so Grady went up to his room and fell asleep. Sunday was a blur. Grady did all his chores with his dad, but he was operating on muscle memory. Tom recognized that Grady was in a funk, but he was not working with dangerous machinery, so Tom just assumed his son was dead tired from staying up too late.

Back to School

The holiday break was over and it was back to school for the final semester of Grady's entire secondary education. It was difficult to imagine that graduation was almost here. Just a few months from now several important life decisions would be made. The biggest decision was where he would go to college. The scouts would be calling soon.

Grady met Gabby at her locker and walked her to class. The way they looked at each other was different than before. Their eyes betrayed their New Year's Eve secret. Grady told her it was the best night of his life. Gabby smiled and let him know more nights like that were in his future. He loved her so much and was annoyed for having nagging insecurities.

He thought about his doubts. She was with him, she wore his ring, she made love to him, what more proof did he need? Maybe it was her hesitation when he would tell her he loved her? Maybe it was her sexual experience? Maybe it was how she liked attention from other boys? Grady knew he worried too much, and then had to remind himself it was all the demons in his head. Why did he think so much? He had a gorgeous girlfriend, a great home, a great prospect for the future, a truck, and he was doing well in school, even math. Still, he always felt like he was waiting for the other shoe to drop.

Day after day, Grady's early mornings and late afternoons were becoming increasingly filled with farm chores. The arrival of spring was the most demanding time on the farm. They were preparing for planting and tending to newly arrived livestock. Despite the workload, Grady loved this time of year. Everything was renewed and the sleepiness of winter was over. He could smell fresh grass, blooms, and pollen. He also enjoyed more sunlight. Spring was time for baseball too.

Grady was as good in baseball as he was in football and today was Pineville's baseball tryouts. He was not worried about making the team since he had been the starting catcher for three years and was named to the Tri-Parish All-Star team last year. He enjoyed tryouts anyway, because he liked to see the new talent. For one more sport season, he reminded his dad he would be home a few hours late because of practice. Tom already anticipated losing his farmhand to baseball, which is why he had been pushing so hard the past few weeks.

Mississippi

He met Gabby at her locker as usual. His feelings were overwhelming. He loved being with her, and he loved making love to her. They were two healthy young adults at their sexual awakening. The physical chemistry between them was obvious to their friends. This morning, however, her joy was less enthusiastic.

"What's the matter?" he asked gently. "Did something happen at home?"

She told him it was nothing.

Grady asked again. "Are you sure? Did I do something wrong?"

Gabby would not make eye contact with Grady. She said it was nothing, and then said they better hurry to class. Grady thought if it were bad, she would tell him, so he let it go. He reminded her that today was baseball tryouts. She nodded dismissively.

During lunch break they went out to the bleachers to enjoy the springtime warmth and be away from the crowd. Finally, Gabby told him what was bothering her. She received a package on Saturday from Mississippi State. She applied for early acceptance because of their science programs.

"Grady, they accepted me." Her eyes filled with tears.

Excitedly he said, "That's so cool! You're in. Far out!" He was excited for her, but she sat there sulking.

She wiped her eyes. "I know, I know, really groovy, right?"

Grady hugged her.

She pulled away and looked in his eyes. "Everything is happening so fast. All day yesterday and today I kept thinking after this summer, our time will be over."

Grady asked, "What do you mean? You cannot know what the future holds. I could get recruited by Mississippi State or a nearby school. We could have a long-distance relationship. Anything could happen!" He was genuinely happy for her but had not really thought about what she was saying, and his pep talk did not cheer her up. They sat quietly for a while, each in their own thoughts, until it was time to go back inside.

After school, Grady went to baseball tryouts. The coach told him to suit up and catch for him as he worked the infield. Several guys were trying out for each position. First base and third base were locked up by returning seniors. Grady felt sorry for new guys trying out at those positions, but shortstop and second base were wide open.

Coach Johnson was working with the pitchers and catchers. Grady saw some of the players trying out for catcher pointing at him and talking. They were wondering why he was catching for the head coach at home plate. They would know soon enough. Second-string catcher was a good position anyway, in case Grady got hurt, and they would be starting catcher next year. Grady noticed a few new guys who had skills, and thought Pineville should have another winning season.

After practice the coach asked Grady to come to his office. He walked in when all three coaches were talking about the tryouts. Coach Finnick informed Grady he was selected as team captain. He then asked Grady to share his thoughts about the tryouts; who had a good tryout and who should be given a second look. Grady hid his elation, but he was beside himself with pride to be in the coaches' inner circle. He had an opinion about each player, good and bad. The coaches agreed on every account and appreciated his insight. He walked out of the office and closed the door. Looking back, the coaches were nodding and closing their books. Grady was excited to get home and tell his dad.

The Draft Letter

Grady came home excited to tell his parents about what happened after practice. Tom and Gloria were sitting at the table quietly eating dinner. Grady's place was set. His mom asked him to wash up and come to dinner.

"Sure, Mom. I have something to tell you about baseball tryouts." When he sat down it was silent. He fixed his plate, prayed, and started eating. After a few moments his dad mentioned to Grady he got a letter from the Selective Service.

"Should I open it now?" Grady asked.

Tom told him to finish his supper. Tom and Gloria exchanged looks of concern.

Tom asked his son, "So, what happened at the tryouts?" Grady forgot about the letter and told them what happened, and how proud he felt when the coaches invited him in. Tom told him it meant he has earned the coaches' trust and should always strive to keep it.

The rest of dinner conversation centered on tryouts and the day's activities, which lightened the mood in the Cordeaux kitchen at least for an hour or so. After dinner, everyone cleared the table and Gloria finished the dishes. They went into the living room to watch television, but more importantly, to open the letter. Grady opened it and read it to himself. When he finished, he could see his parents were waiting.

He told them. "It says that they received my registration for the draft, and they thanked me. It also explains how a new system, the draft lottery, will work and that everyone must comply with the instructions of the Selective Service System in accordance with federal law. If I am selected in June, I will be notified by mail where and when to report to my draft board. It also explains the different categories of people and reasons for deferment, including health, religious convictions, and college, as decided by the draft board. I have nothing to worry about because by that time I will be on my way to whatever college offers me a football scholarship." Grady got up, gave them a peace sign, and went to his room to do homework. Tom and Gloria sighed relief.

By mid-March, the days seemed to be flying by. Grady helped his dad as much as he could, but with homework, baseball, Gabby, prom, trying to improve his grades, and waiting for the scouts' phone calls, he stayed too busy to help.

The biggest concern for Grady was that several of his football teammates had already been recruited. A few had even signed letters of intent. He expected that Josh Hamler and Steve Griffin would have been offered scholarships early in the process, so they were no surprise. He also figured that he and Roger Delion would be the first two on defense to sign. Last week, Roger accepted an offer from Georgia Tech. Grady heard that other lesser players were being contacted as well. He knew too that Vinnie accepted a wrestling scholarship at Mississippi State.

By mid-April, his worry was making him sick. Maybe he had missed a call, or they did not know how to get in touch with him. Grady decided to meet with Coach Cramer and find out if he had heard anything.

Grady poked his head into Coach Cramer's last period class. All the sophomores got quiet when Grady entered the room. Cramer told Grady to meet him in his office after school. He nodded and closed the door, but something about Cramer's response did not sit well with Grady. He thought about it and slowly began to sweat. Why did the coach not seem surprised to see me? Why did he have a look of dread? Grady's mind began to spiral up until a gentle touch on his arm brought him back to the moment. Gabby found him wandering in the hall while his mind was off in space. Grady told her he was going to meet with the coach to find out if he knew any reason why he had not heard from any schools. She hugged his arm and told him to not worry so much. "Call me tonight, okay?"

Coach's Admission

Coach Cramer spotted Grady through his office window. "C'mon in, son," Coach yelled to him. "What can I do for you?"

Grady was surprised by the question. He got straight to the point by telling the coach he has not had a phone call, a letter, or anything from football scouts, even though most of the top senior players already had signed letters of intent. He asked the coach if he knew anything about it. Coach Cramer drew a long breath and rubbed his eyebrows. His awkwardness and avoidance were obvious.

He told Grady to shut the door. "Son, I don't know what to say."

Grady was confused. "What do you mean, Coach? What do you have to say?" Grady could feel his anxiety rising.

Cramer hesitated. "Grady, I have been making phone calls on your behalf for the past month after one of the scouts mentioned something to me. Son, I'm going to tell you something in confidence and you are not going to like it, but I need you to remain calm, okay?"

"Yes, sir," Grady choked back.

Cramer continued. "LSU was interested in you, but they received a call from someone at this school who told them bad things. You know we tried to keep your bonfire incident last fall quiet, don't ya? Well it seems someone told a few football scouts that you are a real hothead and troublemaker with a police record who put a boy in the hospital. These people all talk to one another. College football programs deal with bad behavior from their star players, but there ain't too many that want a troublemaker right out of high school."

Grady sat there trying hard to hold back tears. He put his hands over his face to hide his rage. "Who told the scouts, Coach? Who made sure they knew about the bonfire? I want to know!" Grady's voice was filled with anger.

Coach Cramer shook his head saying he did not know. He said it would be better if Grady did not know either because no good could come out of it.

Grady looked up with tears in his eyes. "How can one person have the power to destroy my life? Why would someone want to do that to me? My life is shit now! My parents can't afford college!" He began yelling, "I could get drafted into the Army!"

He stormed out of the coach's office. His truck tires squealed out of the parking lot and flew down the road, onto highway 28 where he drove for an hour heading nowhere. He finally pulled off the highway onto a levee heading into the bayou. He parked there for hours yelling, crying, and punching the steering wheel and dashboard. Then he got out of the truck and kicked it several times, denting metal.

It was dark when he finally calmed down enough to get back on the road and go home. Grady forgot about baseball, Gabby, dinner, everything. His anger and anxiety were exhausting as he collapsed on his bed.

Tom came upstairs and knocked on Grady's door. "Everything all right, son?" he asked.

"Dad, I'm not feeling good, okay. I just need some sleep." Tom Cordeaux could tell something was wrong, but he hoped his son would tell him when he was ready.

The next afternoon, the phone rang at the Cordeaux house. Gloria answered, "Hello?"

"Hello, Mrs. Cordeaux, this is Gabby. May I please speak with Grady?"

"Hello, Gabby, how are you, dear?" she asked. "How is your family?"

Gabby understood southern etiquette and remained polite despite her urgency to speak with Grady. "Oh, they are fine, everyone is fine," she replied.

Cordialities completed, Gloria finally told her that Grady was still at baseball practice. She said, "When he gets home I will tell him you called."

Gabby said, "Yes, ma'am, thank you very much, goodbye." Gabby did not know what to think since Grady was not at practice. He did not come to school today. The only thing she did know was that one of her friends saw Grady fly out of the parking lot yesterday like he was on fire. He did not call her last night and he did not show up at school today. She was genuinely worried.

Grady rarely let his anxiety take total control, but Gabby could think of one thing right now that might send him to a dark place; not getting a scholarship. It would be the only reason he would disappear in despair, unless he was in an accident and could not call. Gabby thought his mother would have known if he did not come home last night. So, he left home this morning, but did not show up for school. The only thing she knew to do was ask his friends if they had seen him or wait by the phone. She called his closest friends, but no one knew Grady's whereabouts. Roger told her that Grady was very angry about not getting any offers, but that was all he knew. She waited by the phone.

Later that evening, Gabby was taking a shower when she heard the phone ring.

"Gabby! It's your boyfriend," her sister announced throughout the house.

It was a little late for a phone call, but she yelled to her sister to hold on for a minute. She threw on a robe, wound a towel around her hair and raced to the phone. "Hello, hello?" She said, out of breath.

Grady's voice was low and slurring. "Hi."

"Grady? Where have you been for two days? You missed school, you missed practice, you had an exam today, and you did not call me! What happened? Where have you been?" she demanded.

"I've been around."

"That's it? You've been around? That's all I get? I have been worried that you rolled into a ditch somewhere. Gina told me you peeled out of the parking lot after school yesterday. What happened?"

"Nothing," he said in a hushed monotone. "I just decided it was a good day to get a bottle of whiskey and go fishing!"

She asked him in disbelief, "You missed everything today to go fishing? Grady, you need to tell me what is going on, right now."

He slurred a little, "Let's just say some sombitch decided to ruin my life and send me to Vietnam, probably get me killed."

Gabby could not decide if he was drunk or sleepy. He was not making sense and she was annoyed at his listlessness and non-answers. "How could anyone send you to Vietnam? The draft board does not decide until this summer and you will be heading to college by then. I will see you at school tomorrow. It's Friday, we can leave after lunch, and you can tell me what you are talking about. I will see you tomorrow. Good night."

She hung up angrily. Grady hung up and went to his room. He avoided his parents, except to yell to them that he was going to bed.

Why No Calls

Grady met Gabby the next morning at her locker. The look on her face let Grady know she was not happy. Before he could say anything, she shut him down telling him they would talk after lunch. Then she turned and headed toward her next class without knowing or caring if he was following.

Grady was exhausted. He looked like he had rolled out of bed and thrown on whatever clothes were lying on the floor. Gabby was certain he had not showered that morning, but she hoped he had brushed his teeth, at the very least.

The fresh air and sunshine coming in the classroom did not make the time go by any faster. Students were catching spring fever and everyone was anxious to be outside, especially the seniors. It was their last semester of high school and the summer could not come fast enough. It just made Grady more tired.

The end of fourth period bell rang and Gabby was at Grady's locker. They left school. He knew he was in for a lecture, but he was not in the mood. To his surprise Gabby did not say anything the entire ride. They arrived at their spot overlooking the pond and he cut off the engine.

She turned to him. "Okay, will you please tell me what has you so freaked out? I'm scared Grady! Now I'm wondering about your mental stability."

"Oh, that's exactly what I need to here! Thanks, Gabby! Thanks for being on my side!"

She stopped him. "Then tell me what happened!"

There was a long silence while Grady gathered his thoughts. "I talked with Coach Cramer after school to find out if he heard anything from college scouts, or if he knew any reason why they hadn't called me. He had a hard time telling me. Coach finally admitted that an LSU scout confided in him that someone was telling colleges I was trouble, I had a criminal record, and I almost killed a kid. Now, schools will not look at me! Coach tried to stick up for me, but they found out about the bonfire incident."

Grady's eyes began to tear up. He looked at Gabby through crying eyes saying that somebody ruined his chances for going to college. She knew with no chance of college and with his record, he would be in the draft for sure. Gabby just sat in disbelief, tears filling her eyes. Nothing she could say or do would take away his fear at this moment. She moved closer and he wrapped his arm around her. The two of them sat quietly in each other's arms, terrified of the future.

Grasping at Straws

The next few months Grady desperately tried to contact colleges and scouts. Gabby wanted to help in any way she could but there was little she could do. It was exhausting for her to maintain her academics and lift Grady's spirits all the time. As much as she tried, she could not escape the harsh reality that time was marching on. Grady felt it too, but could not deal with one more thing on his plate. Neither one wanted to say it aloud for fear that it might make it true. Their time together was coming to an end. Gabby was going to Mississippi State, and Grady was going nowhere, or as far away as the Army could send him.

One afternoon much to his surprise Grady got a call back from Louisiana State University. He did not recognize the caller's name as one of the primary scouts, but Mr. Jones was on the football staff.

After weeks of no responses, Grady was not prepared when he was able to actually speak to someone.

He spoke in a flustered voice. "Mr. Jones, I am Grady Cordeaux, a graduating senior from Pineville High School. Thank you very much for finally returning my calls. Sir, I think LSU should know how badly I want to play for the Tigers, and I am willing to do whatever it takes!"

Mr. Jones interrupted, asking if he could hold for a few minutes. "Mr. Cordeaux, thank you for holding, I have your file in front of me. Apparently, LSU was interested in you, but determined that you were not a good fit for our program. I'm sorry."

"Wait, Mr. Jones, I don't know what that means. I was an All-State standout linebacker for two years, so I don't know how I'm not a good fit? Three of your linebackers graduated. I have studied your program, and I know you are looking for linebackers. How am I not a good fit?"

Jones responded hesitantly, "Mr. Cordeaux, I'm truly sorry. These decisions are made by the program, looking at the needs of the team and weighing many different considerations. It is out of my hands."

"But wait a minute!" Grady said, with desperation. "Can someone please tell me why I was being looked at by at least five schools last year, and this year, no one will talk to me, even though I had a breakout season? No one will have the decency to tell me why."

"Son, I am not at liberty to discuss the decisions of the program. However, I think you can figure things out for yourself. Let me say this: the integrity of our program is shaped by the integrity of the individual players. We have had athletes who have dealt with personal issues, and we helped them, but we try to not bring new players into our program that already have issues. I am sorry."

There it was! He told Grady why no school was going to recruit him without actually saying it. Grady was almost in tears. He asked

Jones. "Mr. Jones, did you ever get into a fight? That's all it was, a fight!"

"Mr. Cordeaux, like I said, I am not at liberty to discuss any of this with you. I understand how you must feel. I'm sure there are other schools that want your talents and are willing to overlook your police record. We also have information from one of your teachers about your poor academics, especially in math. I'm very sorry. I wish you the best of luck."

Grady hung up the phone and he began seeing red as adrenaline coursed through his body. He could feel every muscle tense up, and he let out a curdling scream from the deepest part of his lungs.

His mother hurried downstairs. "Grady, Grady what's wrong? What happened? Are you hurt?"

He was sitting at the kitchen table with both fists on the table. She was relieved to not see blood.

"Grady, what is it?" she demanded.

"Nothing, Mom, nothing!"

With a raised voice and look of concern she shot back, "You let out a roar that shook this house and you tell me nothing is wrong?"

Tears began to fill his eyes and roll over his cheeks. He had so much anger and emotion in him at that moment, he could not move.

Tom Cordeaux came in from the barn looking for supper. He saw Grady at the table with fists clenched and his mother standing over him. "What's going on?"

Mother said, "I don't know, Thomas, he won't tell me."

Grady mumbled in a satanic voice about knowing why no schools have called him.

Tom did not understand what he said. "What's that, son? What about school?"

"Dad, I was just talking to LSU and the guy told me that Mr. Kenner told them about my math grades, and who knows what else. I'll bet that prick told them about the fight at the bonfire too. I know he did! That's what he meant when he said something to me after the exam. The son of a bitch ruined my life."

Mrs. Cordeaux yelled to him, "Grady Cordeaux, this is a Christian house and we don't use that kind of language!"

Grady did not say any more, but the rage in his eyes worried his father.

"Grady, you don't know if Mr. Kenner said or did anything. Tomorrow I will go to the school and talk with the principal. We will figure this out together, you hear me son? I don't want you doing anything that could make this situation worse. Do you understand what I'm telling you? Grady?"

Grady just stared without saying a word.

Pushed Too Far

The bell rang and Grady sat down in Kenner's class without a word to anyone, ready to snap like a bear trap. Gabby tried all morning to calm him down. It took every ounce of Grady's energy not to say something to the measly little man with his little bowtie and sweater. Grady did not hear a single thing in class the entire hour. All he could do was focus on trying to keep calm.

Finally, the bell rang. Ambling out the door among other students, Grady looked over his shoulder, locked eyes with Kenner, and sneered. His dislike for the puny little man was obvious. Kenner was standing at his desk.

Before Grady was out of earshot, Kenner smiled and said out loud, "Mr. Cordeaux, how are those athletic scholarships coming along?"

Kenner had tripped the wire. Grady dropped everything, turned and charged at Kenner through several students. Rage coursed through him as he tried to reach the little man. Kenner saw Grady's rage and recoiled in fear into the corner behind his desk and file cabinet. He hoped the students could hold Grady back.

Kenner kept screaming, "Mr. Cordeaux, Mr. Cordeaux!" Everything went black.

Grady's entire body felt heavy. He heard, "Mr. Cordeaux, Mr. Cordeaux. Can you hear me? Can you hear me?" The voice was becoming clearer.

He opened his eyes. An EMT was trying to revive him. "Mr. Cordeaux, can you hear me?"

Grady was completed confused until he became aware he was in the ambulance bound for Dallas. He felt more chest pain than when they started out.

Grady whispered, "Are we there yet?"

The attendants were busy with his IV lines and monitors. He was still heavily sedated and confused.

The EMT told him that whatever he was dreaming had him on the verge of a heart attack. "Your heartbeat and pulse were spiking, so we were trying to determine if your sedative was wearing off. Sir, we still have a long way to go. We are going to administer some more sedatives to help you relax, okay? Please just rest and try not to worry; everything will be fine."

Grady could feel the sedatives immediately go to work. He was out again.

Part 3: Enlisted

Basic Training

"Jesus H. Christ! What in the hell has my dear Uncle Sam sent me today? I must be on someone's shit list because all I see in front of me is a bucket full of peckers and crotch stains. Is that what you are, a bucket full of peckers? No, wait a Goddamn minute. I think I see a pussy. Are you a pussy, son?"

"No, Sir!"

"What the fuck did you call me? You better drop and give me twenty."

The overweight young man got down on the ground and tried to do push-ups, while the group waited.

"Count them off, fat ass! I want to hear every time your nose hits the dirt! This pussy is doing push-ups because he called me sir! I am not a sir; I work for a living. From now on you will address all officers as sir, and you will address me as sergeant. You will answer any question I ask with an affirmative or negative response followed by sergeant!

"Do you limp dicks know what an affirmative and negative response is?"

"Yes, Sergeant!"

"I can't hear you!"

"YES, Sergeant!"

"Very well! When I ask a question, I expect my fucking uncle Ho in by-God Vietnam to hear you. Do I make myself clear?"

"Yes, Sergeant!"

"Out-fucking-standing! The corporals are here to train you to act, think, breathe and piss like a unit, and you will obey every order they give to you. From now on there is no 'you', there is only your platoon. Is that clear?"

"Yes, Sergeant!"

"Corporal Mulkay?"

"Yes, Sergeant Turner?"

"Take this sorry scrotum sack of pus monkeys over to barracks 21, make sure each crotch stain gets his G.I. issue, and then take them over to get that hippy hair shaved and off my base. I want to see some skulls! Have them ready for barracks inspection at 1400 hours, and muster formation in front of barracks 21 by 1405 hours. If they miss their formation at 1405 hours because one of these commie-loving, hippie pukes is not squared away in my barracks, they will have a five-mile run this afternoon. Do I make myself clear?"

"Yes, Sergeant!"

"Get them out of my sight!"

Grady was lucky to not have been singled out by the sergeant today, but he knew his time would come. It was late June 1970 in Fort Bragg, North Carolina and the first time Grady had been out of Louisiana. The judge gave him a choice to enlist in the Army or go to jail for the assault on Mr. Kenner. Once enlisted, he had to be a model soldier, or he was going to jail. There were no football scholarships, no college, and no draft. He was enlisted in the Army and shipped out to Fort Bragg two weeks after graduation. The only things he had to look forward to for the next eight weeks were drill sergeants and letters from Gabby.

Grady did not understand why he had to take a four-hour plane ride on a DC3 to Fort Bragg when Fort Polk, Louisiana was only 45 minutes southwest of Pineville and did basic training. Someone said Fort Bragg took all the special cases, but another guy said the Army does whatever it wants, without regard to whether it makes sense or not. The two things he knew for sure were that he did not like plane rides, and he was a long way from home.

Corporal Mulkay shouted at the men to get their shit and follow him to in-processing. The recruits were issued uniforms, bedding, and gear. They stood in line to get their heads shaved, get deloused, given a quick once over by overwhelmed unenthusiastic doctors, and then turned back over to Corporal Mulkay.

The corporal did not look to be much older than most of the high school graduates in the platoon, but his demeanor and confidence let you know he had been in the Army long enough. His lean, muscular physique was hardened by Army training, but the intense look in his eyes came from something much more intense. Mulkay looked like a thin G.I. Joe. He was clean shaven with a crisp crew cut, and a uniform that was creased, spit-shined, and polished everywhere. He was the poster boy for Army standards, except he was no boy. During the eight weeks of basic training the recruits learned that Corporal Mulkay had experiences in Vietnam few others lived to tell about. Grady noticed Mulkay's military bearing. He did not speak unless directed to do so, nor did he show emotion. He followed orders from Sergeant Turner. Turner was the leader of the 80-man platoon, and Mulkay was one of his subordinates who assisted in the training. He was in charge of the men who had arrived with Grady.

The corporal barked out an almost unintelligible command and watched disgustedly as the men tried to get in formation in front of barracks 21.

"Ten hut! I am Corporal Mulkay, and you are worse than dick cheese. When I ask a question you will answer the question, followed by my rank. Do you understand?"

"Yes, Corporal!"

"When you answer my questions, you will be very loud and clear, because I have listened to the same bullshit so many times from other sacks of scum like you, I cannot hear well. Is that clear?

"Yes, Corporal!

"Very good, shit birds! In the next eight weeks I will not be your friend. Do any of you limp dicks know why I am not your friend? I will tell you why. Friends exchange smiles, smiles lead to holding hands, holding hands leads to kissing, kissing leads to fucking, and there will be no fucking in my squad or in this platoon! Is that clear?"

"Yes, Corporal!"

"Very well!" screamed Mulkay. "What I will be for the next eight weeks is your mother, your father, and your savior. If you do exactly as I tell you to do, in the precise moment I tell you to do it, I might be the sumbitch that saves your life in combat. Do I need to repeat that?"

"No, Corporal!"

"Are you sure?"

"Yes, Corporal."

"Good! My job is to train you to be soldiers. You will learn how to march, how to stand in formation, how to address your fellow soldier depending on his rank. You will learn discipline, responsibility, structure, and how to be part of a unit. You will learn how to use a weapon to kill the enemy. You will learn how to stay alive. I will work you hard to turn your body and mind into a fighting machine for God and country! Is that clear?"

"Yes, Corporal!"

"There will be no discussions, no debates, nothing except compliance. The reason for this strict rule is that when I tell you to drop, if you hesitate for one split second, one of the many weapons of war designed to turn your head into pink mist might find its mark. Are we clear?"

"Yes, Corporal!"

"It is now 13:17 hours; that is 1:17 in the afternoon for you dumb assess who have not yet figured out military time. You will learn it! When I say you are dismissed, you have exactly 13 minutes to be dressed in your new fatigue uniform given to you by my dear Uncle Sam, with your new boots on, and your bunk will be ready for inspection. Is that clear?"

"Yes, Corporal!"

"Dismissed!"

The men tripped over each other scrambling to gather their things and get into the barracks. They had just a few minutes to claim a bunk and get dressed. At exactly 13:30 hours, Corporal Mulkay stepped into the large dorm room with 40 sets of bunk beds and 80 footlockers.

"Every one of you pukes drop and give me twenty push-ups, now!"

"Yes, Corporal!"

Each man fell to the ground and tried to do push-ups. The corporal continued yelling. "When I tell the platoon to drop and give me twenty, I want twenty push-ups, in unison, with every man counting out in the same sequence. Is that clear?"

"Yes, Corporal!"

"A push-up begins with your prone body face down, palms on the ground under your chest, your arms fully extended, your back straight and your toes on the ground. You bend at the elbows until your nose touches the ground, then you return to the previous prone position, and repeat twenty times, or until I tell you to stop. Is that clear?"

"Yes Corporal!"

"Does any man in this barracks know why you are giving me twenty push-ups? What is your name soldier?" Mulkay screamed at the recruit nearest him.

"Grissel, Corporal!"

"Did you say grease ball? From now on you will be known as grease ball. Recruit Grease ball is giving me twenty because when I or any other senior ranking soldier (which is everyone to you pukes) walks into this barracks, one of you will yell 'ten hut'! It means come to attention. At that moment, every man will snap to attention in front of his bunk. You will stand erect, chest out, with your arms down at your side, in a dick rigid position. Is that clear?"

"Yes, Corporal!"

"I can't hear you!"

"Yes, Corporal."

"Now, since your ignorance caused me to have to explain what happens when a higher ranked soldier walks into this barracks, you are late for formation in the front of this barracks. I have no choice but to lead you on a five-mile march. After five miles in new boots you will absolutely know for fucking certain if you have the correct size."

Mulkay paused for a moment. He looked around at the men and screamed out. "Well, what the fuck are you waiting for? Get your sorry assholes out of my barracks and in formation. Now!"

Grady made it a point not to stare the wrong way, say anything, or do anything that would make him a target. He had been warned that this was how life was going to be in boot camp, and you only had to endure it. It was like early season football practice two-a-days on steroids. He knew that every man in the platoon was going to be made an example of at some point in the training. It was about breaking down the individual and forming them into a unit. It was also about teaching soldiers how to stay alive in combat. Grady worked hard to absorb everything he was being told, but Gabby was always in the back of his mind.

The training was grueling. By 4:30 a.m. the recruits were outside doing physical training, they would come in for breakfast, and go back out again for different physical training. By 9 a.m. the North

Carolina summer heat would beat down on them, and then the bugs would come out. Grady had dealt with mosquitoes in Louisiana, but in basic training you were drenched in sweat which attracted the mosquitoes and no-see-ums. They were tiny bugs you could not see, until they bit you, leaving a welt. Each morning, noon, and night the men hurried to get in formation, and were made to stand and wait. This was when the bugs were the worst.

The first week was spent mostly doing physical training, learning how to stand in formation, march, salute, and getting used to following commands. The men were also tested for intelligence, strength, and aptitude. Every week after was built upon the previous week's training, adding more intensity and demanding higher results. After several weeks, the recruits learned about weapons, particularly the M16 rifle, grenades, combat tactics, and hand-to-hand combat. Every week several men were picked out to perform some ridiculous duty, like base perimeter patrol, or kitchen patrol. The "shit" duties were meant to perform a menial but necessary responsibility, deprive men of any sleep opportunities, and remind recruits they belonged to Uncle Sam.

Mail Call

It seemed like forever to get through the first two weeks of basic training. Only then did the Army allow recruits to start receiving mail. It was also the only morale boost since they arrived. When the sarcastic Army clerk called out recipients for their mail, he usually had a nasty comment to go along with it. Often, he would throw a letter to a recruit declaring that it was another "Dear John" letter. When the clerk called out Grady, he butchered Cordeaux. It sounded like "Cor deo ux." The men laughed at the mispronunciation until the clerk tossed a bundle of eight letters to Grady. From that moment on, the envious pals in his platoon began calling him "lover boy." Grady sat alone that night amongst eighty men, in his bunk before "lights out" and opened each letter.

My darling Grady, I can't tell you how much I've missed you these past weeks. I am having a hard time not seeing you every day, and still preparing for college. All my plans are different now. I thought we would have the whole summer together to talk about our future and make love in our special place. I thought, at the very least, you would be at a nearby school where we could see each other on weekends, or I could come to your football games. My heart hurts and I cry every day you are away from me. Oh Grady! Why did you have to go after Kenner? I wish I could have stopped you. I am trying to figure out how I can see you before you ship out. It will all depend on my schedule at State. I don't even like saying the words "ship out." It already makes you sound so far away. I love you so much, and I will wait for you forever. Your eternal love, Gabby

Her letters were filled with words of love, longing, sadness, and devotion. He wanted them to go on forever because it helped him feel closer to her. Some of the letters were so sorrowful, but they filled his heart anyway. He loved her so much and missed her terribly. He longed for the intense feelings of a first love and the perpetual euphoria of being with that person. He wrote her back in the quiet of the night when the Army gave basic trainees a few precious moments of personal time.

After the first mail call, Corporal Mulkay told the men to forget about those girlfriends back home because they will not be there when the men return. He uttered under his breath that each man would not be the same person anyway. When Mulkay said things like that Grady just ignored him, thinking Mulkay did not know the kind of true love between him and Gabby. Grady fell asleep exhausted every night but was always dreaming about the day he would come home to her.

The weeks passed quickly, and before he knew it, basic training was over. He endured the tempest with little trouble. Toward the end, the men learned to respect and appreciate Corporal Mulkay. He gradually became someone who wanted them to be their best, rather than someone who tormented them. The men worked hard learning what the Army was teaching. They all came to understand it could mean the difference between life and death in a firefight. The last week, the platoon listened to lectures from soldiers just returned from Vietnam. They told the men how nothing was as it seemed over there. They described firefights in deep jungles at night, knowing that any villager could be the enemy, being shot at by women and children, seeing the horrors of what people do to one another, and having to take orders from officers who could not find their way out of a paper bag. All their testimonies were disgruntling and filled with contempt. They failed miserably if their intent was to give a pep talk. Each man in the platoon followed the nightly news too, thinking that as the politicians in Washington talked more often about ending the conflict in Vietnam, maybe they would not be sent over.

After basic training, the recruits became the Army's newest privates who were issued their next assignments, which dashed their hopes for the war ending quickly. Grady learned during basic training that there would be additional follow-on training. He was disappointed to learn that basic training and any additional training did not count toward his one-year tour in Vietnam. He would have to spend at least two years in the Army and one of those was going to be far, far away from home. On the day they graduated from Basic, the men were handed their Military Operational Specialties. Most of the them were designated Infantry 11B, and then sent to other military bases for Advanced Individual Training (AIT) Infantryman for another eight weeks. Private Cordeaux was disappointed he was being sent to infantry training at Ft. Riley, Kansas. He hoped to be closer to home, and Gabby.

Settling In

While at Ft. Riley, Grady did everything exactly as he was told so he could master infantryman. He was settling in to the ways of military training, but he still wrote Gabby every night from his bunk. Her letters to him became less frequent as she was settling in at Mississippi State in Starkville, Mississippi. She professed her love, but she filled more pages describing the excitement of finally being at college and her new experiences. She talked about her new classes, how grown-up she felt being on her own, and how the professors did not check homework. She wrote about classes with so many students they were held in auditoriums and taught by graduate students, rather than professors.

She also described living in a co-ed freshmen dorm where the girls lived on one floor, and the boys lived on another. She said Vinnie lived a few floors below her, and it was nice to have someone from Pineville nearby, and not be totally alone the first semester. She assured Grady not to worry about Vinnie because he was a nice guy and he was very much in love with Trisha. Unfortunately, Trisha graduated valedictorian of Pineville High School and won an academic scholarship to LSU, four hours away from Vinnie. They were only able to see other when they went home during breaks. Vinnie was spending a lot of time with the wrestling program and found it difficult to keep up his schoolwork too, so occasionally he and Gabby would study together. Gabby's mention of Vinnie so many times in her letters, along with telling Grady not to worry, meant that she was aware of how it sounded. Grady got angry and wondered if she actually thought about how her letter impacted his emotions, or if she was just that obtuse.

She finished each letter by swearing her undying love, but Grady sensed changes in her devotion by her word choices, the length of her letters, and the inclusion of insignificant details. He hoped it was all due to the newness of college life, but it gave him twinges of doubt, wondering if filling letters with insignificant babble was her unconscious device to maintain the level in a cup of evaporating love.

Vietnam

Grady stepped off the aircraft in the Republic of Vietnam in September 1970. He gasped trying to suck in enough of the humid, petroleum-filled air from the jetway to fill his lungs. The Army told him about the tropical climate, but he never imagined how stagnant and humid it would be. He was now in Vietnam, an Army private 2nd class, about to begin his one-year tour. *Alle-fuckin-luia*! he thought to himself.

His second thought, after the humidity scorched his lungs, was that it will be 364 days and a wake-up until he could get the hell out of there. All he wanted to do was get back to Gabby and go to college. One good thing about the Army was they would help him pay for his college. Grady's third thought was that it was going to be a very long year if all he did was think about leaving.

He followed the line of soldiers to an in-processing building on the flight line. Several of the guys in the line were talking about their previous tours. He could not believe soldiers would actually return for another tour, but he heard one soldier mention R&R in the P.I. He did not find out until later that the P.I. was the Philippine Islands, and that some of the guys went there for "Rest and Relaxation or R&R." He also found out that R&R in the P.I. really meant Filipino hookers instead of Vietnamese hookers.

After in-processing, a sergeant asked Grady and the other men if they were the recruits coming in to 47th Infantry. The sergeant did not look like the other battle-hardened men he saw on the flight line. He was wearing a clean regulation uniform. The guys coming off R&R were wearing things that looked like they might have been part of a uniform at one time. The haircuts, anti-war slogans and various patches were not regulation. After several months of strict Army training, Grady found their appearance to be confusing and distracting.

"Yes, Sergeant," the new arrivals replied.

"Alright." He told men to come with him. They boarded a small bus and rode over to a helicopter sitting on the tarmac.

Grady asked, "Where are we going? And how did you know we were the guys?"

The sergeant answered, "You are going to the admin HQ of the 9th Infantry Division, 2nd Brigade River Raider, 3/47th Infantry, and I knew it was you dipshits because nobody stands out more in the Nam than green recruits."

Forty minutes later when the helicopter skids touched down at another U.S. military compound, the pilot yelled to the men over the drone of the rotors, to get out.

The UH-1 huey helicopter lifted up as soon as the men cleared the rotor blades. The group walked to the nearest building that looked like a terminal for flight operations. A specialist E4 met them at the door and asked to see their orders. He brought them inside, told them to have a seat in a temporary lounge area, and to get a coke or smoke.

They waited until he returned. Everyone they had met so far was terse and emotionless. There was no gunfire, no bombs, no one rushing around, no one bleeding. The atmosphere was both very businesslike and unfamiliarly casual and undisciplined.

"Okay, you men seem to be where you are supposed to be, which is unusual for the Army, but that's just my opinion. You are to report to in-processing, Building 203, just down the flight line. You will be issued bunks and gear. You will be taken to a barracks. This is the main operating base for the 9th Infantry. When you are not on a swift boat, or on patrol, this is where you will call home. This is where you will get your mail. When your tour is over, this is from where you will depart. The good Lord and Uncle Sam willing, you will be home by the 1972 football season."

The specialist looked at Grady. "Did you play ball, Private...Cordex?" he asked Grady, trying to read his name on the clipboard.

"Yes, I did, Specialist Edwards. My name is Cordeaux." Grady sounded it out phonetically, 'Kor Doh'.

"I don't give a rat's ass how to pronounce your name," Edwards said matter-of-factly. "You look big enough to have played high school football with some authority. What happened, Cordeaux? Not smart enough to get a scholarship?"

Grady looked at him, surprised at the informality. "A little trouble at home is all."

"Ah, southern justice sent you here to serve your country; I get it. There are a few more like you here, and you don't have to say my rank. You are no longer in basic training; you are in the shithole we call Viet fucking Nam. Listen, Cordeaux, and the rest of you pukes too. Keep your heads down! Do everything your sergeant tells you to do and nothing else. Stay away from the heavy drugs; they are everywhere. Stay sharp and I'll see you come back through those doors in 365. I will be handing you orders to go home. Maybe next year, Cordeaux, I can watch you play for Alabama, huh? Just don't get killed!"

Edwards walked out and left the men to find a bunk and get settled. It did not take long to find the toilets and the chow hall. Grady looked for the mailroom. He asked around and found a mail clerk, who already had three letters for Grady. Two were from Gabby and one was from his parents. He read through them in his bunk and began to feel overwhelming anxiety. There was nowhere to run. This was it.

He had been too busy training the last few months to let it get to him, but when he finally had a moment to catch his breath, anxiety hit. He had to either plough through and think of something happier or hijack a plane back to the States and go AWOL. He thought about all the tender moments he and Gabby had shared earlier this year. Now it seemed like an eternity ago. He hoped the next year would go quickly. His eyes watered as he read her letters. He wanted her so badly, just to be able to hold her and smell her hair. He closed his eyes and slept for the next two days.

First Firefight

"Check your fire! Check your fire!" Sergeant Williams yelled to his squad. The firefight was over as quickly as it started. The squad was humping through swamps and rice paddies for two days until they came upon the Viet Cong village they were ordered to search out and destroy. It was Grady's first enemy encounter and when it was over, he did not expect to ever get over what had just happened.

"Gimme a headcount," Williams yelled with a voice trailing off in submission.

Each man grunted at the sarge to let him know he was still alive. They were one man short. Grady looked behind him for JT, a new guy who had come into the squad the same week he had arrived. Grady, still in shock from being shot at and firing his rifle at another human being, crawled back to find JT lying face down in the mud. He pulled at him, but JT did not move.

"He's not moving!" Grady yelled in desperation.

One of the other men in the squad crawled over and turned over JT's limp body. Blood, intestines, and a liver slid out from his torso. It was Grady's first casualty.

He started gagging and vomited, repeating "Oh God! Oh God!" He was in shock and pissed in his pants. He had never seen a dead person, let alone someone disemboweled. The sight and the smell were permanently etched in his mind. He was too numb to even cry.

Suddenly, Corporal Jones, the short timer in the squad, grabbed Grady's shoulder. "Listen 'greeny', shit happens! It happens when new guys don't hit the dirt the second the gooks start shooting at ya."

Jones let go of Grady. He turned to the rest of the squad. "God dammit! I'm so fucking tired of this shit. I'm tired of seeing brand new 'greenies' going home in a body bag not one month in country. I hear the whole 9th is gonna be getting outta this motherfucker real soon too. I hate this fucking place!"

The sarge broke in, "All right, enough of this shit, tag him and bag him. Cordo, stay close to me and do exactly what I tell you to do! We move out in ten."

Grady could not wrap his head around what just happened. Five minutes ago, JT was alive, now he is not. His eyes are lifeless, his corpse is growing cold. He will not be going home to tell his mother or father how much he loves them. He will not kiss his girlfriend anymore. Everything that he ever was and ever will be is gone. Grady did not know the guy, but they talked once or twice. None of the other men in the squad talked to JT or Grady. He learned it was bad luck to talk to a new troop. New recruits or 'greenies' were more likely to get killed in the first two months, and the men did not want to tag and bag someone they just met.

Everything seemed to be happening in slow motion. His anxiety was pounding inside his head causing all his senses to be hypersensitive. Each snapping twig or leaf movement caught his intense scrutiny wondering if an enemy soldier was aiming a weapon at him. In his mind, the jungle was alive with VC. He carried the fears further down a rabbit hole thinking about the letter his mother would get from the Department of Defense. He imagined Gabby sobbing. Back in reality, no one noticed the wetness in Grady's pants because of the sweat and mud. They would not blame him anyway, not for this. Every combat vet knew that the shock and horror was too much for a human brain to process, especially the first time. Many grunts on patrol in the bush had gone through what Grady was experiencing. They understood he had to get through it and come out in his own time. Getting over your first kill or your first casualty was like getting off drugs; you had to suffer through it. The ones who did not react to the blood, gore, and inhumanity were abnormal. Horror becoming routine was a scary thing. No man wanted to see that in himself. It meant he was changed forever.

The sergeant radioed to HQ his report on the village for follow-up mortar attacks. He also reported the one KIA (killed in action).

By the fall of 1970, American ground troops had been waging full on, boots-on-the-ground war for five hard years, and death was all too frequent. Even the battle-hardened Non-Commissioned Officers (NCOs), 26-year-olds who looked 40, never got accustomed to losing men. Some of the them were on their second or third tours in the Nam, but death was never acceptable or easy to deal with. The worst part was when the policymakers demanded numbers of dead to measure successes or failures. War-weary G.I.s were required to walk through battle-damaged areas and killing fields to count numbers of charred, fly infested, dismembered corpses so someone could call our strategy successful. Even these NCOs still shook their heads at the senselessness.

Every now and again if you listened to the chatter while on patrols, in the sandbag bunkers, trenches or foxholes, you heard the frustration. Back at the main post, where men had time to reflect, they bitched about the way the war was being fought, or why America was in the fight. Low morale, drugs, and lack of support at home were taking a toll on the morale in the Nam.

Grady was told he was engaging in "Vietnamization." It was President Nixon's, and the U.S. military's word for transitioning South Vietnamese to be able to defend themselves. The reality, at least in the Mekong delta, was that the U.S. 9th Infantry was still hunting Viet Cong, and bombing the hell out of Cambodia to take out NVA resupply lines.

It did not take long for Grady to be confused about who he was fighting, on what side of the border he was fighting, and where he would go if the 9th Infantry, 3rd Battalion pulled out of Vietnam. One thing he knew for sure was that he did not want to tag and bag anybody.

When Grady's squad came in from river patrols, he looked forward to mail more than anything. Most of the soldiers would get cleaned up and head into Saigon for some female attention, but not Grady. He would get his mail and open each letter from Gabby by the date of the postmark. It was his second month in country, and he was getting a letter every week.

My darling Grady, how are you doing sweetheart? I can't imagine what you must be feeling over there. I hear that Vietnam is a very dangerous place right now. People are protesting against Nixon, and the possibility of involving Cambodia in the war. Please write back as soon as you get this, so I know you are okay and that you still love me with all your heart. I would never be able to go on if something happened to you. I cry myself to sleep most nights after I hear the stories on the evening news about what is going on over there. It seems wrong that we are pulling our military out of there, but you had to go in. I even heard someone say they were thinking of stopping the draft. Not fair! I'm trying very hard to keep up on all my studies, but college is hard! There are so many papers to write, and lots of other things going on that keep us busy. High school was pretty easy comparatively. It has been a blessing to have Vinnie to talk to when I get sad. He seems to be having a difficult time with Trisha too, so he talks to me about her as well. They seemed like such a great couple, but I think she has found a lot to do at LSU and is too busy for Vinnie. Perhaps, it's just her course load, I don't know. Anyway, that is enough about them. A few guys have asked me out, but don't worry my darling, I let them know right away that I'm your girl. Please don't worry. I'm yours forever. There is not as much protesting going on about the war at State, but lots of other troubles seems to be flaring up. The students hate Nixon. The nation is in turmoil and racial riots are going on everywhere. I'm scared. My darling, please hurry back to me in one piece so we can start our life together. I will write again tomorrow; got to study now. Sweet dreams, my love. Think about us at our favorite spot. I love you. I'm yours forever, Gabby.

Mekong

Almost all her letters were similarly formatted, but he treasured each one individually. Reading them brought back his sadness about being so far away, but holding the letters made him feel like he was holding a small part of her. It was all he had right now. He could not write back to her saying where he was, or what he was doing in Vietnam, for security reasons. She was correct, though. Vietnam, especially the delta, was a dangerous place.

The Army moved more troops south in 1970 and took the fight into the Mekong delta region because of the heavy Viet Cong presence. The Mekong delta was muddy, hot and humid! The worst part about the war for Grady was he never really knew who the enemy was. The Riverines would patrol up the delta in swift boats and attract gunfire from both sides of the river. It seemed like every village they encountered was occupied by Viet Cong.

Grady quickly caught on that everyone who was not American could be the enemy, and that thought kept the patrolling GIs on high alert at all times.

Boredom became another dangerous enemy because it fostered complacency. After a month of patrols up the Mekong river with little activity, the men were lulled into a false sense of calm. Grady felt most on edge during those times.

The next several months went by with only a few river patrols involved in gunfire. Up in the North highlands, west of Da Nang, the North Vietnamese regulars were engaging U.S. troops every day, but in the Mekong, things were eerily quiet despite the 9th getting reports daily about VC reinforcements.

Grady was getting into the routine of being an infantry riverine. He knew his job and he became good at it. However, as the holidays approached, so did his depression. A few days before Christmas he was back at his base, My Tho, where he received a package from home. His parents and Gabby had put together a box full of Christmas cookies, shaving kit items, socks, a few small presents, and many letters. Gabby was home, on break.

Hello, my darling, I pray that this letter finds you safe and well in that awful place. Sweetheart, I'm doing well in school, but it has been so unbearable not having you near me, especially when I come home for breaks. Vinnie and I have been riding together to save on money and gas when we come home. He's been a real friend. I keep thinking back to last fall and Christmas when we had so much fun, making love at our spot, or the time all of us got together on New Year's Eve and I slept in your arms all night. This year it's very different. I cry myself to sleep sometimes and my roommate keeps asking what is wrong with me. I go out with other girls to try to cheer up, but it rarely works. It is getting so hard to be away from you, lover. I have been to your house several times to see how your parents are doing. Your dad is looking older trying to keep up the farm, but he says it's only a short while longer. We put together a Christmas package for you. I cried when I was shopping to find you a present. My present will be when you come back to me. I'm not sure how much longer I can take this heartache. My parents took me to church so I could talk to our Priest. He told me to try and live one day at a time. He also said I was too young to be feeling this sad. I told him about you, and we prayed together. Honey, all our old friends came home for the holiday break and are having a lot of parties and get-togethers. I have gone to some, but it doesn't feel right without you. Some of the couples we knew are still together, but I just heard that Vinnie and Trisha broke up. It was more her than him. He is pretty torn up about it. He is as sad as I am now. I have heard that there are lots of beautiful women in Vietnam who want to find a nice American. Grady, please don't find anyone else. It would break my heart. My best thought is that you are halfway through your tour and will be home by next summer. I can't wait. You have, and will always have my love, Gabby.

As Grady read each letter, a nagging feeling of doubt began to foment in his mind. She was talking more and more about not being able to stand the loneliness, and going to parties, and how sad Vinnie felt. He did not give two shits about Vinnie! It was the same loneliness for him too, except he wasn't going to parties to ease the pain. The only parties he went on were VC hunting parties, and killing Charlie did not make him feel any better.

While seeing Grady's reaction to one of the letters, one of his squad mates told him he needed to get laid. When the GIs went off post they would buy any one of the thousands of prostitutes on the street for less than $5. The girls were beautiful, but it was a little dangerous because of all the diseases. One type of syphilis was incurable. The Army doctors had their hands full dealing with venereal cases, and if a soldier got the wrong kind of VD, he would never be allowed to leave Vietnam. Grady was afraid of those kinds of risks, and more importantly, he did not want to cheat on Gabby, no matter how lonely he got. The guys would tease him a little, but most of them understood. Every man had his own way of dealing with the loneliness.

Thuc Pham's

On New Year's Eve, Grady's squad was going to one of the classier clubs in Saigon. Since it was not a pussy-shopping trip, Grady decided to go along too. The guys neglected to mention that the club had some of the most beautiful women in Saigon. They wanted to celebrate the new year, and getting out of the shit in the next six months. The word had come down that the 9th Infantry was pulling out. The men who still had time on their tours would be transferred to other units. It was an excellent reason to celebrate. They carried "beaucoup dollar" because this part of town was high-priced. Grady's only goal was to drink away his pain.

Grady had been downtown a few times before, but he had never seen it this crowded. They took a bus to an intersection, and then rode part of the way in covered buggies pulled by motorcycles. The roads were jammed every night with cars maneuvering through the motorbikes, cabs, pedestrians, vendors and whores on streets with no obedience to traffic laws. Tonight's traffic was much worse because of New Year's. The group arrived at Thuc Pham Le' Versailles in the heart of Saigon by late afternoon. The first thing the guys did was book rooms for the night. The restaurant and club were on the first floor of a five-story building with hotel rooms above.

They tried to arrive early so they could get a good table in the restaurant, but by 1700 hours only a few tables remained. They got one of the last available and began ordering drinks over the roar of the crowd. The short timers knew, by looking over the crowd, this was going to be one hell of a party. The patrons were a mix of Vietnamese civilians and noisy GIs with beautiful Vietnamese women on their arms. The New Year was still seven hours away, but the party was in full swing.

Grady's buddies were pounding liquor, while he was nursing a beer. Back home he was a beer-drinking redneck, but in his current state of mind, the overwhelming amount of activity around him made him nervous and wanting to keep his wits. GIs were briefed all the time that VC could be sitting next to you in a bar downtown and you would never know it. The men also were briefed on which bars to stay away from. Thuc Pham's was too upscale to be on that list.

After the first round of drinks, everyone ordered food and the party kicked into high gear. The food was delicious, the pours were generous, and the party was loud. Grady slowly began to lighten up until, for the first time in country, he did not feel sad.

One of the guys, Joe Pataglia, explained to Grady about Pham's. Joe had 29 days and a wake-up left in the Nam. He came here tonight because it was the best place in Saigon, and he wanted to remember something good about Vietnam before he went home. A wealthy Vietnamese family owned Thuc Pham's. It was rumored they had old money and political ties going back before the French. The restaurant had been in operation since the 1940s, with a reputation for excellent food and discretion. It was rumored that Thuc Pham could go anywhere in Vietnam and be treated with honor and respect. Grady thought it strange how business transcended the violence of war, but here was a perfect example.

The men finished their meals and were ready for more liquor, when a young Vietnamese woman asked if everything was to their liking. Every man in the restaurant noticed her as she made her way around the tables. Something about her was different. She was stunningly beautiful, even more so than the other young women. The way she held her head, the way she carried herself, even her aura made it clear she did not put up with inappropriate behavior from customers. She was somebody, and though she was young, she commanded respect from the staff and clientele.

She was at Grady's table and asked the men if they were enjoying themselves and if everything was to their liking. She made brief eye contact with every man at the table. When she looked at Grady her gaze held on him. He looked back and was awe-struck. He had seen beautiful Vietnamese women, but none like her. There was no mistaking her high class. She wore a baht chain of solid gold around her neck worth more than all their paystubs combined. Her fine clothes were hand-tailored to accentuate her perfect figure. She had to be a member of the Pham family.

Both their eyes betrayed themselves by revealing interest meant to be concealed. She politely asked Grady in near-perfect English if there was something else she could get for him. He was caught off guard and mumbled that he was fine for now.

"Hey, don't worry about him, sweetheart," Tony Rice said. "He's already madly in love with a girl back home, but I'm available."

She politely smiled at the abrupt rudeness, then turned and walked away.

When she was out of earshot, one of the guys said, "Did you guys see that? Miss Vietnam and Grady were salivating over each other while the rest of us were chopped liver. What's going on, lover boy?"

"What is it about you?" Pete asked.

Grady, just coming out of her trance, leaned in to reveal his secret. "It's because I'm saving myself, they sense it, and they can talk to me without worrying about my hand sliding up the back of their leg to grab their asses."

The men burst out laughing.

Grady joked outwardly, "You guys are too obvious, try being subtle." Inside, he was trying to make sense about what had just happened. He felt thunderstruck.

"Says a guy who doesn't get laid," Joey said. They laughed and continued partying into the New Year.

New Year's Patrol

The next morning, January 1st, 1971 began with hangovers, empty wallets, and painful urinations. Grady rolled out of his bunk, got cleaned up, and headed to the chow hall for breakfast.

His sergeant approached him. "Cordo, tell the squad we got a mission brief at 1500."

"Roger that, Sarge." Grady said.

He thought to himself. *Shit! It is the first day of the New Year, the entire division is supposed to be drawing down, and we are going on a mission.* Mission briefs were at least 12 hours before deployment, so he knew that meant they would be heading out early morning. The VC had their own New Year called Tet, that was celebrated sometime in January or February depending on the moon, but they also celebrated January 1st with the Americans. Maybe they would be hungover too. Grady shook his head and went back to his breakfast. He would tell the squad about the mission pre-brief after coffee and breakfast.

"Happy fucking New Year!" he mumbled to himself.

It was eerily quiet on the river. The squad expected to encounter enemy resistance somewhere upriver, or so they were told. The helmsman yelled to the Navy lieutenant that they reached the go/no go point, the hallway point of their fuel supply. He got on the radio and relayed to the two other swift boats.

The infantry guys knew what it meant. They had gone over twenty miles upriver and saw no evidence of resistance or the enemy's weapon resupply lines. Grady heard chitchat earlier about "beaucoup" weapons coming in from Laos and Cambodia. Instead, it was another shit day on the Mekong with little to show for their efforts.

Deep down, the men were grateful that they did not encounter the enemy this day or any other. The lieutenant and their crews turned the boats around for the long patrol back to base. The return trip was always more tense than the trip in because villagers who saw the boats going upriver reported them to the VC. They knew the Americans had to come back out.

Ambushed!

Despite the thick tension, two of the squad on stern watch were dozing, while Grady and Big Jim took watch on port and starboard midship. The navy crew settled into their tasks of operating the vessel and manning the .50 caliber gun. Two hours of eerie quiet had passed. Big Jim was whistling to himself unfocused, and Grady's eyes were glazed over from scanning the miles and miles of overgrown riverbanks.

In an instant, a piercing whistle followed by an explosion rocked the bow of the boat. A round struck the front bulkhead directly behind the gun. The grotesque screaming sound of metal melting instantaneously, with fire and smoke filling the horizon all in the same exact moment, was too shocking to comprehend. Another explosion two seconds later sent metal shards and bodies flying in all directions. The instantaneous release of so much destructive energy was too much for the victims to organize in their brains. Shock and survival instinct took over. Grady did not know he was thrown from the boat. When he came to, he was under water. The air in his lungs forced his body to the surface. Confused, he grabbed the nearest thing.

He regained his wits in a few moments, but it seemed much longer. He could feel warm fluid on his face and saw the red as he wiped his forehead. A searing pain shot through his thigh. He was in shock. He reached out to something floating near him. It was Big Jim, face down in the water. His survival instincts were returning as he pulled the big man to the exploded remnants of his boat.

Coming out of shock, Grady realized they had been attacked. He reached over the splintered gunwale and pulled himself aboard, scraping his torso and legs on the sharp wooden edges. Then he heaved Jim's limp body aboard, while bullets were flying over their heads. His hearing began to return, and he could make out gunfire. Grady's vision was limited by blood streaming over his eyes, but he moved to the bow to check for survivors. He saw a navy crewman pinned under metal and wood splintered debris.

Using all his strength, he pulled up a metal plate allowing the crewman to crawl free. He yelled at him to get the engine started. The two men ducked the small arms fire spitting over their heads pinging metal. Grady looked around and saw two more bodies floating. He dove into the river and pulled each one back to the side of the boat opposite the incoming rounds.

He was fully cognizant by now and saw the other two boats engaging the enemy. After pulling the bodies aboard, Grady crawled to the mangled .50 caliber. He set it atop a metal brace and returned fire. The hull was engulfed in smoke, and the smells of burning oils, wood, metal, hair, and flesh were beyond nauseating. All three swift boats were now shooting at a well-armed enemy unit on the bank. Grady shot into the trees where he saw tracer rounds coming at them. Suddenly, a huge explosion shook the shoreline and a massive fireball rose above the trees. Someone must have hit an enemy cache of ammo or explosives. The soldiers continued shooting until someone yelled, "Check your fire, Check your fire!" When the shooting stopped, the enemy had vanished into the jungle.

One of the boats pulled astride the shot-up exploded hull. The lieutenant yelled for a crew count and damage report. Grady and seaman Brooks looked around for the other three sailors. Big Jim and two infantrymen were vomiting and spewing river water. Their injuries were severe, but they were alive. The other boat crews searched the river for the two sailors and skipper.

A crewman assessed that a mortar round hit the boat directly in front of the cockpit and blew up the ammo storage. The impact point was in front of the skipper's position. The men knew there would be little left of him to find. The other crewmen were blown out of the boat and there were no signs of them. The two undamaged boats took on the survivors. The lieutenant ordered them to scuttle the wreckage and get the hell out of there to where they could rendezvous with a rescue chopper.

Less than three miles downriver the boats pulled ashore where they could get the wounded men onto the choppers. Grady was able to get to the chopper on his own, but a medic met him halfway. He saw Big Jim and Joey carried on litters. The medics were stuffing Joey with gauze and hanging saline bags. The chopper with the sailors and Sal lifted off. Grady tugged at one of the medics asking if Big Jim and Joey were okay.

The medic just said, "I want you to hold this on your head, okay?" He applied a gauze pack to Grady's forehead. "Your buddies are going to make it; we got them in time." As Grady applied pressure to his head, he also felt intense burning in his leg. He closed his eyes and passed out.

Laid Up

Grady opened his eyes suffering an intense headache. It took a few minutes to absorb his new surroundings. He went from being wet, bloody, and smelly in a helicopter, to a dry, warm hospital bed with twenty other guys in a big room. A nurse saw that he was conscious and came over to check on him. Grady noticed she was pretty, and very serious.

Looking at his chart without lifting her eyes she said, "Good morning Private—Corde, Cordeaux? How do you feel? I am Lieutenant Shehan and I will be changing your dressings today. Do you know where you are?"

Grady was embarrassed about being naked under the thin gown, exposed to the female officer. He tried to cover himself up as he answered. "Yes, Ma'am, I'm in a hospital somewhere in Vietnam."

"Excellent, Private, that is exactly where you are, and you needn't worry about your modesty here. Most men have injuries far too serious to worry about modesty. We are professionals who are here to get you well, okay? So just relax and let us take care of you. It is the least we can do for a hero."

She turned away and moved down the row of soldiers in the ward. Grady looked around for Big Jim, Joey, or Sal.

He yelled to the lieutenant. "Ma'am, Ma'am? Do you know anything about my buddies who were brought in same time as me?"

She looked back at Grady, shook her head and continued her rounds.

Grady looked at the bag of fluids hanging above him and the line going into his arms. Remembering what happened on the river, in a panic he reached down to check for his leg. Feeling his thigh wrapped in dressing brought him huge relief. He wiggled his toes and closed his eyes in gratitude to God. Grady glanced discreetly at other men on the ward, after thinking how thankful he was to have all his parts. He felt guilty for thinking it, but it was honest. The sedative that Lieutenant Shehan pushed through his IV was kicking in. He fell back into a deep sleep.

It had been three weeks since the swift boat attack. Grady suffered serious injuries, but the doctors were able to stitch him back together. Some of his squad got a ticket home. Big Jim sustained broken ribs, a collapsed lung, and shrapnel in his chest. They estimated it would take six months of rehab before he would be able to walk upright again, if ever. Sal was not as lucky. When the explosion threw him out of the boat, he impacted something solid in the water causing a cracked skull and brain contusion. The doctors did not know if he would ever regain full mental or physical capabilities. The Army decided Jim, Sal, and Joey were done. The only cost Joey had to pay was two fingers and a thumb. He would be okay, but the Army did not want infantrymen who could not pull a trigger. Grady never got a chance to say good-bye, but he was glad they got back to the world.

He wrote several letters to Gabby and his parents while he was in the hospital, downplaying his injuries so they would not worry. He hoped to get mail while he was laid up, but the Army did not reroute that quickly. He missed reading her letters, even if the frequency was dwindling each week. He was sympathetic to how busy she was her first year of college, but it hurt that school was a higher priority than him.

When the doctors finally released him, the first thing he did was get his mail, go to his bunk, and read through Gabby's letters one by one by postmark. He had been in the delta for a week, and in the hospital for three weeks, so he expected many letters. He was disappointed only six letters were waiting for him. Three were from Gabby and three were from his parents. He took a deep breath, and then tore into her letters. Her tone was becoming less personal. Instead, she filled the pages with the activities at school, politics, demonstrations, and the mood of the country toward the war.

His anger rose with each paragraph. Surely, she must have known that he did not want to hear about his countrymen disagreeing with the war. Toward the end of her first letter, she mentioned she missed him and couldn't wait until his tour was over, but something bothered Grady. She used the right words, but they conveyed no feeling. The words were from someone pre-occupied.

He wondered if his perceptions were skewed because the war was getting to him. The growing doubt about her devotion made him feel completely alone. He wondered how it was even possible. After all, only he knew her so completely, only he shared secret memories, and only he received her affection. He felt sad and helpless not being able to hold her, kiss her, or hear her say the words. His emptiness created plenty of room for imaginary doubt, or was it real?

Military Honors

A flurry of activity on the post the next morning annoyed Grady as he went through his personal hygiene routine. Newly-arrived troops scurried around painting things, shining things, and sprucing up. He wondered if the 9th was preparing to pull out.

Sometime mid-morning, Grady was told to report to the Company Commander's office. The commander, Lieutenant Colonel Jamison, informed Grady to be in dress uniform tomorrow because the Commanding Officer in Vietnam, General Abrams was coming to the post.

Colonel Jamison said all the men of the company would be on the parade ground for the ceremony. The Army held ceremonies occasionally to award medals, but Grady had not seen this much fuss about one. He knew it must be big if the four-star was coming in. He saluted his colonel and waited to be dismissed. Jamison returned the salute, and ordered Grady to meet him tomorrow in front of the parade grandstand before the ceremony.

Grady felt intimidated and nervous. Typically, all his orders came directly from his sergeant, who got them from the lieutenant. This was the first time he met Lieutenant Colonel Jamison. He departed the Command Center now knowing why the post was abuzz with activity. It seemed inconsistent to him that men were being killed in the bush, and yet the Army still had time for parades, painting buildings, and ceremonies.

The next day, in his dress uniform, Grady reported to Jamison on the platform in front of the parade area. He saluted smartly.

"Reporting as ordered, Sir!"

The colonel returned the salute and invited Grady to sit with him on the platform. Grady was completely puzzled by the invitation. The ceremony began when General Abrams arrived in a staff car and came to the platform with a small entourage. An Army major stood at the podium welcoming the general, distinguished officers, and troops. He then began the ceremony.

General Abrams walked to the front of the stage as the major called on Private 1st Class Grady Cordeaux to front and center. Shocked, Grady got up and marched crisply to the front where he delivered a smart salute to General Abrams and returned to attention. The major called "Attention to Orders!" All the men in formation at the ceremony snapped to attention.

The major read a citation describing "extraordinary heroism, risk of life while engaged in combat with the enemy," etc.

Grady was too nervous to comprehend the entirety of the citation. He understood what was happening though when the general pulled a medal from its box and pinned the United States Army Distinguished Service Cross on Grady's uniform. General Abrams told Grady that the President, the country, and the 9th Infantry Division were proud of him.

The general leaned in toward Grady's ear, "Son, this is the second highest award a soldier can earn, and the first one usually goes to widows, so on behalf of a grateful nation, we thank you."

The general stepped back and stood at attention in front of Grady. Grady again saluted the four stars in front of him. General Abrams returned the salute and shook Grady's hand. He turned and walked off the platform to his staff car. The whole affair lasted only a few minutes.

Grady was completely surprised. The Army had just recognized and awarded him for his actions on his swift boat. They said he saved men's lives under fire and returned fire while wounded. Grady's memory of the event was fuzzy, and it happened so fast he could not recall the details. He acted instinctively, and certainly did not think he was heroic. The general had also given him a Purple Heart medal for being wounded in combat. In just half a year, Private Cordeaux was promoted to private 1st class and had earned a small rack of medals and ribbons on his chest. After the ceremony, Lieutenant Colonel Jamison requested Private Cordeaux to report to his office at 1500 hours.

Grady left the ceremony receiving pats on his back, high fives and lots of comments from troops in his platoon. He smiled and joked, but inside he was unsure how to feel. On one hand, he was proud to have done something good for his buddies, and proud to be recognized by the Commanding General of the Southeast Asian Theater. On the other hand, the enemy was still there, men died anyway, and Grady was still in Vietnam, while his girl was back in the world going to frat parties. He wanted to get drunk, but he had a meeting with the colonel. He got back to his barracks, into his fatigues, and sacked out.

Meeting with the Colonel

"Cordeaux, we're proud of you, son. The other men are grateful for their lives, too," Colonel Jamison told him.

He invited Grady to take a seat. Grady was uncomfortable being informal with a high-ranking officer, so he responded to the colonel with, "Yes, Sir."

"Not many men get the Service Cross. You probably could've got the Medal of Honor if it had been a major engagement. I don't make those decisions, son. I guess politics reach all the way back here to the Nam, but we are damn proud of you."

Jamison paused for a moment and said, "Let me get to the point! The 9th is going to be shipping out in a month. The politicians want to reduce the U.S. presence in this god-forsaken place, so the 9th is going back to Kansas. The men who still have time left on their tours will be reassigned to other units in country, or in the European theater."

"Cordeaux, you almost earned a free ride home and an Honorable Discharge because of your injuries, but the doctors said you were still combat-qualified. However, because of your heroic actions under fire, I will do whatever I can to see that your last six months in Vietnam will not be on the business end of an AK-47. We need men like you in the rice paddies, but you've earned your keep."

Jamison continued, "So, think about it, ask around, see the detailer, and let me know in a week where you might want to go or what you want to do. Do you understand me, son?"

"Yes, Sir!" Grady replied. He stood up and saluted the colonel.

Jamison returned the salute. "Dismissed."

"Oh man! You got a horseshoe up your ass, hero," one of the guys said when Grady told him about the offer.

Most of them were going home when the 9th Infantry left Vietnam, so they were not envious of him having to finish out his tour, but they were glad for him to get out of combat.

"You won't have to deal with black pajama gooks shooting at you from every bunker and tunnel complex in the bush," a buddy said.

"Man, you done made the grade!" another said.

Grady did not feel so privileged; he still wanted to go home, but at least the second half of his tour would be less dangerous. Jamison was giving him his choice, but Grady did not know about other divisions or units in Nam. He had a week to figure it out or the Army would figure it out for him.

A few days passed and Grady still had no idea where he wanted to be reassigned. He was enjoying the time to relax, take hot showers, eat hot meals, and read his mail. He wrote letters home, explaining his situation without too much detail, except to say his mailing address would be changing.

His disappointment with Gabby's letters was growing. Each letter was short with little substance. She wrote that she loved him, but her words felt obligatory rather than sincere. She mentioned the stress of her schedule and homework.

In comparison, Grady's only stress was an enemy he did not know who was trying to kill him. He did not point out to her the absurdity of her perspective compared to his situation, because there was no way she could fully understand the danger he faced every time he went on patrol. He was beginning to see her total lack of empathy. Grady shared with his parents sparse details about life in the Nam, and while they were overwhelmed with running the farm, their letters were still filled with words of love, encouragement and caution for him.

He assured his mother he was well. He even wrote about learning to manage his anxiety. Up to recently, it plagued him, but after talking with Lieutenant Shehan, he had a revelation. She had a few psychological sessions with him pointing out that his actions in combat and in crisis mode were not hindered by anxiety and fear; under extreme stress he actually was very much in control. She helped him to see that his illness had not constrained him when courage was needed. The realization was so liberating that it made his anxiety nearly impotent. It allowed him to release his demons. After closing the letter to his parents, he focused on getting through the second half of his tour and coming home.

Grady was napping in his bunk when he felt someone tugging on his boot. He was alarmed to see Sergeant Williams standing over him. "What is it, Sarge, we got a mission?"

"No, Cordo, you ain't going nowhere for a while, but I got some Intel to pass on."

Sergeant Williams took a minute to allow Grady to wake up and listen carefully. The sergeant told him about a military unit in Saigon that did interesting stuff with planning and training the Army, Republic of Vietnam (ARVN). The sergeant heard it was a really good outfit.

Sergeant Williams got close to Grady's face as if he was entrusting him with a secret. "Listen, Cordo, nobody knows what's going to happen in this damn war. Some people are saying it could be the first war we ever lost. I don't know about that, but what I do know is that instead of sending more poor white boys and brothers to fight this yellow man's war, the man is sayin it's about time they fought for themselves. And we have to train them.

"Something's going down too, some Lam Son bullshit, real soon. I also know that the 9th is pulling out. Hell, we had 500,000 men here a few years ago, and now we got less than 90,000. I hear those dudes will be leaving too. I think if you got to be here anyway, you might as well do something to help the ARVN. You dig? We are getting out of here and no man wants to be the last to die, so don't let it be you!" Before Sergeant Williams walked out he told Grady to think about it.

In January 1971 with 201 days left in Vietnam, Pvt. 1st class Grady Cordeaux climbed aboard the UH-1 helicopter headed for Da Nang to join the Screaming Eagles 101st Airborne Division. He had decided to help train ARVN troops to fight for themselves. The 101st assigned him to the Special Ops Group, I Corp. Grady jumped off the helicopter on the tarmac and an Army specialist yelled, asking if he was Private Cordeaux. Grady nodded.

The specialist yelled, "Jump in the jeep, Major Reese is expecting you."

Special Operations Group

The two men walked toward a Quonset hut on the edge of the flight line. Specialist Grainger knocked on the door. A no-nonsense deep voice shouted to come in!

Grainger opened the door and snapped a salute. "Private Cordeaux reporting, Sir."

Reese was a middle-aged, 6-foot, 2-inch 275-pound balding man with a thick moustache and hairy forearms as thick as a woman's leg. His brown eyes were deep set under thick eyebrows, looking down a wide crooked nose. Grady looked at him and immediately knew the major played football.

He grabbed the bowl of his pipe in his palm and spoke in a deep southern accent. "Thank you, Grainger. Stand by."

"Yes, Sir," Grainger replied, standing at ease in the corner.

Without looking up from his paperwork, Reese said, "Have a seat, Private."

Grady sat a full minute until the major finally put down the reports and made eye contact. Grady knew it was a power play, and he immediately formed an unfavorable opinion of the man.

"Before we get down to brass tacks about why you are here, I have to dispense with a formality." Thinking he was supposed to hide in a corner somewhere out of the way, Grady replied, "Yes, Sir."

Major Reese reached into a drawer and came from behind the desk to the middle of the room.

He nodded to Grainger, who called, "Ten hut!"

Grady snapped to attention. Reese's tone changed. He read, "Attention to Orders. The United States Army recognizes and promotes Pvt 1st Class Grady Cordeaux, of Special Operations Group, I Corp, to the rank of E-4 Corporal, effective immediately."

Grady was dumbfounded. He saluted the major, who returned the salute and shook Grady's hand. When it sunk in a few minutes later, Grady became suspicious about the kind of assignment for which a promotion might be needed. Did this mean he had classified clearances? It did not take long for his curiosity to be satisfied.

"Talk to me, Cordeaux. I've read the file about how you saved men on your swift boat, and I know you are a good GI, but tell me about home. Do I hear a Dixie accent?"

"Yes, Sir," Grady replied. "Born and raised in central Louisiana."

Reese smiled. "I knew you were a good ol' boy when I read your file. I'm a Bama boy myself. You play football in Louisiana?"

"Yes, Sir! I was waiting for college offers, but I got into a scuffle and wound up here."

"Yeah, you look like a ball player. Linebacker, right?"

"Yes, Sir," Grady replied.

"Me too. I played for Auburn, and then ROTC called me to fight for my country. I'm not sure the ARVN can handle two ol' football boys from the South."

After the informalities, Reese got down to business. "Corporal, we are going to work together very closely for the next several months. I need you to help me help these ARVN infantry boys do the best they can against the North Vietnamese Army (NVA). Oh, by the way, part of that promotion comes with a security clearance, so everything I tell you from now on is not to be discussed outside of these walls. Got it?"

"Yes, Sir."

"Alright, Grainger will get you settled in your new hooch. Get cleaned up, get a shower, eat something, and meet me back here at 1400 hours. Dismissed."

"Yes, Sir." Grady saluted and headed out the door. He waited 30 seconds outside, until Grainger pulled up in the jeep.

Grady said, "Fast door to door service." He then asked, "Can you make sure I get my mail?"

"I sure will," Grainger replied, arriving at a hooch.

Grady jumped off the jeep, opened the door and saw one bunk, a locker, a closet, a desk, a fan and small fridge. It looked like an officer's quarters. He came out to ask if he was in the right hooch, but Grainger was gone. The hooch had plywood walls covered by canvas on the outside, a sturdy roof, and electricity. It was the Ritz compared to some of the bunkers and tents where he slept in the forward areas. Whoever assembled this place knew where to find resources.

Grady noticed a folder on the desk with his name on it. He was pleasantly surprised how efficient things were in I Corp. Flipping through the folder, he saw a map of the base. Someone highlighted the showers, toilets, mess hall, and supply center. He stowed his duffle bag and headed to the showers.

Warm showers were hit or miss in the Nam. These showers had water tanks with pull chains above the stalls. The water, which came from trucks parked alongside, was not boiling, but it was warmer than he had felt in a long time. After enjoying the luxury, he got into clean fatigues and went to chow. Even the food was better.

Not long after he sat down to eat, everyone started moving out. Something just happened. He had a feeling the major would tell him in a few hours. It preyed on his mind, but Grady was able to eke out a few winks in his new bunk before his 1400 meeting.

"Corporal, I guess you have been wondering why you were assigned to us?" Reese did not wait for a response to his rhetorical question. "I'm going to brief you on a classified mission. These plans have come from the top, and you are not to repeat anything after you leave this office. Don't mention it to a buddy, to a girlfriend, parents back home, to your girlfriend off base who 'love you long time', and certainly not to the guy sitting next to you in a bar. Are we clear?"

Grady nodded.

"Corporal, I need a verbal acknowledgement that you understand what I have just told you."

"Yes sir, Major Reese, I understand!"

"Very well." Reese lit up his pipe. "On the 29th of January, U.S. forces in I Corp will join the ARVN in an offensive named Lam Son 719. We are going to assist the ARVN in invading Laos. The objective is to stop the NVA from resupplying their forces in the Mekong. We know that hundreds of tons of supplies, arms, and food make its way from Hanoi to the enemy in South Vietnam via the Ho Chi Minh trail.

"ARVN wants to destroy the trail where it goes through a strategic village called Tcehpone, in Laos. U.S. forces will clear the way up Route 9 to the border. Their troops will go the rest of the way to Tchepone, backed by U.S. air support. No U.S. ground troops will cross the border. We expect heavy enemy resistance. Success will be measured by the destruction of the trail, and the supply line in Laos, to kill as many enemy as they can, and then return safely. The U.S. will assist in the exit and provide transportation for the wounded."

Grady's Role

Reese paused for a minute allowing Grady to absorb what he had just been briefed. "Any questions?"

"Yes, Sir," Grady answered. "What will my role be in this mission?"

"I'm glad you asked. I am an Intelligence Officer and a commo expert. I requested a ground pounder to be at my side the duration of the offensive. You will be with me in a chopper monitoring the entire mission from treetop level. I need you to identify what weaponry and unit strength the enemy deploys against the ARVN boys so we can put the right amount of kinetic energy where they need it. Can you identify a piece of mechanized artillery, towed artillery, or any other kind of shit-hit-the-fan, pray-to-Jesus kind of weapon these Godless communists might bring to the fight?"

Grady nodded adamantly, "Yes, Sir!".

"Goddamit, Cordeaux, they told me you were a hardened soldier. I like your attitude son!" Reese was smiling and yelling. "We have two weeks to prepare for this mission. I think that is plenty of time to get ready. Take a few days R&R. Once we kick it into gear, this could go on for several months. There are a few choppers leaving for Saigon. Go get drunk, get laid, then get back here. Any questions?"

"No, Sir," Grady answered.

Reese smiled. "Dismissed!"

Grady went back to his hooch. He was looking forward to mail from Gabby. An hour later Grainger came by to tell him that there was no mail for him. His mood plummeted. He assumed the mail transfer from IV Corp up to I Corp was slow, but not dead.

"You'll probably get something later this week," Grainger said offhandedly, jumping into the jeep.

Grady missed his girl. He was in a new place, with no friends, a new mission, and no connection back home. However, he decided rather than wallow in self-pity, he would take the R&R that Major Reese suggested. He made a phone call to Reese's staff, and his orders were cut. He packed a small bag, swung by to pick up his orders and headed to the flight line to catch a ride to Saigon for a few days. At least he might see some of his buddies. *They are probably all getting ready to transfer back to the world,* he thought. Grady jumped aboard a huey to Da Nang Air Base, then another hop to Tan Son Nhut Air base near Saigon.

R&R in Saigon

Bars and prostitutes were on every corner of Saigon. They stood on the streets showing potential customers what they were selling. Every GI was a target for hookers, pickpockets, beggars, hustlers, and drug dealers. As long as a GI had money, Saigon provided the urchins willing to take it. Grady disadvantaged himself by being alone. It was too easy to become a victim with only one pair of eyes on the lookout.

The only place he could think to go was Thuc Pham's. He got out of the jeepney at an intersection near Thuc Pham's. It was the high-class neighborhood which usually meant the patrons had deep pockets. Grady was unaware that a group of street kids were ready to liberate his wallet and watch. Seconds before the thugs were on him, an arm pulled him in under the protective canopy of Thuc Pham's.

He resisted, shouting, "Whoa, wait a minute, I don't want any boom-boom long time!"

After he said it, he looked at his accoster and saw that she was not a street girl. The well-dressed, beautiful Vietnamese woman glared at him in anger. "That is the thank you I get for saving you from being robbed. Next time I will mind my own business and see how you do. Au revoir." She released his arm and turned to go back inside.

"No, wait!" Grady grabbed her arm. She jerked away. The look on her face let him know the damage was done.

"I'm so sorry, I did not mean to insult you. It all happened so fast with so many people around I did not see you. Please believe me, I would never have said anything like that to someone like you."

Her facial expression did not change. If his apology meant to thaw her, his last comment sent her back to a chill. "What do you mean, someone like me?" You mean someone Vietnamese?"

"No, no…I, I meant someone so, so beautiful. I mean someone so out of my league." Grady fumbled his apology. He did not know how to talk to a foreign woman who obviously came from a social class so completely different from his own.

Her face began to soften. She asked what he meant by 'out of his league'. Grady did not know how to explain the sports analogy.

He answered. "Someone better than me. You're the one the other guy gets… oh never mind."

She wondered if he recognized her. She confessed, "I remember you from New Year's. You were here with your friends. They found girls to be with, but not you. Why not? Are you married?"

Grady asked if he could come in and sit down. She immediately turned into the gracious hostess of the establishment. "Please come in." She explained, "I saw you coming up the street. Those boys were going to rob you, so I grabbed you before they did. I did not mean to scare you."

"No, no it's fine. You saved me. Thank you, again," he said sincerely.

They looked at each other for a moment, not understanding what was happening, until it became awkward.

Grady answered, "Um, yeah, no, I'm not married, but my girlfriend is back in the States. She is waiting for me to finish my tour and we will get married. What about you? Oh, I'm sorry. Is that a question I can ask without offending?"

She was sitting next to him. "Oui! Yes, it's fine. My family owns this restaurant and many others in Vietnam. When the time is right, my parents will find a suitable Vietnamese man for me to marry to bring into the family businesses. The time is not right. With the war going on I do not think it will ever be right. I'm sorry. I do not know why I told you so much."

He had a quizzical look. "Don't you want to find your own husband?"

She responded, "It is a long story. Our culture is very different from yours. Americans can do whatever they want, but in Vietnam I must obey my father and mother. They like the GI for business, but not for marriage. Americans bring many good things but also bad things. You do not act like most soldiers. You are quiet and polite. What is your name?"

"Oh, right…. Um, I am Grady Cordeaux, from Louisiana, it's nice to meet you."

Grady stuck out his big farm hand to shake hers. She just laughed. "Did I do something wrong?" he asked.

"No, Grady Cordo," she said. "You have very big hands. It's okay."

She placed her delicate hand in his. "I am Tien du Cuc Cho Pham."

Grady was confused when she said her name.

She knew right away and said, "You can call me Tien."

He felt relief. "It has been my pleasure to meet you Tien. Would it be all right if I stayed here and had a beer? I'm on leave and I'm waiting to see if any of my friends show up tonight."

She smiled. "Yes, of course. Please enjoy. Let me know if you need anything. If you would like to eat here, that will be fine. I will check on you later."

Grady was not comfortable with what he was feeling. If he was being honest, it was nice to meet a Vietnamese girl who was not interested in his money or ID card. He eased his guilt by convincing himself that she was only being a very professional hostess, and it was only a friendly conversation. He ordered a beer and watched the crowd file in for the night.

Lam Son 719

The chop, chop cadence of the UH-1 hueys was an unmistakable sign the operation was underway. Grady sat on the right-side rear, behind the M60 machine gun protruding out the open door. His helmet and headset allowed him to communicate with Major Reese on the left side rear. It was the second week of February and Lam Son 719 had begun. U.S. forces helped clear a path on Highway 9 in Central Vietnam to the Laotian border. South Vietnamese mechanized forces continued the push down the highway in Laos, with the objective of destroying the Ho Chi Minh trail through Tchepone and seizing all the weapons caches. It was one of the largest air mobile operations in history. For the next six weeks, Reese and Grady looked out the open doors of the UH-1 reporting NVA positions and strength along the way to Tchepone. U.S. artillery units provided support from the border. Little bird choppers flew at treetop level to draw fire.

Grady was able to identify most of the individual elements from five NVA divisions, including tank regiments, artillery regiments, and antiaircraft artillery sites. Their chopper took small arms fire every day and occasional anti-aircraft artillery fire, but they made it back to base every day to do it again tomorrow. The odds of a huey gunner surviving his tour were low, but the pace of the operations never allowed Reese and Grady time to dwell on the dangers. They knew each time they went up their chances of coming back were getting thinner, but both men and the crew had a vital mission from which they could not waver. Grady overcame his fear each morning by calling up the most intense concentration he needed to pinpoint enemy units while flying overhead at 50 miles per hour. After a few sorties when the helicopter got shot up pretty hard, Grady thanked God when his boots touched ground again. He would go to a quiet place to try to reconnect with his human side and unleash the fear that had been buried deep in his soul. When he did, he vomited everything in his stomach. Men in war can go to their highest highs and the lowest lows, but when the hormones return to equilibrium, there is a reckoning.

Not long into the campaign, the ARVN got bogged down in the mud along the narrow Highway 9. This stall provided ample opportunity for heavy enemy fire from the jungle on both sides of the highway, making forward progress nearly impossible. Grady and Reese witnessed over and over again the column of vehicles being overwhelmed by NVA on the flanks. They would call in artillery support, but the responses were weak.

Additionally, the NVA struck some of the ARVN fire support bases, preventing them from providing the much-needed artillery support. The ARVN lacked the necessary amount of anti-tank weapons to counter the NVA armor. ARVN units often ran out of ammunition. Their inability to return fire allowed the enemy to capitalize on their weakness and inflict heavy losses.

By mid-March, when it appeared that the offensive would fail, ARVN finally broke through to Tchepone. It was a disappointing victory because the weapon caches they captured were minor, and they paid a heavy price in manpower. U.S. helicopter rescue forces also suffered heavy losses. The NVA shot down 66 UH-1s. The South Vietnamese and American politicians were desperately trying to demonstrate the ARVN's ability to win the war without U.S. presence, but the only thing Grady and Reese witnessed was failure.

Retreat

On the 20th of March, Grady boarded the chopper with Major Reese, as he had done every day for the past month. Grady was no longer providing reconnaissance, he was assisting rescues. ARVN forces were retreating from Tchepone and the NVA were backfilling every step of the way. The beleaguered ARVN troops were still being attacked from both flanks as they tried to retreat. There was no semblance of order, only chaos. Most helicopter rescue flights were being overloaded with retreating soldiers desperately hanging on to anything they could, including the landing skids. Overloading made the choppers easy targets. NVA soldiers with rifles were picking off the strap hangers, while antiaircraft fire was knocking the overburdened choppers out of the sky.

Grady's helicopter was to ferry troops from ARVN Fire Base Bravo in Laos back to the border. The chopper approached the landing zone, but desperate soldiers were amassed on the landing pad. The pilot hovered five feet off the ground as Grady and Reese yelled to the men to back away so they could land. NVA were assaulting what was left of the Fire Base. and the soldiers knew if they did not get on the next helicopter, they would be captured, tortured and killed.

The soldiers panicked, grabbing the skids of the helicopter to climb aboard. Grady and Reese did not want to throw them off and defeat their rescue objective, so they pulled as many men inside the cabin as they could. Eventually the chopper became overloaded as more men tried desperately to climb on. The pilot lifted the chopper with men clinging to the landing skids.

NVA shot at the men hanging below the skids. All were hit by gunfire and fell to their deaths through the jungle canopy. Two soldiers standing atop the skids were hit but managed to hang on. The chopper strained to maintain altitude with the heavy load.

Major Reese yelled to the terrified soldiers, "I think we are going to make it!" Grady saw the major's mouth move but could not make out his words. Just then he looked out the open door and spotted the contrail of an anti-air missile.

The missile struck the rear rotor housing causing the huey to spin under the force of the main rotor blades. The pilots held the control sticks as best they could, guiding the spinning chopper in a semi-controlled descent into the jungle canopy. It hit the treetops hard breaking the cockpit glass and sheering off the tail section. A few of the men were killed on impact; the survivors were in shock. Both pilots were impaled by tree branches breaking through the cockpit canopy. Grady regained consciousness abruptly when the fuselage broke loose from its precarious position 30 feet in the trees and fell to the ground. An ARVN soldier was crushed under the falling fuselage. Several others were injured worse upon ground impact.

Although dizzy and vomiting, Grady unbuckled his seat belt and fell out of the open fuselage door. He went back into the helicopter to get the major and any survivors. Major Reese was unconscious and bleeding from his head and arm. Grady unbuckled him and lifted him out of the cabin onto the jungle floor.

Before the missile struck, Grady knew they were only three kilometers from Highway 9 where the whole ARVN army was retreating back to South Vietnam. They needed to head east immediately before the NVA swarmed their crash site.

Grady could only assume there was enemy between them and Highway 9. He made a quick assessment of the condition of the survivors, and their weapons and resources. Knowing the extreme difficulty of carrying an unconscious man through thick jungle, Grady tried reviving Major Reese. An ARVN officer told Grady that

Reese's head injury was bad, and he would be unconscious for a while. Grady asked him his name.

"I am Lieutenant Tran Pho, of the 357th Medical Battalion, ARVN."

Grady replied, "Well, Sir, you are the ranking officer at this moment. What are your orders?"

Pho asked Grady for his name.

"I am Corporal Grady Cordeaux, an infantry specialist."

Pho asked, "Do you know how far we are from ARVN forces, or NVA?"

"Sir, before we were hit, we were three clicks from Highway 9 due east of our present location."

Pho asked one of the soldiers if his compass was intact. It was. He handed the compass to Grady. "Corporal, I will leave it to you to lead us to Highway 9."

Pho pointed to two soldiers who were the least injured and barked an order. "You two carry the major. We should go now, as quietly as possible."

Grady was surprised and relieved at Pho's leadership and his men's discipline. He had witnessed the courage and determination of ARVN soldiers in battle for nearly a month, but he did not expect it from a doctor. The ARVN soldiers were often poorly equipped, but their courage was remarkable, and it earned Grady's respect.

Escape and Evade

The soldiers quickly made a litter out of cut bamboo and straps from the helicopter to carry the major. In less than five minutes, they headed east into the jungle. Grady was impressed and relieved at how stealthily the soldiers moved through the jungle, even while carrying the litter.

Every 500 meters they stopped to absorb 360 degrees of their surroundings. They could hear soldiers running through the jungle 100 meters to their north and assumed it was NVA soldiers rushing to the helicopter crash. It would not be long before they tripped the claymore mines hastily set around the downed chopper. Grady and the survivors were more than half a kilometer from the crash site when they heard the detonations of the claymores. At least three of the six exploded, and the other three would go off soon. The survivors smiled, except Lieutenant Pho.

The squad cut through nearly two kilometers of dense jungle when Grady began to feel numbness in his unsteady legs. He was moving on pure adrenalin, but with each step the pain and lack of control in his legs intensified. Pho noticed the change in Grady's gait. He whispered to one of his soldiers to keep an eye on Grady in case he faltered. Pho suspected that Grady's spine might have been injured in the crash.

Suddenly, Grady held up a closed fist indicating a halt. He sensed something ahead and everyone stayed still for several minutes.

Pho moved to Grady to find out what he had seen. "What it is, Corporal?"

Grady did not turn his head or move a muscle. He was in too much pain.

He whispered. "Something to our south does not look right. Whenever the little hairs on the back of my neck stand up out here in the bush, I pay attention."

Pho understood. "Are you wounded?"

"Lieutenant, honestly I feel like my Goddamn lower half is not attached to my upper half. I'm losing feeling below my waist. I would not know it if I shit my pants, or if my dick was shot off. Right now I want two of your men to come with me; send them up here, quietly! We're going down this ridge real slow like we're stalking turkey and circling back around our southern flank. Tell the rest of the men to stay put and face south with rifles ready!"

Sergeants Quang and Tran crouched low as they moved up to Grady. He told them his plan, then they slithered down the ridgeline 200 meters out of sight. They stayed low, moving around a small knoll south of where Pho and the men were holding. The thickness of the jungle made it hard to detect terrain elevation changes, but Grady could distinguish high ground from low ground by the type of trees and vegetation.

As the three men circled around directly south of their unit, halfway up the hill they could hear the enemy. It was a squad of eight NVA infantry positioning to attack Pho and the survivors. Grady's men heard the NVA unit saying they had to advance slowly 200 meters ahead, and since it was a U.S. helicopter that crashed, the survivors were probably Americans, which excited and unnerved them.

Grady instructed his team to move quietly behind the NVA squad. When they were 200 meters from Pho, Sergeant Quang would be directly behind the NVA; Grady would go to the east side; and Sergeant Tran would go to the North. Grady and Tran would get the NVA in a crossfire, Pho and his men would counterattack from the east, and Quang would get those retreating back down the hill. Grady ordered Tran not to attack until he heard Grady fire.

After the battle, they would rendezvous with Pho. If they got shot, the squad would try to get to them, but not knowing how many other NVA units were nearby, they might be on their own. Then Grady and Tran split off from each other crawling to their objectives. Grady could see the NVA clearly from his position. They were heavily camouflaged and moving quietly. When they were less than 30 meters from Pho's position, Grady saw one of the NVA soldiers signaling that the enemy was in sight, and getting ready.

The NVA raised their rifles to take aim on the unsuspecting group of crash survivors. Before they could find the enemy in their rifles' sights, the crack of Grady's M16 rifle report sounded through the bush, opening the chest of an NVA soldier nearest to him. In less than the first bullet's echo, the jungle spit bullets from three sides of the NVA eight-man squad. The firefight lasted less than 30 seconds, but eight NVA soldiers lay dead in the jungle. Grady had taken out two, Tran killed two, and Pho's group killed the rest. One of Pho's men was wounded in the arm, but the rest of the unit was unscathed. Grady, Tran, and Quang rejoined Pho. They moved out knowing that nearby NVA would come running.

Grady heard heavy equipment. It was the retreating ARVN forces on Highway 9. The group emerged onto the highway to guns pointing at them. They identified themselves and were welcomed to join the column. When they fell in behind a deuce-and-a-half truck, Lieutenant Pho yelled in Vietnamese to stop the vehicle so Major Reese could be uploaded into the truck, and for a doctor to treat him. They also radioed the Americans to advise them of the situation so they could provide medical evacuation for Major Reese.

Pho ordered Grady to get into the truck with Reese to speak for him. Grady told Pho he would stay with the truck but preferred to walk with the ARVN soldiers who were at his side in the bush. The ARVN men heard this and were honored that Grady wanted to walk with them. He heard them telling other soldiers what had happened, and how Grady had planned the flank attack. As the word spread, Grady felt he was held in high regard.

The ARVN column was nearing the border when Grady began to stumble. He thought he had the stamina but he was losing control of his legs. Pho saw this and yelled to the men. They grabbed Grady and lifted him onto a truck.

"I don't know what is wrong with me," Grady said.

Pho looked him over quickly and noticed Grady's crotch was wet.

Grady said, "I don't remember doing that either."

Pho tapped the shoulder of the doctor, an ARVN major, tending to Reese. The two spoke in Vietnamese.

The doctor told Grady, "Corporal, you will go with your major when the helicopter comes. It should be very soon now. I want you to tell the American doctors you were in a very serious helicopter crash. I want you to tell them that you cannot feel anything below the waist. Understand?"

Grady replied, "Yes, Sir, but I just got the wind knocked out of me."

The doctor said, "Corporal, the crash was very hard on your body. An impact like that could break a man's spine. If that happened, you would not be able to walk. However, you do not have feeling below your waist, so it is likely you have damaged vertebra or a disk, enough to cause you to lose feeling at the rupture point and below. The American doctors will want to x-ray you for this. The lieutenant told me you fought bravely and led these men out of danger. Now your body is telling you it is time to heal."

Within minutes the men secured a landing zone for the incoming chopper and loaded Major Reese, Grady, and Private Lin-dou, who had taken a bullet to his left shoulder.

Respect

It was early May, but already hotter than hell. "Ten Hut!" a voice barked from the platform on the flight line. All the men snapped to attention. Grady stood on the platform holding crutches under his arms. He moved to the center of the stage beside Colonel Bridges. "Call to Orders! For distinguishing himself through gallantry, heroism and valor by leading the evacuation of a wounded U.S.

senior officer, a squad of friendly forces, and himself through many miles of hostile enemy territory while under fire; for planning and leading a successful offensive assault against the enemy during that evacuation; and for maneuvering the squad to safe territory, all the while wounded and in extreme pain, Corporal Grady Cordeaux, by orders of the President of the United States, the Commander of Armed Forces, Republic of Vietnam, and the United States of America is hereby awarded the Silver Star."

Colonel Bridges pulled the medal from the box and pinned it on Grady's uniform already decorated with several medals and ribbons. Grady saluted the colonel as best he could while on his crutches, then accepted a handshake. "Gentlemen, honored guests, if you would indulge us a little longer, Corporal Cordeaux will be further recognized." A major read off citations for a Purple Heart for being wounded in combat, an Expeditionary Medal for participating in the Lam Son 719 campaign, and the Medal of Gallantry from the Republic of Vietnam. Grady spent nearly a month in traction and rehab at the hospital trying to recover from a ruptured lumbar disk and pinched nerves. He walked with great pain for several weeks and was only now feeling capable. Grady did not care much for the medals. He understood the motivational factors for awarding them, but he did not know how to feel. The whole crash and escape lasted only five hours, and it was almost an out-of-body experience when it was happening. But lying in a hospital bed unable to move with time to think, he relived every second it took to escape, and then the hundreds of opportunities a bullet, landmine, or punji stick could have ended his life. During the escape, everything was a fight or flight mentality. When he had solitude and time to reflect on the reality of the situation, he caught his breath and sobbed uncontrollably alone.

After the ceremony, the men headed to the mess hall where Grady was buying. All U.S. air bases in Vietnam had beer tents, and Da Nang had one of the biggest. The guys were breaking Grady's balls about the rack of medals on his chest, but he earned them. He had not been in country a year yet, and he had seen more shit than most. His buddies wondered if he was lucky or unlucky. He demonstrated extreme courage under fire, even though he had anxiety. It never stopped him from running right into the hornet's nest when the bullets started flying. Most men cower in those moments, but Grady found something deep inside that pushed him onward.

As the celebration wound down, Reese sat with Grady. He was healing nicely from his wounds, thanks to Grady. "Corporal, the minute I heard your southern drawl I knew you were the kind of man this Army, and our nation needs. I am damn proud of you. Thanks for getting me the hell out of there.

"Listen to this. After at least two intense engagements in combat where you showed extreme heroism while wounded, and after a month and a half in traction to get your legs back, the U.S. Army, in its infinite wisdom, has decided that you have had enough. Son, they are sending you home a few months early. I have orders on my desk that say you get to leave 5 June. You are going home, son. Congratulations!"

Grady stared at Reese. Finally, he spoke. "Are you shitting me, excuse me, kidding me, Sir?"

"Nope." Reese shook his head. "It's for real! You have served your country enough. Hell, word is that if you stay any longer, they will probably promote you again. I thought you had a girl waiting for you back home? Oh, which reminds me, someone dropped off a stack of mail on your bunk the other day. I know it has taken a while for the mail to catch up to you in Da Nang, but that's the military. I'm going to go hit the rack. I think they are deciding if I get to go home too. Come by my office tomorrow, and I'll give you your orders."

"Yes Sir!" Grady saluted, grabbed a few beers and hobbled to his barracks with a shit-eating grin on his face.

Mail Finds Grady

Since arriving at Da Nang in February, the mail came to him in spurts. He got ten letters at a time, then none for three weeks. He wrote to Gabby as often as he could, between missions, and then from the hospital recovery unit.

Grady turned on the light over his bunk, popped open a beer, and lay back to read her letters one at a time. The postmark of the most recent was April 26th. Usually, even though they came in bundles, the last postmark was closest to the current date. Now they were weeks behind. He might be back home before her next letters reached him.

He read the oldest letter first. These quiet moments engulfed in her letters kept him sane. He was so anxious to hold her once again in his arms and make love to her in their special spot under the moonlight.

He imagined her pouring her heart into every word. Unfortunately, by the third letter, her lack of emotion was obvious. Grady wrote her about feeling close because they might both be staring at the same moon, or remembered how she felt in his arms. In contrast, she wrote about war protests, how students were tired of the war, and the U.S. involvement over there was wrong. She mentioned how difficult the spring semester was, but the fraternities' parties relieved the terrible stress. She told him he had no idea how hard it was for her in college.

He was in disbelief she could be so self-centered to even say such a thing to him, considering his circumstances. Her vocabulary was changing too, saying things like everyone was tuning in, dropping out, or sharing free love; everyone except her. She told him about the racial troubles they were having with radical black groups. Since she was Hispanic, she did not feel like she belonged anywhere. It went on and on, each letter repeating the same thing. She wrote very little about her love for him, or their plans when he got back. His annoyance was at its peak, but rather than stop, he opened the last and most recent letter.

Dear Grady, for some time now I have been trying to figure out a way to tell you something. We have both gone through so many changes in our lives this past year. I feel like the whole damn world has gone through so many changes. I fear that those two young lovers, who parted in Pineville last summer, no longer exist. Some nights I look in the mirror and I don't recognize the girl staring back at me. I'm so scared because my heart is being torn in two. I loved you so very much when we were in high school. I don't think anyone could have loved so deeply. But time apart, the terrible loneliness, and the social change that we've been caught up in has led me down a different path.

I'm so sorry, but I have to be honest and tell you I have been seeing someone at school. He is a nice guy. Ironically, you might know him and even have been friends with him. Do you remember Vinnie? We became good friends and he would keep me company sometimes. I relied on him to get me through tough times.

Well, he won't even talk to me or be my friend anymore. He says I should not have let this happen. He was looking out for you, because of how you are over there fighting for us. He said you don't deserve this. Grady, please believe me, I didn't mean for this to happen; it just did.

I met Jim and started talking to him because he said he knew you from playing football against you in high school. He said you were the best defensive player in Louisiana. We had a class together here at State and one thing led to another. I guess Vinnie saw it coming. Every time Vinnie sees Jim and me walking, he looks like he is going to kill Jim.

I'm sad I lost Vinnie's friendship, but more than anything, I'm sorry I couldn't hold on to our love. It's the war and how wrong it is. I will never be as strong as you, and I don't deserve you. Grady, the tears are falling freely now that this letter is coming to an end, as is our love.

If you still want to write me, I will continue to do so as your friend forever. If I don't hear from you, I will understand. Please stay alive and come home to all of us. I only wish the best for you and hope that one day you will find it in your heart to forgive me so that we might see each other again.

Until that time, I remain as always,

Gabby

Grady read each word again and again hoping somehow he had misread something. He stopped because of the torrent of tears, and the anger inside. He threw a beer bottle against the wall, and then buried his face in the pillow screaming guttural yells from the bottom of his lungs.

He wanted to shoot everyone in the shithole country for taking him away from his true love. He imagined getting on a plane to Mississippi to shoot some fucker named Jim who stole his girl while Grady was protecting Jim's right to protest and fuck someone else's girl. He slurred Jim's name through tears, sweat and spittle, imagining that doing so would wound the little frat boy. He wanted to squeeze Jim's little leftist radical head until it popped like one of the pus zits on Jim's pimpled, peace loving face.

Grady's fury was raging even more intensely than at the bonfire, except now he had the experience of snuffing out a human being with a weapon. It was a dangerous familiarity. He imagined walking onto the campus of Mississippi State and emptying his M16 clip into Jim's torso so blood and limbs splattered on the ground. These thoughts of revenge brought a wild sneer across his face, and he began breaking things in his hooch.

Two soldiers who had been at the beer tent earlier with Grady were walking by when they heard the commotion. They rushed into his hooch and wrestled Grady to the ground. He was so amped up he almost lifted both of them. After they subdued Grady and got him calmed, they saw the letter on the bed and knew exactly what had happened. Dear John letters were an everyday occurrence in the Nam.

The three soldiers talked about those fucking hippies and cheating girlfriends back home. They told Grady to forget the little bitch. There were too many women to worry about one college girl who spread her legs for every swinging dick, flower child, commie hippie on campus. Every other guy in Vietnam got the same letter. After considerable consoling, Grady agreed to join his buddies off base and drink away his heartache.

Grady was not paying attention to his pals negotiating with some girls, but he did get drunker than ever before. The three men woke up the next day in a small room above a bar outside of Da Nang. A naked Vietnamese girl was asleep on top of Joey on the floor. The men eventually pulled themselves together, paid the girl, and struggled to get a jeepney back to base. On the ride back, Grady made up his mind about what to do.

My Decision is Final

Grady made an appointment the next week to meet with Major Reese. Reese was expecting Grady to pick up his orders and go back to the world. It was perfectly timed. Americans were leaving Vietnam anyway, as the U.S. policy was to pull out with dignity and leave the fight to the ARVN. President Nixon planned to leave fewer than 60,000 military and civilian personnel to assist with logistical and training issues, but all U.S. combat support was to stop by late 1971. While the registration for the draft remained in place, the U.S. had discontinued drafting men into service. Grady's year had been one of the last years men were drafted and sent to Vietnam.

He knocked on Reese's door and walked in. They exchanged salutes and Reese invited Grady to sit. "Corporal, I have your orders right here. We might do one or two more recon missions, but for all intents and purposes, your tour is completed. Thank you for honorably serving your country. Some fucking war, huh?" Reese said, handing the orders to Grady.

Grady did not take the orders from Reese's hand.

Instead, he said, "Sir, I would like to extend my tour another year."

Reese stood stunned for a moment. "Corporal, what are you talking about? You are a hero; you have nothing more to prove, son. Go home, go to school, play football! For God's sake, do anything else, but don't stay here on this sinking ship! Don't you see what is happening here?"

"Yes, Sir! That is exactly why I want to stay. I feel like it is our duty to see this through. We have both witnessed the bravery of those men, Sir. We know they are going to lose this war if we abandon them. I want to stay just one more year to see it through."

Reese paused for a moment. His tone and stature changed to a father figure. "Grady, what happened? You were writing your girl. You wanted to go home. We talked about this. Remember? You're a decorated war hero. You are pushing your luck too far, son. Go home!" Reese was almost begging.

"Sir, I don't have a home to go to anymore," Grady confided.

"What happened, son? Are your parents alright?"

"Yes, Sir, my folks are fine. It's my girl."

"That's what this is about? Your girlfriend broke up with you? Oh, for God's sake, Cordeaux, it happens here twice a week and every other Sunday. Forget the girl! You still got your parents who need you on that farm, you got friends back home. Now you can afford to go to college and meet hundreds of girls who would love to get their claws on you, a war hero. C'mon, son, grab this bull by the horns, take Uncle

Sam's gift and ride out of here a few months early. If you don't, you or your parents could regret it. Please!"

Grady stood up and came to attention. "No, Sir. My mind is made up. Major Reese, Corporal Cordeaux requests another one-year tour in the Republic of Vietnam. Sir, will you forward my request?"

Reese understood Grady's formality and was resigned to the fact that he had to consider the request, sadly. "Corporal, I will make my decision by the end of next week. Dismissed."

Grady saluted, turned about face, and left the office. Reese could approve the request right then, but he wanted Grady to think it over.

A Good Man Gets Out

It was barely mid-morning, but the tarmac was already scorching hot in the June sun. Several soldiers including Grady came out to say good-bye to Major Reese. He was recovered enough from the crash to go home. The Army reassigned him to an administrative billet near his hometown of Tuscaloosa, Alabama. It was a joint military posting at an Air Force Base, but Reese did not mind. He was happy to get home to his wife and girls.

After handshakes, Reese said to Grady, "Now look, hero, I still do not agree with your extension request, but I got you a billet to keep you out of the line of fire. Those were my terms, got it? So, when you get down there to Saigon, things will be a little different. Okay? Just do what they tell you. From now on, we are less of a fighting force, and more of a civilian functionary. Then, when it's done, promise me you will get the hell out of Dodge. Comprende?"

"Yes, Sir, roger that!" Grady nodded.

Reese looked back out of the huey. "Alright! Men, it's been one fucked up war!"

He buckled up and lifted off for Tan Son Nhut Airfield. It would be his last stop in the Nam before boarding the plane out to San Francisco International Airport, and then to Alabama. Grady smiled because a good man was going home alive.

One week later, Grady boarded the same flight to Tan Son Nhut to begin his second tour in Vietnam with a special operations unit in Saigon.

When U.S. boots hit the ground in Vietnam in the early 1960s, the military had a strategic plan. However, by 1971, evolving politics and pressures at home had the military fighting the war one day at a time. Hundreds of combat troops were shipping out of Vietnam every day, and the remaining military was supporting the ARVN, so they could do the fighting. The strategy had changed. The GIs remaining in Vietnam were becoming eyes and ears on the ground.

A Nurse in Need

Air Force Lieutenant Michelle Grissom arrived at Tan Son Nhut in September of 1970, assigned to the Medical Battalion in Saigon. Her responsibility as a nurse was to help young men learn to cope with missing body parts so they could go home and face whatever was waiting for crippled veterans. Some men lost limbs, some lost the will to live. It broke her heart every day to see young men, good men, broken and struggling to learn how to be whole again. After she introduced them to physical therapy, they still suffered, sometimes worse, from the mental aspects of sudden disfiguring disabilities. Not long after initial treatments, they were deemed capable of travel and were shipped to stateside hospital wards for wounded veterans.

After only three months in country, Lieutenant Grissom felt defeated. She worked tirelessly to introduce hope to her patients, but their injuries sustained in an unpopular war, serving in a military ill-equipped to care for their numbers, were too much for amputees and paraplegics to emotionally heal. When they finally got home, many were angry and bitter about sacrificing so much, only to be spit on and called "baby killers" by soldier-hating Americans. For her part, Michelle was overwhelmed knowing the insurmountable obstacles these brave boys would face every day for the rest of their lives.

In March 1971, she treated a young corporal with lumbar disc ruptures. Corporal Grady Cordeaux needed aggressive physical therapy and traction, but unlike many others, his spirit was not broken. During the physical therapy sessions, he talked about anything that came to mind, especially his girl back home. It took his mind off the pain. Lieutenant Grissom was supposed to stay focused on the therapy, but once in a while a topic would catch her attention and she would engage in conversation if nothing more than to be understanding and sympathetic with her patient. With the corporal, she shared her story to let him know she understood his sadness of being apart. Instead of the caregiver helping the patient, they consoled each other.

Michelle Grissom was more concerned about treating patients than marching in formation or worrying about military politics and rank. Although an Air Force officer, she retained her civilian nurse caregiver bearings. She was far more attractive than many of the nurses. Her education and rank betrayed her age, but she could have passed for a college senior. Her silky blond hair in a shag cut fell on the back of her neck. She had blue eyes, soft cheek bones, and full lips that attracted stares from an entire ward of wounded soldiers. Her small figure was perfectly toned and taut from a healthy diet and exercise, and although she had earned her nursing degree in Chicago, she looked more like a Florida beach girl.

Sometime during Grady's physical therapy, Michelle found herself attracted to his sensitivity and emotional vulnerability. She struggled to deny her feelings, knowing that a relationship would be inappropriate on many levels. He too was finding comfort and attraction in her care. In conversations, they delicately danced around their feelings, respecting officer/enlisted and doctor/patient boundaries. Still, it was impossible for him to ignore her looks, her intellect, and her humor, nor could he ignore her body pressing against him during therapy. They held their feelings in check throughout his 60-day therapy, and then he returned to Da Nang.

It was July by the time Grady began his new assignment in Saigon. He learned all the basic responsibilities of his position within a few weeks and was ready to take on the more physical demands of the training, until his commanding officer, Major Johnson, observed him in action. The major immediately ordered Cordeaux to go back for more physical therapy.

Michelle was surprised to see Grady again. When she asked about his injury, he described a minor but constant pain in his lower back, and a new pain shooting down his legs. She listened and designed a much more aggressive physical therapy treatment.

While working with him, Michelle inquired about his girlfriend. Without thinking, he told her about Gabby's last letter. Michelle listened intently to his story, and could almost feel his broken heart. Ironically, she too was heartbroken recently after finding out her boyfriend in Chicago was cheating with a coworker. Her ending the relationship was not as painful as Grady's breakup.

She found herself drawn to Grady even more and pondered once more a physical relationship with him. She rationalized it would be alright because her tour was ending in three months and it would not be a forever thing. The circumstances were perfect for both their needs.

When Grady's therapy was almost over, Michelle asked what he did for fun. It struck him odd that he did not have a good answer. He told her sometimes on weekends he would go downtown to drink and watch floorshows. After he said it, he thought, *how pathetic!* Everyone in the Nam knew about floorshows. A few cities in the Far East were infamous for their sex floorshows. Saigon was on top of the list. He was embarrassed.

Surprisingly, she laughed. "Well, maybe one weekend, when you're not at a floorshow, we can have a drink?"

Grady suggested they meet at the Tao Gate Friday at 2000 hours.

She smiled. "You're on, soldier. We'll keep it casual. Okay?" She did not want the impropriety to ruin things. He smiled and walked out, feeling much better.

During that week he thought a lot about her question. It bothered him that he did not do anything for fun. His time in the Nam was spent being a soldier and thinking about Gabby. He had no life other than killing VC and pining away. His cloistered living probably was a blessing in disguise. When GIs were not on patrol, they were trying to lose themselves in alcohol, sex, drugs, or worse.

After enough physical therapy, Grady finally began his new assignment with vigor, settling into Special Operations. It was a potpourri of different assignments that did not fit neatly into any one category. He was detailed to the ARVN NCO Military Training Academy two days a week as an advisor in civilian clothes. Once a week he reported to U.S. Military Operations, SPECFOR Command HQ in Saigon, where he did administrative work, wrote situation reports, and reviewed operational data.

The remainder of his week he engaged in civilian interaction. It was military jargon for socializing off base and keeping his eyes and ears open for information on enemy activity. It was made clear that information-gathering was always passive for Grady. For his protection, he was never to engage a source. He had no training or tools in spy craft. He was merely a GI in Saigon.

On Friday night, Grady waited outside the gate for Michelle. It was humid, but the forecast called for a light breeze. Grady appreciated the breezes blowing in from the ocean because it helped him sleep. Tonight he tried to look his best in khaki slacks, a short sleeve button down shirt, a clean shave and a splash of cologne.

He glanced toward the gate and saw her walking past the guards. Until now, he had only seen her in army fatigues and hospital scrubs, but tonight there was nothing uniform about Michelle Grissom. Standing 5'8" in heels, she wore a low-cut sundress covering a toned body begging to be seen. Her hair was soft, her make-up was light, and her skin smelled of lavender.

When they met she smiled and took his arm. "Let's go, GI and get off this street."

He hailed a cab and told the driver to go to Le Hue San, a part of town with upscale bars and restaurants. They arrived and went to the first restaurant they saw. It was a French-Vietnamese lounge with a good crowd, and a glamorous Vietnamese singer covering French classics.

The couple was barely seated when Grady asked. "So, Lieutenant, what are you expecting from this evening."

Michelle was surprised, but also glad he was bold enough to ask. She pulled a little closer to him at the table. "Tonight I'm Michelle, a girl in a foreign country who met a boy I like from home. I'm a few years older and I'm okay with it, and I don't want forever, but I need right now." He thought about her reply.

"Okay, it's my turn," she said. "What do you want?"

They locked eyes in silence for a few moments. Finally, he said in a soft voice, "Michelle, I don't have a lot of experience with girls, so I'm not sure if I know what I want or if I could handle it when I get it."

She studied the honesty and vulnerability in his face. She liked it. "So be yourself with me, be honest, and let's not judge."

He thought for a moment and nodded. Then he added, "I want that feeling between a man and a woman that happens when they get so close, they can't get any closer. I want to feel like I'm the only man in the world. I want my heartache to go away, and at least for tonight, I want to forget about the rest of the world."

He surprised himself by the honesty and knowing what he wanted. Then he wondered if he just ruined the evening. Michelle did not blink. She stared into his eyes and moved toward him slowly until her lips touched his.

"Ahem!" The waiter excused himself politely to get their attention. "May I bring you something to drink?"

They ordered wine, hors d' oeuvres and cheese. The remainder of the evening they ate a main course, listened to French love songs and enjoyed easy conversation. Michelle's remaining short time in country came up briefly in conversation, but nothing more needed to be said. They both understood the situation. Late in the evening, she leaned over and gently kissed Grady's ear lobe.

She whispered, "Does this restaurant have a hotel?"

Many of the restaurants in Saigon were hotels too. Grady was enjoying her tongue caressing his ear. He paid the check, and they strolled to the lobby where he got a room. No words were necessary as the two slowly made their way up the stairs.

Their bodies glistened from the intense passion of their lovemaking. She enjoyed his stamina; he enjoyed her enthusiasm. It had been a long time for both, and they needed the intimacy to remember what it felt like to have rather than to want, to love rather than hate. Afterward, she lay in his arms, head on his chest listening to his heartbeat. She did not overthink it. He felt good and that was enough. This was going no further, but it was everything right now. Lieutenant Michelle Grissom was breaking a strict military code of conduct as an officer by fraternizing with an enlisted man, but she did not care. All she cared about was feeling human again, even if it was for just tonight.

The next few months flew by as the two strangers spent every weekend in each other's arms. Their passion was secretive, intense, and finite. They both knew there would be no long-distance relationship, no promises, and no tearful goodbyes. It was just something to fill the emptiness. The day she was leaving, he went to her and kissed her goodbye. At the Flight Operations Terminal they gave each other one last look, and then she was gone. Grady went back to work and tried not to think of her. Michelle was only his second lover, so it was impossible to get her off his mind, but he knew what it was. And it was over.

Alone Again

A few weeks later, Grady went off base with his buddies. They stopped briefly at several corner bars, and then stumbled past the restaurant where Michelle and Grady had their first date. He smiled to himself. No one noticed. After an hour in a bar with cold beer, they looked for a bar with entertainment. Grady noticed they were across the street from Thuc Pham's. He had forgotten where they were in Saigon.

He wanted to go in alone, so he told his buddies he was heading back to the base. After they gave him a significant ration of hazing for wimping out, Grady finally broke away from the pack. He waited for them to be out of sight before crossing the street.

It was Friday night and the club was crowded. The staff scurried around trying to wait on everyone. Grady sipped a beer at the bar, all the while looking for Tien. The crowd was different this time. There were fewer obnoxious GIs, and more civilians with money. He finished his beer and asked the bartender if Tien was here.

The bartender asked, "Can I help you?"

"No, no, it's not that, everything is fine. I just wanted to say hello."

"Oh, okay. She is upstairs in the business office. I will call her to come down," he said.

Grady wondered if it was a good idea. Before he could stop the bartender, Tien was standing behind Grady asking the bartender who was asking for her. The bartender looked at Grady. She moved to his side to see his face.

A smile of recognition came over her face. "Bon Nuit, Grady Cordo, you are back at Thuc Pham's? You have not been here in many months."

Grady was excited she remembered his name. He answered, "Actually, Tien, I came here to see you!"

"Oh okay, Grady Cordo, why do you want to see me? Do you want to have a big party, or do you want to rent a room in the hotel? Anybody can help you with it."

Grady did not know how to respond. She did not get the hint he was interested in her. And it did not matter anyway, since her responses made it clear she was not interested in him. His look of disappointment was too obvious to hide. He was equally embarrassed that he completely misread the eye contact they had during their first meeting.

He answered her. "No, it's nothing like that, it's just...um, nothing. Sorry, I didn't mean to bother you."

His entire demeanor had changed and his rejected look said it all. He turned away from her toward the bar.

She did not want to assume she knew his intentions, but she asked him, "Are you here by yourself?"

He nodded.

"Have you eaten tonight?"

He mumbled, "No, but I'll probably grab a bite at the base."

She said, "I am going to have dinner very soon. Would you like to join me?"

Grady was completely confused. He decided her offer did not mean anything, but he was hungry anyway, and would rather dine with a beautiful woman than back at the base with sweaty GIs.

Candles on the table enhanced the ambience of the small private alcove. Grady assumed it was an area reserved for family and VIPs. He was neither, but her kindness gave him the opportunity to enjoy the rich life, if for only a meal. She ordered for both of them in Vietnamese. Her soft Asian features hinted that she could have European genes in her ancestry. He thought maybe one of her grandparents had something more than business dealings with the French. It was not unheard of for Vietnamese to have French in their lineage.

He studied her, imagining she could blend in almost anywhere in the Pacific. She moved with gracefulness that came only from formal training. Grady remembered reading somewhere that social graces and music were mandatory training for girls of wealthy Asians.

"Grady? Grady?" she asked. "Are you alright?"

He answered, "Oh, yes. I'm fine, please forgive me."

"I hope you don't mind that I ordered for you? We have some dishes that our chefs prepare only for family. I hope you like seafood?"

"We get seafood back home, and we eat a lot of fish from the Bayou."

Tien giggled. "You will have to explain 'Bayou' to me over a glass of wine."

The two sat for an hour enjoying dinner, wine, and stories about their dissimilar childhood experiences. They laughed at the differences. When the conversation slowed to a natural pause, Tien asked, "How is your girlfriend?"

The question caught Grady off guard. He wondered if she was merely making conversation, or was there another reason? He hoped it was the latter.

His restless body language signaled embarrassment. Tien's eyes locked attentively on him as he searched for the right words.

Finally, he said, "We both decided it wasn't working, so we called it on account of rain."

She cocked her head slightly as if not fully understanding his answer. "Grady, I don't understand why you called it rain and broke up? What did you call it?"

He smiled. "No, it means we cancelled it, like they do in baseball when it rains, and they cannot play."

She nodded. "Oh, so you cancelled your relationship like a baseball game. It is not very romantic to do this, do you think?"

He laughed. "It is not really what happened. I was trying to make the break-up sound casual, that's all. I don't want to be the jerk who got dumped."

She understood the universal law of love that the one doing the breaking up keeps the power and dignity, while the one being dumped is the loser. She thought how sad it was that pride entered the equation, when both people lose equally.

"Yes, I see. She wanted it to be over, but you did not. Perhaps this happened for a reason?"

"Yeah," he said. "The reason was some leftwing swinging Richard, spending daddy's money and protesting the war, was doing my girl."

Tien did not understand this at all, except that it was not a compliment. "So, that would explain why I saw you with a woman last month."

Grady was stunned. "What? You saw me with another woman?" He felt the need to hide the relationship with Michelle. "You must've seen me with my physical therapist discussing my treatment plan."

Tien looked at him again. "Grady, when a woman looks at you the way she did, she was thinking about more than your treatment. Didn't you know?"

He stammered, "No, it wasn't like that; she was just a friend. It doesn't matter anyway. She left a week ago and I will never see her again."

Tien wanted to know more. She and Grady were close in age, she liked his raw innocence, and he had better manners than most GIs. Her family still expected her to marry a Vietnamese boy from a wealthy family, but the war was changing so many things already. She hoped that tradition might change too.

She continued her roundabout probing. "So now you can go with your friends and be with all the Vietnamese girls you want, huh? Not too bad, right? There are so many beautiful women."

Grady shook his head. "Nah, that's not for me. I mean, I like girls; I just don't like girls who don't like me. I'm the kind of guy who wants to get to know someone really well. I think every woman has something beautiful about her. The first thing a guy sees is her looks and body, which determines if she makes the first cut in the tryouts. Some guys go for a homerun after the first cut. I like to know a woman's heart. Is she kind? Is she nice to old people and dogs? Does she get spiteful and vindictive? Can we be our true selves and still like each other? Do we have common interests? I want to know those things before I take it to the next level. You can't do that by paying a girl by the hour. I don't think badly about guys that pay girls, but it is not for me."

Tien listened to every word. She did not understand the baseball analogies, but she understood perfectly what he was saying. He said things that opened a woman's heart to possibilities. She heard him say if she opened her heart, it might get hurt, but it would not be because he was a thoughtless, selfish pig. His heart was open for love's sake, not gratification. He said a lot of the right things.

They started their evening as acquaintances with a mild interest in each other, but before the evening ended, her eyes and heart were opened to new possibilities. She hoped he felt it too. He asked about the check, but she told him there would be no check. He did not want to leave. They got up together and walked to the exit. He told her how much he enjoyed the evening, and she said she hoped to see him again. They parted ways, each thinking about next time.

New Hope, Bad News

Grady went about his duties with renewed vigor. He was still disgusted at Gabby, but after talking with a chaplain, and igniting a spark between him and Tien, he made up his mind to not let it anger him anymore. He owed his parents an explanation about extending his tour. They would not understand it, especially since his father needed him to come back alive and run the farm.

Tom and Gloria pleaded with their son not to put himself in harm's way any longer than necessary. Gloria especially begged him to be careful and come home. She wrote about his father having a difficult time keeping up the farm. Tom's health and the farm were failing. The news troubled Grady, but he believed his dad could hold on another year or so.

The next few weeks at the ARVN training academy were mentally exhausting, as he tried   projecting optimism. The South Vietnamese NCOs were skilled at fighting when they had U.S. resources. However, nothing could hide the truth about the U.S. withdrawal and decreased support. Grady saw the troops' lack of confidence in facing the challenges ahead.

ARVN would have to fight with much less of everything. The U.S. drawdown left 500 out of 5,000 helicopters, 6,000 armed troops, and a small percentage of the original logistical support and supply lines. Meanwhile, the NVA was changing its tactics daily, and gaining new ground. The Soviets and Chinese were supplying ammo, new weapons, and heavy equipment.

Grady's task was overwhelming, but Tien's presence began to enrich his personal life. Their first few dates were at Pham's. It was familiar and safe. Grady accepted that she was expected to marry a Vietnamese man, so he tried to think of her as a friend. He liked talking with her and initially it was enough. Sometimes he entertained thoughts that the war might change traditional expectations demanded of her. It was a question for a different time, a different place. For two months, the pair met for dinner every weekend and learned more about each other. They appeared to be refreshingly honest, which made things comfortable and sometimes surprising.

Grady understood and respected the appearance of propriety under the watchful eyes of her family, if the friendship was to continue. Pham elders would have disallowed the relationship, if they followed closely and watched their expressions, but business kept them preoccupied. Grady's light-heartedness at Pham's allowed Tien's family to lower their guard. If they knew part of his job was to gather information about the enemy, it would be difficult to explain. He had to be careful on two fronts.

A Spark Ignites

One August weekend, Grady went to Pham's to meet her. He had completed a good week at work and was excited about her companionship for the night. Many of his friends went out on the town to get laid. It was not like that for Grady; he kept his libido in check. His only sexual experiences were with Gabby and Michelle. He longed for an emotional connection that could not be bought on the corner in Saigon.

He spotted Tien the moment he entered the restaurant. She looked gorgeous in a white satin dress that flitted in the fan's breeze. Her shimmery raven hair was down her back. Her make-up highlighted sexy almond eyes. She was a beautiful woman, often mistaken as half American, half Vietnamese, called Amer-asian. The combination resulted in some of the most beautiful and sought-after women in Asia, and Grady understood why her family was so protective of her.

They greeted each other at the bar and engaged in small talk about their week. She was ready to get a table until Grady suggested they go out for a change. Tien's expression changed from joy to concern. She was unsure how her uncle Nguyen would take to the idea. She went behind the bar to ask him in private.

When she returned, she smiled. "My uncle has talked with you before. He says you are not like the other GIs, so it is okay to go for dinner, but I must first ask my cousin to help with the restaurant tonight. If it is okay, we can go." She returned smiling and they headed out onto the street.

A taxi took them to a Chinese restaurant a few blocks away. Tien was familiar with it. She told Grady it had good food but was very expensive. He did not worry about the cost. He wanted to be with her without her family watching. Tonight, he wanted to enjoy how she looked and smelled. The August day's heat was oppressive, but the evening had a cool breeze. They sat out on the back patio where cooks were using long sticks to stir meats, sauces, and vegetables on a curved wooden grate over a fire. Tien and Grady picked out their vegetables and meats, then handed them to the chef. It was Mongolian bar-b-que.

The romantic mood set by the breeze, the cool tropical drinks, the exquisite aromas from the grill, and ambience of the torch-lit patio garden was perfect. American love songs played in the background. Conversation came easy and the couple easily melded into the romance they hoped for. They conversed easily and honestly about each other's families, long-term hopes, and dreams. By the end of the evening each learned from the other that they wanted to be cherished by their partner, they both wanted a family and to live comfortably, and they both longed to grow old somewhere that valued freedom and life.

The evening slipped away and they toasted to love, freedom, and peace. They made their way to the restaurant entryway, neither one wanting the evening to end. It was 10 p.m. and the streets were heavily crowded. Tien pushed through the crowded entryway to the street, but lost hold of Grady's hand. When she got through the crowd, she turned around to find him right behind her. Suddenly, she was in his arms and her face was inches from his. Glad for the opportunity, Grady slowly put his lips to hers. She opened her mouth acceptingly. They both were hoping to find acceptance in their kiss. Grady's heartbeat raced when Tien pulled his head closer. She kissed him again, more deeply.

The ride back to Pham's was slow due to pedestrian traffic and street vendors. The couple did not mind the delay, soaking in the warmth of a new ember of love. Their brains were being doused with pheromones like gasoline on a fire, overwhelmed with intense emotions of pleasure and wonder. Her pulse quickened as she got out at Pham's. She gave Grady a long, forbidden look, and disappeared inside. He was left wanting more, but instead, asked the driver to take him to the base.

Doubt

Grady was unable to sleep with too many thoughts and emotions racing around in his mind. The same questions were going around and around in his head with no answers. It was maddening! What was he doing? Was he starting something he could not finish? Did he knowingly allow her to walk right into his heart? How would this play out? The military would never allow it. He liked her too much to hurt her by getting involved and then abandoning her. Why was he being so selfish? Was she playing a game? He liked her a lot! She was so smart, mature and beautiful. She had so much grace and poise in a world that was about to implode. She was perfect. She felt good in his arms, against his body. He wanted her, but he did not want to hurt her. She was foreign, but all her goals and dreams were just like his. They were different culturally, but she was still a woman, and he was still a man. The conciliatory and conflicting arguments waged war in his head most of the night. Exhausted, he finally drifted off to sleep the last few hours of dawn. He had been in country over a year, but Vietnam was aging him. In high school, he had a man's body. Now, he had a man's heart and soul to go with it.

Whispers were whirling around Saigon, keeping Grady busy at work. The buzz was that the NVA was planning another spring offensive to rival Tet 1968. The communists were taking advantage of stalled peace talks and withdrawal of American forces. By the end of 1971, it was projected that fewer than 10,000 U.S. combat troops would be in Vietnam. This was a major concern to the ARVN, who were dependent on the U.S. massive military support. The U.S. presence was shrinking, but the communist support to NVA forces was growing on all fronts.

Grady worked with the NCO academy strategists brainstorming possible NVA offensives and ARVN's counter moves. It was a matter of allocating the right resources to the right places at the right times. Unfortunately, the resources were diminishing, and the planners did not know the right places or the right times. There were only educated guesses as to the full scope of the communists' resources, but Grady doubted the ARVN could hold on for long if the NVA kept advancing. Each day brought new information that made the outlook a little dimmer. Grady tried to stay focused on his job, but Tien was on his mind.

What Took So Long?

By the end of September, all their war planning was done, and Grady earned a free weekend. It had been a month, so he went to Pham's to surprise Tien. Scanning the room, he saw her interacting with a table of soldiers in the back of the dining area. His heart sank. It had been too long, and he assumed she had forgotten about him.

He sat at the bar and ordered a double shot, tossed it back, slapped the money down, and turned to the door.

She grabbed his hand from behind as he walked to the door. "I have waited for you for more than three weeks. You come in, do not talk to me, and then leave without a word. Why are you ignoring me?" she asked quietly.

Grady did not know what to say. "I came here as soon as I could, but I see that you already have new friends." His eyes darted to the table of soldiers.

"So, you see me doing my job as hostess, explaining the bill to drunk GIs and you think they are my friends?" Tien's look and tone let him know the implication was hurtful.

"No, no, I did not mean it like that," he mumbled.

She asked, "How did you mean it?"

Grady did not know how to get out of the hole he had just dug. He shook his head saying nothing.

Tien's eyes watered. "Now I know you think so little of me. Thank you for showing me your true self before I fall for you." She covered her face and ran to the ladies' room.

Grady had blown it, and he did not know what to do. He sat at the bar and ordered another double. A girl behind the bar poured his drink. He guzzled it and slammed the shot glass on the bar.

"Hey, this is water; I wanted whiskey!" he sneered.

The girl, who did not appear to be more than 17, leaned into him. "I know, but you should not have any more whiskey. You need water to clear your head for when you go into ladies' room to talk to my cousin. She has been waiting for you all month to come here, and first thing you do is accuse her? You need to tell her you sorry, and you love her. You need to go now, before she come out and go upstairs."

Grady stared at the young girl in disbelief. She was right.

He knocked on the ladies' room door. No one answered, so he walked in. Luckily, Tien was the only woman in there. She was crying on the couch.

"What are you doing in here? You should go back to the base," she sobbed.

He asked, "Is that what you want? I came here because I wanted to see you. I have not been able to get away from work the whole month, not one day free. There are a lot of things happening. I came as soon as I could. When I saw you laughing with those guys my heart sank in my chest. I was jealous and mad at myself for not coming sooner. I have to work on my jealousy. It's not like I can call you. I didn't want to take anything for granted either and assume that we were…together. I did not mean to imply anything before. It just came out wrong. Tien, I'm sorry. I have been thinking about you all the time I was working. Really!" Grady grabbed her hand. She finally made eye contact with him.

She asked, "You wanted to see me? You were jealous? Were you jealous because you think I am yours?" He nodded, so he would not say something stupid. She leaned over and hugged him. "I was worried. I did not know if you had to go into the jungle, or back to America. I already care too much for you.

"I do not think my elders know about us yet, but my cousin does. She likes you. I don't know where we go from here. I don't know what will happen if the NVA come. My family has important friends on both sides, but it might not matter. Many people will die. I don't know if the future holds a place for me in this world. We started as friends, but now we are more and it scares me."

Tien was saying the things Grady already had in his head. He understood too, that she was trusting him so completely to let herself be vulnerable, confessing her inner thoughts without fear of rejection. The couple's connection grew stronger with each confession. He asked her to be with him tonight. She kissed him and agreed.

In the cab that night, she whispered to him her fears about an NVA offensive coming soon. Grady looked at her and held his finger over his lips. She understood the gesture and was puzzled by it but said no more.

They arrived at a restaurant close to the base. When they were seated for dinner, she looked around and then asked him why he hushed her in the cab? Grady did not know how much to tell her. He wanted to be completely honest but could not.

He told her, "We cannot trust anyone in Vietnam. The cab driver could have been VC. Talking about things could be very dangerous. You might be in danger by being my girlfriend." Tien frowned, but liked that he said 'girlfriend'.

He continued. "You know VC are everywhere? Part of my job is to listen and report things I hear. If you tell me things about the VC, it will be like you are working for me. I never want anyone to think you are working for the Americans. So, it is better if you do not tell me things you hear about NVA plans. Okay? Do you understand?"

She answered firmly, "No."

Grady asked, "What do you not understand?"

She stared at him. "I have a college degree in biology, I speak several languages, I understand everything you said. I am saying it is not okay."

He was confused.

She said, "I am falling in love with you, and I trust that you are not just using me for information. I know it is dangerous for me to be with you. I accept the danger because I think we could become something more. So, if I have information about the enemy that could help keep you safe, I am going to tell you the information. So, do you understand?"

A wide-eyed Grady could not fault her logic.

Gripped by A Moment

They ate dinner and sipped champagne. The conversation centered on Tien's parents and how they might react when they discover she is falling for Grady. She reminded him about her family history and Vietnamese culture. Tradition was extremely important, and her parents were unwilling to change because of social trends.

She knew the only way they would change was if their world collapsed, which she believed was coming. Her parents taught her that the Vietnamese people and culture survived many enemies, occupations, and wars throughout history. She knew their history, but she also knew this enemy was different because when they conquer, they will only accept total obedience from the conquered. She also cautioned her parents that the NVA would kill everyone associated with the Americans, everyone with an education, and everyone with wealth.

Tien's parents did not accept her theory, believing instead their position and business with Vietnamese elites from both sides would secure their safety. She wept talking about her parents not surviving a North takeover. Grady drew closer and held her hand. He paid the bill and they departed the restaurant through the hotel lobby. Tien hesitated, and then looked over at the hotel front desk. Hand in hand, they walked to the front desk. Grady knew what to do. The hotel clerk handed him a key.

Tien reminded Grady she could be a little late but she could not stay all night. He quickened his pace up to the room. Once inside, Tien excused herself and went into the bathroom. Grady sat on the bed, reluctant even now to assume anything. When the bathroom door opened, she walked toward him wearing only a towel. Any doubts he had about her intentions were gone.

Her towel fell to the floor. His heart was pounding as he stared at her naked slender body, thinking she was the essence of femininity. She was so sexy and somehow modest at the same time. He pulled her close enough to smell delicate perfume on her abdomen. She gently pulled him up so she could unbutton his shirt. She unbuckled his belt and slid down his pants, revealing his excitement.

Their naked bodies cast shadows on the wall. They caressed each other, glided into the bed and began making love. She winced. He asked if he hurt her. She whispered it was fine as they slowly moved together in growing passion. Afterward, they lingered in each other's arms until Tien saw the time on Grady's watch. She sighed and whispered it was time to go.

A cab delivered the couple back to Pham's. When they arrived, Tien spied to see if any family members were at the cafe tables or in the entrance. No one was in sight so she gave Grady a deep kiss and got out. On the ride back to the base he relived the evening in his mind. It did not occur to him that Tien gave herself to him tonight. She was so proper and refined, and letting him be her first meant she was giving her most precious gift. He was beginning to understand the totality of real love, to feel a devotion and longing for her that penetrated his core. She was the kind of woman he would be honored to call his wife. He tried to deny his feelings because he was so young. She was only his third lover, and he was changing so quickly. However, he could not deny his feeling that she would always make his life complete, and he would want to do the same for her.

Bridges to Cross

Grady fell into a deep, peaceful sleep that night, and woke up with a new attitude about the Nam. The mission had not changed, but he had a reason to look forward to every day. In the bush, a weekend was just another couple of days, but back at the base, the weekends meant something. Grady got a good cup of coffee and "shit on a shingle" or SOS as the military called it. When they offered bacon too, it was almost like home.

Grady sat down to eat, and it occurred to him that the aviation noise from the flight line was very low this morning. He made a casual scan of the chow hall. It was clear by the low number of grunts coming in from the bush, that the U.S. presence was drawing down. The type of soldier was changing too. There were fewer 18-year old soldiers. The ones he saw were more seasoned veterans staying to help the ARVN.

Grady was one of the younger ones staying on to help with the fight, keeping up a brave face, even though every soldier knew the NVA was slowly closing the noose around the South. Grady did not know how long it would take to cinch that noose. Now he had a reason to worry.

Grady was unsure if falling for her was a good thing. A trained soldier in combat risked his life every day. He knew the dangers, but he only had to worry about himself. Caring deeply for Tien meant he had another person's life to worry about, an untrained civilian, a possible casualty of war and something precious he could not lose. He wondered how he came to this state of worrying about another person. He remembered believing that Gabby was his last first kiss. He never expected to have to start over and meet that special someone again, especially in Vietnam. Tien was happy in her life and not looking for love, either. Ironically, or with fate's intervention, having their hearts closed off to love allowed a true and honest friendship to grow, which deepened into the one thing they were avoiding.

Grady also worried about her family traditions and plans for their daughter. Grady and Tien were aware that Thuc Pham would forbid a relationship between his daughter and an American GI. However, it was too late. There is always a moment when the spark of love ignites. Grady and Tien's moment already happened before either one realized it, and by then, neither one wanted to stop it. Grady resigned himself to cross Thuc Pham's bridge when he came to it.

One final lingering doubt was if this was a tumultuous love born out of dire circumstances. If it was a deeper love, it would have long-term implications for their future. They would have to suffer through family objections, he would have to apply for permission to marry a foreigner and to bring her to the U.S., she would have to leave her home and family. Grady stopped his mind from over-thinking. He took deep breaths and decided to let things happen. In the meantime, until he saw her again, it was time to get back to war.

Back to the Front

By the fall of 1971, chatter on the streets of Saigon, along with intelligence reports, indicated the NVA was preparing for a spring offensive. The politicians were negotiating peace, but the ARVN believed it was a stalling tactic by the North to give them time to resupply. The civilians in Saigon also worried about the nearby VC threat because they were hearing very little about them. Intelligence assessments were unreliable since they ranged from the VC being so badly beaten they were no longer a threat, to the other extreme saying they were ready to strike hard. The truth may have been somewhere in between. Reports about the NVA resupplying suggested they were ready to carry the offensive to the South without the VC. The wide spectrum of data coming into the ARVN communication command center made it problematic to know where to apply counterforce. However, there was little doubt that something big was coming. Grady sensed an ominous threat on the horizon, and it bothered him deeply, in a whole new way.

He was beginning to feel compassion for this place and these people. He was not blind to the many things wrong with South Vietnam, especially government corruption, fragility of the economy, and drug markets. Conversely, Grady saw bravery and patriotism in the ARVN troops and he came to respect them. Like in the U.S. military, the ARVN had draftees who did not want to be there, but the NCOs, officers, and volunteers were impressive and disciplined. Sadly, Grady believed they were going to pay a heavy price very soon for their allegiance.

The fear that weighed heaviest on his mind was the safety of Tien and her family when Saigon fell. What would happen to her? She was not a collaborator, and her family was in business with people from both North and South Vietnam, so they might be safe. But, if Tien were implicated with an American GI, the enemy would assume she was collaborating. One did not need a crystal ball to know that the future for South Vietnam was bad. Grady knew he had to search deep in his soul to decide what would be best for Tien, and he did not have a lot of time to do it.

He was distracted all week while working with ARVN strategic planners because his mind kept drifting to her. He loved her past the point of turning back, yet his love would endanger her. He made the painful decision, for her sake, not to see her anymore. It was far more bittersweet than he expected, but he had to do it.

Her parents knew the threat, which probably was why they never wanted her dating an American. Grady understood their wisdom now. His decision would hurt her deeply, but at least she could survive heartache, as opposed to the treatment she would endure as a collaborator. He debated telling her or just not seeing her anymore. It would be cowardly and cruel to cut her off without an explanation. His heart told him the right thing to do was tell her face to face, but seeing her one more time could make it too difficult to end. He took time to think it over.

The hectic pace of mission planning settled down at the training academy, finally giving Grady a chance to catch his breath. He had not seen Tien in a week, but the guys in his detachment talked him into going out for a few beers after work. He told them he would get cleaned up and find them. The setting sun put on a beautiful display of pinkish hues across the sky as he walked to his hooch. He loved the colors of the sunsets and the unique aromas in the evenings, like grass burning, exotic foods cooking, and gunpowder. Grady was perplexed on day one by the breathtaking landscape and scenery of Vietnam disturbingly juxtaposed to the destruction, debris and death of the war.

Within sight of his hooch, he saw a woman standing there. "Tien?" he asked. "What are you doing here? How did you get on base? How did you know where to find me?"

She wrapped her arms around his neck and kissed him. "Are you not happy to see me?"

Grady pulled her tighter. "Of course, I am happy! I am ecstatic! But how did you get here?"

She said, "If you invite me in, I will tell you."

They went inside and Grady quickly tried to neaten up. With nowhere to sit except his desk, they sat on his bunk. He offered her snacks and bourbon. "I'd like to offer you something better, but I did not expect company."

Tien began, "You asked how I found you. The leaders of the Army of South Vietnam know my father. It is easy for me to get papers to come on base. I asked a soldier where you live, and after he asked around he told me.

"My mother and father went to Thailand on business. I told my uncle I am going to visit a friend. I think he knows where I am, but he said okay, anyway. He thinks it is better for me to be with you, because our way of life might be gone soon, and you have a future. May I stay with you in your room, not in a hotel?" She looked right into his eyes. "I love you and that scares me."

Tien had never disobeyed her parents. She was leaping into a relationship with Grady that could define the rest of her life. Her intuition told her Grady was a kind man of honor and deep integrity. He would love her, take care of her, and devote his life to her. She prayed she was right.

Grady did not know what to say. He had been thinking all week about ending their relationship for her sake, but at this moment his selfishness and his heart would not let her go. The room darkened with the setting sun. They sat for hours having an honest conversation about each other's intentions and possible future. Sometimes words were hard to find because they did not know their own truths but talking it out brought them closer in mind and body. Slowly, after enough was said, the talking turned into lovemaking. They lay together terrified about their spoken and unspoken commitment. The next morning, Grady awoke knowing in his heart he loved her too much to let her go.

His second tour in Vietnam seemed to be going by much faster than his first. The weeks turned into months. His opinion of the country changed completely too. He liked working with the South Vietnamese soldiers, and the training staff. He found it exciting being at different places in Saigon trying to pick up local chatter.

One of the things he did not like was not knowing if the information collected was any use to the intelligence analysts, but his reports went up the chain anyway. Grady understood his minuscule role as one of a thousand people collecting information on a very large, complex puzzle. But he also believed that it only took one piece to complete the picture.

The biggest reason Grady no longer hated Vietnam was that his heart was full. He spent every spare minute with Tien. Always conscientious of the possibility of the enemy identifying them together, they did not go out on the town very often. However, they spent an increasing amount of time together in private, growing deeper in love every day. Their passion was intensified by its secrecy and perishability. In their world, tomorrow was not guaranteed, so they lived and loved in the moment.

Grady Restrains

One night Grady visited Pham's restaurant to see Tien. She was working and could not go out for the evening. He took a chance she might be free, but since she was not available, he ordered dinner and sat in a back corner. Grady stayed awhile after dinner, sitting at the bar while she tended to patrons. He could at least spend time with her from afar.

Three U.S. junior officers were in the restaurant becoming drunk and belligerent. When Tien was taking their food orders, they made loud crude comments about Vietnamese girls. When she helped serve the food at their table, one of the men reached around and put his hand under her skirt grabbing her inner thigh at the crotch. She dropped the plate of food and reeled away from the customer, cursing loudly in Vietnamese. The officer laughed and gestured with his hands he did not understand why she was complaining.

Tien's cousin, Jun and Grady at the bar both witnessed the incident. Tien was furious, but more than that, she was afraid Grady might intervene. She knew if an enlisted man struck an officer, he would be court-martialed. The officer's friends would back up his story. Tien's uncle and her large cousin rushed over to the table to see what happened. Tien told her uncle in Vietnamese what the man had done.

The drunk officer told uncle Nguyen that this whore told him he could touch her pussy for two dollars, but she got mad when he tried to put the money where it belonged. Nguyen and his son grabbed the man to throw him out of the restaurant. Grady was standing near them with a beer bottle upside down in his hand. Jun had grabbed his arm before he could strike the man. She pleaded with him to stop!

He looked at Tien and her eyes said it all. He stopped in his tracks.

The drunk lieutenant asked, "Who are you, pretty boy, and what do you think you're gonna do? Huh? Is this your whore?"

Before Grady could speak, a voice came from behind him. Grady whirled around to see a distinguished man in an ARVN officer's uniform with an impressive rack of ribbons.

"I am Colonel Tam Song, of the Command Planning Staff, Saigon, ARVN. What is your name, soldier?"

The lieutenant looked at him. "Uh, who's asking? Did you say Colonel Charlie Gook?"

The officers laughed, but customers in the restaurant gasped. The insult came out in a drunken slur, but it was clear enough. Colonel Song was one of the most respected commanders in Saigon. The U.S. Command thought very highly of him. He had recently been promoted to general but had not yet pinned on the rank. The colonel told the four men, "We will find out your names soon enough." He ordered his guards to take the men to ARVN HQ.

"They are under arrest for drunk and disorderly, and for insubordination to a superior officer."

Colonel Song then yelled something in Vietnamese and the guards jumped. The three officers were dragged into the street by the colonel's guards. They thrashed and yelled that the ARVN soldiers were making a career mistake by messing with American officers. The last thing anyone heard as they were tossed into ARVN cars was something about being Americans.

Colonel Song apologized profusely to Tien and her uncle for the insult to her honor. He assured them the men would be dealt with harshly. He asked them if there was anything he could do to make it up to them. Tien and her uncle politely refused and thanked him for his intervention.

Before Colonel Song returned to his table, he approached Grady. "You are Corporal Cordeaux? I know of you and the support you have been giving our planning staff. I have heard good things. I also know that you have reason to be very angry with those men, especially concerning one of Thuc Pham's daughters?" He winked at Grady.

Grady did not know how to respond, so he nodded. He was still in awe at the reverence the ARVN commander showed the Pham family.

The colonel continued, "Corporal, I think you showed much restraint and wisdom tonight if I correctly understand the situation. I am very impressed. Please enjoy your evening and rest assured those men will be punished."

Jun walked Grady back to the bar. A half an hour later, she leaned over the bar and whispered something to Grady.

He went to the back office. Tien threw her arms around him and sobbed. He hugged her back. "It's okay, those men won't bother you anymore."

"Oh Grady!" She sobbed. "I was so afraid you were going to do something that would get you in trouble. I was scared for you, for us."

He admitted, "Yeah, I wanted to take that asshole outside and beat him, but I saw the look in your eyes which made me think twice about it. I thought about not doing anything that would hurt us. I knew you would get justice because those guys will not make it out of Saigon alive tonight."

Tien stopped sobbing and kissed him. "Thank you, darling. Thank you for being calm and thinking of us."

Lying in his bunk that night, Grady could not sleep. He was agitated by the event, but satisfied that he had held his temper. He knew it could have gone very differently. It was another example of how Vietnam was changing him.

One morning at the Planning Staff meeting there was an awards ceremony. Grady did not know about it, so he sat in the back of the room. When the staff members were in place, a small parade of senior officers came through the door of the conference room. General Song was the last to enter. An ARVN lieutenant colonel asked the attendees to be seated.

"Gentlemen, we have among us, a soldier who has distinguished himself in his duty. Corporal Cordeaux, would you please come forward."

Once again, Grady looked like a deer in headlights. He was caught completely unaware of what was about to happen. He walked to the front of the room and stood at attention. The lieutenant colonel directed the men to come to attention as he read the citation. "The Armed Forces of the Republic of South Vietnam recognize and do hereby award for outstanding attention to duty, for exemplary action above and beyond, and for exceptional reporting of enemy activity with one of the highest ratings of reliability, the South Vietnamese Medal of Excellence in Intelligence, to Corporal Grady Cordeaux, U.S. Army."

General Song removed the medal from its box and pinned it on Grady's uniform. Grady saluted the general and they shook hands. When the ceremony was over, the men on the Planning Staff congratulated Grady and reminded him they would see him later in their mess hall, where he would be buying drinks for everyone.

A future

Tien and Grady were spending as much time together as their jobs would allow. They were growing deeper in love every day and finding it difficult to sneak around her parents or hide their feelings. She hoped they would respect her desire to be with someone of her own choosing. She knew the old ways, but every explosion or death in the streets was a reminder the old ways were dying. Grady and Tien were at the point in the relationship when they began planning a future together, even though the chances for peace or prosperity in South Vietnam were weakening every day.

In the uncertainty, they desperately sought comfort with each other during the brief encounters stolen away. For a long while, the excitement, newness, and forbidden passion was enough, but by fall 1972, their love and emotions were being smothered. She was becoming the most important thing in his life, and he was hers, yet their circumstances were suffocating. They yearned to move forward.

During the fall and winter of 1972, the North Vietnamese kept hitting ARVN forces in attacks along the Cambodian and Laotian borders, in the South, and in the North highlands. The ARVN retaliated against the enemy's sporadic incursions, to little avail. The North was probing for weaknesses. However small, the totality of the enemy actions was ominous. Grady and Tien envisioned the big picture and felt uneasy about everything.

One evening, Grady told Tien he had a long stretch of R&R due and wanted to go somewhere for a holiday. She tried to smile, but sadness showed on her face.

"When will you be back?" she asked.

He squeezed her. "Darling, I want to take you with me. We can go away together. Let's go to Thailand!"

Tien squeezed back but said nothing. Her silence confused him.

He asked again what she thought.

"Grady, how will I ever be able to go away with you? My mother and father would never approve! They know about you, and they tolerate us knowing each other hoping that one day you will just go away. They are very old-fashioned about such things. It would be highly improper for Thuc Pham's daughter to go on a trip, unescorted, with a man. I know things feel very tense now, but I cannot imagine any circumstances when it would be acceptable to be gone for a week with you."

Grady was disappointed. He was hoping she would at least dream about it before being so pragmatic. He was holding her close, and rather than spoil the moment, he said nothing more about it. The evening wore on and they lay in each other's arms until it was time for her to go. He walked her to the front of the base. When she got into the cab, Grady asked her once more to think about Thailand. She smiled faintly and disappeared into the busy street.

He stayed busy the next week with the Planning Staff, tracking down leads about upcoming NVA movements. Friday was an especially exhausting day, so when it was over, he was relieved to be able to enjoy a long shower and relax in his hooch with a beer.

As he dozed off into a much-needed nap, a gentle knock on the door aroused him to his feet. He knew that knock. He swung open the door and she rushed into his arms, pushing them both backward into the hooch.

When they stopped kissing, Grady opened his eyes to her wide-eyed smile. "What is it, darling?" he asked. "What has got you in such a great mood? I like it, and I need good news."

"Grady." She hesitated for effect. "I can go to Thailand!" She squealed saying it.

He lifted her and whirled around in excitement! "You can? How? What changed? It is wonderful news! We will have the most romantic time ever! Tell me how this is possible."

Bangkok

Tien explained to Grady what transpired that week at the restaurant. As if fate was playing a hand, her parents and two aunts had plans to go to Hong Kong on business in December. They asked uncle Nguyen to take care of the family and manage the business while they were away. As soon as the opportunity presented itself, she asked her uncle if she could go away for a week. Uncle Nguyen liked Grady, and thought he was good for Tien. However, it was not appropriate for a younger brother to go against the eldest brother's wishes. Nguyen thought long about her request.

Going against his elder brother would create an enormous break in the family unity and trust. It also would go against generations of tradition. However, the old ways were fading and nothing in South Vietnam was traditional anymore. Nguyen was an educated man, and a student of history. He believed their traditions and lives were going to be changed forever.

He knew that communist takeovers throughout history involved bloody purges of the privileged class. The Pham's were almost aristocratic. Thousands of people, especially government employees, educators, and businessmen would be eliminated. For these reasons with slight trepidation he gave permission to Tien.

She sensed he did not want to disobey his brother, but something more profound was driving him. He told her to tell no one. His secret hope was that Grady would take Tien away from Vietnam forever. She did not dwell on her uncle's rationale. All she thought was Thailand was on!

The first week in December could not come soon enough. Grady planned their entire trip. He booked a beautiful hotel in downtown Bangkok near a temple garden. This R&R was going to be about romance and love, rather than the usual GI jaunt to Thailand. He steered away from areas with red lights, brothels, bars, and neon.

The day they were to leave, Tien met him outside the base with a small suitcase in hand. She hugged him, but the look on her face was less than he expected. He assumed she was overwhelmed with excitement and maybe a little afraid. In reality, the worry on her face was something else.

"Everything will be fine!" he assured her.

She was not as confident. She sat quietly during the two-hour flight. Grady asked if she had ever flown before. She nodded yes. They arrived in Bangkok just as darkness was pushing away pink and red hues of the Thai sunset.

They caught a cab to the Bentakiti hotel in the Sinsamut Gardens Village. Tien smiled when they entered the lobby. She did not think Grady could afford such luxury. Every piece of furnishing and finish was exquisite. The open lobby allowed the breeze to blow through without disturbing the elegance. It bustled with well-dressed men and women, and neatly uniformed staff. A bellman in a police-like white uniform took their luggage and escorted them to their room. It was on the third floor with a balcony overlooking the gardens. Grady tipped the bellman, closed the door and kissed his Vietnamese princess.

He was madly in love. This feeling was not the same feeling he had for Gabby. He realized what he felt for her was being in love with his first sexual experience. With Michelle, they both acknowledged their desire for human contact, and neither one had enough time for anything deeper. They liked each other and shared intimate secrets together, but love requires so much more. The emotions he had with Tien were pure, intense, with real life-altering consequences. He felt like she brought out the best in him. He believed she would be a good wife, a good mother, and a partner who would work together with him to enrich their lives. Grady had already entertained thoughts about proposing to Tien, but the uncertainty of the future held him back. The idea crossed his mind now as he held her. He was not ready, but he knew he loved this woman more than anything and wanted her in his life. She was kind, loving, attentive, smart, gorgeous, and would be a wonderful mother.

Grady popped the cork in a bottle of champagne and poured two glasses, handed Tien her glass, and raised a toast to romance, and to the Paris of the Far East. He took a big gulp. She was amused and put her glass on the table.

Grady said, "So, you don't want to drink with me? What's the matter, darling? You have been quiet since we left the base. Is this too much?"

She just looked into his eyes. "Hey, handsome GI, ladies do not gulp champagne, especially right before they are going to make love."

As she was talking, she pulled the strings at the top of her dress allowing it to fall to the ground. Grady forgot everything he was saying. He watched her seductively remove the rest of her clothing. Her body was beautiful in the shadows. She wrapped her arms around his neck and started gently kissing his mouth while unbuttoning his shirt. She helped him undress. They fell to the bed without a care in the world; in Grady's mind at least.

They lay in bed enjoying the afterglow of their lovemaking. Eventually, Grady thought about food and Tien realized she was hungry too. They showered and opened their suitcases to get dressed. Grady's suitcase was too big for only going away a week. But when he pulled out a long flat box, she understood.

"Grady, what did you do? she asked with a girlish joy in her voice.

"I bought you the most beautiful ao dai I have ever seen. It was in a shop window in Saigon."

He pulled it out of the box. Tien could not believe how beautiful it was. It was a full length v-neck ao dai made from the finest Ha Dong silk. The red silk ao dai had a hand-painted, golden sacred lotus flower along the entire right side and ornate gold thread embroidery on the front panel. Her smile lit up the room. She tried it on and stood in front of the full-length mirror. It fit perfectly. Suddenly, as if a light switch had been flipped, her facial expression turned to sorrow. Grady furrowed his brow in complete confusion. She was the most beautiful woman in the world, and he wanted to show her off in Bangkok. Why would she be upset?

She sat on the edge of the bed and broke down, holding her face in her hands. Tears streamed down her face.

She sobbed, "Oh Grady."

He dropped to a knee and pleaded with her to tell him what was wrong.

"Grady, everything is so perfect! The trip, the hotel, the setting, you, this dress, everything is perfect." Her tears continued.

"Then what is it?" he pleaded.

Tien wiped her tears with a tissue, grabbed his hands and with a deep breath whispered, "I'm pregnant."

Panic filled her as the words left her lips. She knew this was the worst thing that could happen if she ever hoped her parents would accept Grady. She would bring shame upon them.

Then, too, she was uncertain how Grady would react. Unplanned pregnancy was common between Vietnamese women and American GIs. Mostly, the GIs did not react well. Sometimes, women did it purposely to hitch a ride out of poverty to the land of the big "BX." Tien was not a street girl looking for a way out of the country. She did not need to hitch her wagon to an American GI. In truth, she would be poorer with Grady than with her family, and he knew it.

Her confession stunned him for a moment as he processed it in his mind. Instead of fearing the news, a rush of joy filled him like never before. This amazing woman, who gave him her love, was going to give him the most precious gift ever. His heart pounded and his mind raced

Tien was uncertain and anxious. She begged to know what he was thinking. He returned to the moment and embraced her tightly, burying his tearful eyes in her hair on the side of her face.

He whispered in her ear, "I love you more than I have ever loved anyone. You are so beautiful! I love you so much it hurts."

Tien cried. They held each other in tears and silence. When the noise from the street began to invade their sanctuary, they let go and gathered themselves. Grady suggested they get dinner and talk. She did not feel presentable, but Grady assured her she was the most beautiful woman in the world.

A Picture to Remember

When Grady and Tien started down the lobby's grand staircase, several guests looked up at them. She looked like a princess. Grady motioned to the hotel photographer at the concierge desk. He asked him to take her picture. She quietly and properly protested because her eyes were puffy and she did not want her picture taken.

When the photographer saw them coming down the staircase, he already decided he was going to photograph her. He thought she was Asian royalty. The photographer posed her at the end of the ornately carved railing. He imaged her in full length, to capture the elegant ao dai, but also her subtle smile. She was so breathtakingly beautiful. He told Grady it would be one of the best portraits he had ever taken. Grady asked for two copies. The photographer said the pictures would be available at the hotel desk at check out. As other hotel guests looked on, the handsome couple headed out for dinner and important conversation.

Grady asked the doorman where they might find the best restaurant within walking distance. The man pointed to a bright sign two blocks down the avenue; "Grand Buddha."

The Grand Buddha was an elegant restaurant, featuring a big band and a vocalist. It was so popular that it was nearly impossible to get in without a reservation. Tien and Grady walked into the lobby. The maître d' greeted them and escorted them right to their table. Unbeknownst to Grady, their hotel concierge had called ahead explaining that an Asian princess and her escort were coming their way for the evening.

The restaurant was ready. When the couple was seated, the waiter presented them a bottle of champagne for their approval.

"Oh, I did not order that," Grady said.

The waiter replied that it was complimentary. Thinking it was not good enough, the waiter suggested he could bring another bottle if they preferred?

"No, no, that will be fine," Grady replied.

Tien smiled and graciously accepted the pour.

The waiter gave them a few minutes and returned to describe the chef's recommendation for their dining experience. Grady nodded his approval. While waiting, the couple held hands across the table listening to the band. They each had hundreds of thoughts going through their minds, but neither one said a word. Grady was waiting until after dinner to begin the conversation. He had no doubts about what he wanted. He hoped she wanted it too.

The food and the entertainment were exquisite. They were seated off to the side of the dining room, where the lighting was soft and the music was just quiet enough to enjoy conversation. He commented that she had not touched her champagne. She tilted her head slightly downward and gestured with her eyes. Grady remembered and smiled. He moved from his side of the table to right next to her.

"Sweetheart, this news of yours really messes up my plans."

Tien looked at him with sudden confusion.

Before she could say anything, Grady said, "I have been wondering how and when I was going to tell you how much I love you."

She jumped in, "I love you too, very much! Telling me it messes up your plans is not what I need to hear right now, Grady Cordeaux!" Tien was ready to cry.

Grady squeezed her hands. "Listen to me! If a guy wants to ask a girl to marry him, but she tells him she is pregnant, it seems like he is only asking because of the baby. Having our child only makes me love you that much more. I wanted you to come to Thailand with me because I was thinking about asking you to marry me."

Tien looked at him in bewilderment. Her expression made him think she did not understand what he was telling her. After an awkward silence she said, "Well?"

Grady did not understand. "Well, what?"

She whispered to him, "Are you going to ask me?"

For a moment he had to think about what she meant. His unique smile grew across his face. With watery eyes, he dropped to one knee and held her hand.

"Tien, I have loved you since I first met you. You are the most beautiful woman I have ever known. When you finally agreed to go out with me, I was in heaven and that feeling has grown each day. When I am with you, bad things go away, and life is hopeful once again. I would be the luckiest man in the world if you would be mine forever. Tien Pham, will you marry me?"

She leaned over to whisper in his ear, "Grady Cordeaux, yes, I will marry you." They kissed, oblivious to the applause from restaurant patrons.

The jeweler directed the couple to a beautiful two-karat emerald cut diamond in the display case. Tien's eyes opened wide. Her smile said it all. Grady gulped, knowing that this was one of the obstacles they would have to overcome. A diamond of that size would be too expensive for his corporal's pay. Trying to appear to be a savvy shopper, he asked the jeweler what other rings they might see. Tien cast a tiny typical frown. The jeweler showed them several others until Tien sensed Grady's restlessness. He was fidgety and awkward. She thanked the jeweler and led Grady out of the store. He did not understand what had just happened.

They walked silently hand in hand for a few minutes. Finally, she asked what he was thinking. She wanted to know if his anxiety was coming out. Grady did not know how to start the conversation for fear it might spiral into a fight, when it should be a time for intense joy. Despite his worry about an argument he decided it would be better to start out their new life with total honesty.

"Tien." He hesitated. "You understand that as long as I am in the Army, we will never have the kind of money your family has. We will never be poor, but we will never be rich, either. I come from a farming family who did not have much. I'm not saying we will always be thrifty, but right now we might not be able to spend as much as we want. Does that sound like someone you could spend the rest of your life with?"

Then she asked him, "Is that why you were nervous in the jewelry store?"

He nodded. "One day I will buy you a big, beautiful diamond to wear proudly on your hand, but for now I cannot afford 2500 dollars U.S. I'm so sorry."

She said, "Grady, I don't need a ring. I wasn't even thinking about the cost. I'm so sorry to make you feel that way. Please forgive me. I know you are a man who works very hard and will provide for our family. My father will see it too."

Grady had not yet thought about Tien's father. It made his heart pump faster. They went back to their hotel where she helped him forget his worries for that night at least.

After five days the couple returned to Saigon before Tien's parents were back from Hong Kong. There was no evidence that Tien ever left and her uncle and cousin would never say a word. When her parents did finally return from their business trip, Tien set a date when Grady would meet her father.

Le Thuc Pham agreed to make time to have a special dinner with his daughter, unaware there was an ulterior motive. Le Thuc was an important businessman. Most of his days and evenings were spent in meetings, dinners, or parties with business associates, politicians, high-ranking military officers, and wealthy social elites. He was the patriarch of the family, but his wife's role was to take care of family matters. However, when his favorite daughter requested personal time with her father, he made time.

Meeting Thuc Pham

Grady sat at the bar trying to be calm. He wore his best suit, a clean white dress shirt, and a thin dark tie. Even his shoes were spit-shined. He could not sit still, repeatedly picking up his drink without taking a sip. He reached his finger in around his collar several times to loosen it. Beads of sweat were on his forehead. Tien's plan was to loosen up her father by chatting with him over a nice daddy/daughter dinner, then excuse herself and bring Grady into the private dining room.

When she finally came out to get Grady, his throat went dry. She grabbed his arm asking, "Are you ready?"

He steeled himself momentarily, rose off the barstool, and walked with her to meet Le Thuc Pham. Tien escorted Grady into the private room, said something to her father in Vietnamese, and then said in English she would like to introduce someone.

"Cha," she said, "this is Corporal Grady Cordeaux."

Le Thuc looked at Grady unimpressed. He wondered why his daughter was introducing a GI he had seen in the restaurant. It was not until Grady sat to eat that Le Thuc began to understand, and his expression went sour.

Grady told Le Thuc it was an honor to finally meet Tien's father. The old man shot back that he did not know someone was waiting to meet him.

Grady continued, "Mr. Pham, I have known Tien for over a year and have become very fond of her. In truth, sir, I have grown to love your daughter very much."

Grady saw Le Thuc's jaw and eyes tighten.

Grady pressed on, "Sir, I would like to ask for your permission and blessing to marry your daughter. I will love her and take…"

Before Grady could finish the sentence, Le Thuc stood up. He glared at Grady, and then spoke harshly in Vietnamese to Tien before storming out of the room.

Tien began to sob until she burst into tears, disbelieving that her father would be so inflexible about her being in love.

Grady hugged her. "What did he say to you?"

Through her sobbing, she told him her father said she was a terrible disappointment. Grady did not know what to do to comfort her. She told him to go back to the base. She would see him as soon as she could. He did not like the uncertainty of that comment. He kissed her, told her he loved her, and then disappeared into the street.

Grady got back to the base, grabbed a few beers, and sat in his hooch wondering what would happen next. He loved Tien. He wondered if her parents could prevent her from marrying him. He did not know much about Vietnamese culture, but he did know that thousands of Vietnamese girls married GIs all the time, and marrying him would not be such a terrible thing.

Grady worried that Le Thuc thought his daughter would be taking a huge step down in social status by marrying him. He worried that Tien would eventually hate him for it. They loved each other so much now, but later when the bills came in, or when they could not afford to go to dinner parties every weekend, would it matter? He could not get Le Thuc's reaction out of his head, and it was spiraling him into doubt and anxiety. He finished the beer, grabbed a bottle of bourbon from his locker and drank himself to sleep.

Every day since her father's refusal, Grady hoped Tien would be waiting for him at his hooch. He could not focus at work. It was good that he was not in combat anymore. Being in the bush with your head somewhere else was how guys got wasted. Going to meetings, talking with informants, and listening to conversations these days did not require pinpoint alertness to stay alive. In the middle of the week he went to DaNang to work with an ARVN group, and welcomed the distraction. He returned the next day to more meetings and training until Friday afternoon. He left work hoping she would be at his hooch. He jumped in a jeep and rode down the flight line to his quarters. As soon as his hooch came into view, Tien was standing there.

New Plans

When he got close, he saw a look he had not seen on her face before. It was as if life had been sucked from her soul. Her joy was gone, her posture was hollow and defeated. Two small suitcases at her feet said it all. Grady rushed to her. She held onto him as if she would never let go. He kissed her over and over telling her how much he loved her and did not want her to ever leave him again. She sobbed uncontrollably.

"Let's go inside and you can tell me what happened," he whispered.

They went in and sat on the bunk in silence until she regained her composure.

She stopped crying long enough to say, "My parents disowned me!" As soon as she said the words out loud her tears came even harder.

The couple clung to each other. He felt adrenalin surging through his body. He also knew he could not let his weakness present itself; not now! She needed him to be strong for both of them. Seeing fear in him would crush her completely.

Subtly, he drew deep breaths and focused on her, pushing out the panic, and regaining control. He began to assess the situation in his mind like he would assess the enemy. He dissected the whole, and then thought about the individual parts, one at a time. It was how he managed in the Army; it could work in everyday stressful situations too.

Tien would be terribly hurt if she could read his mind and see the compartmentalizing under way, but it was his secret strategy to look at things in parts, and then as a whole. The overwhelming whole was that Tien and the baby were his responsibility now. The individual parts were easier to handle, one at a time. They could live in an apartment off base, they could get married, they could have the baby, and he could end his tour and bring her back to the States. He could handle each one of these things separately without feeling overwhelmed and anxious.

Grady finally achieved enough calm to ask Tien how the conversation went with her parents. She started telling him and her emotions took over again.

When her tears subsided, she began to tell what happened. "It was so awful after you left. My father went upstairs and yelled at my mother. He accused my uncle of allowing our relationship to go on under his nose. He was angry with my cousins and employees. My mother came to my room and yelled at me. She was angrier than I have ever seen. She asked me how I could do such a thing and shame them that way, telling me I was destined for so much more."

Tien's expression punctuated her next statement. "Grady, I have never seen my mother with so much hate in her eyes. I could not stop crying, but she did not care. She was too angry to feel sympathy for me. When I told her how much I loved you it was as if I put a knife in her heart. She cursed me and said terrible things. Spit was shooting from her mouth like a snake. She told me I destroyed the family and should live the rest of my life in shame."

Tien continued. "She pushed me so hard that something in me snapped. I was a tiger cornered in its cage, so I lashed out. I told my mother I was ashamed. I was ashamed of her because of her lack of understanding about love. I told her she should be ashamed at how little she loves a daughter, and how little she understands about love between a man and a woman. I said all she cared about was obedience.

"She just stared at me with knives in her eyes. I let my anger out on her. I told her if she is any kind of mother, she would stand up and defend me instead of cowering in the presence of my father. All she loves is the power and prestige of her position. I told her that very soon all that status would be gone, and she will be a poor peasant woman in a rice paddy with the other comrade farmers under the Minh regime."

Tien said, "Grady, you do not know our culture, but a daughter would never talk to her mother like that. Family traditions and obedience are very important in Asian culture."

He was in disbelief at how she stood up to her mother, and he knew what it meant.

Tien continued, "After I had said enough and the damage was done, I told her I was pregnant, but she would never know her grandchild. My words pushed the knife deeper into her heart and twisted it."

Grady hugged her tightly as the anger seeped out of her body. She had just lost everything in her life except him. All he could do was hold her, and let her know she was safe. The couple clung to each other in bed and fell asleep from emotional exhaustion.

They awoke at midnight, hungry and in need of a shower. Grady grabbed a robe and his shower kit. He put his robe on Tien and led her to the showers. It had semi-open stalls, but at this hour it was empty. Soldiers out on the town might be returning to base soon, but most would be too drunk to notice anything. Tien showered while Grady stood watch. He showered in the next stall when she was almost done.

Refreshed, they made their way back to the hooch, slipped out of their shower clothes and made love. It was one thirty in the morning.

Lying there, Grady whispered, "What did your mother say when you told her about the baby?"

Tien closed her eyes. The silence let him know she did not want to talk about it anymore. After many moments she said, "I have never seen that look in my mother's eyes. She was so cold and without any love in her heart. She told me I was not her daughter. When she got up to leave my room, she told me to be gone by morning or she would have the police remove me. She said no daughter of hers would shame her so much by being an American whore. The last thing I heard my mother say was that she would never speak my name again."

Tien swallowed hard and closed her eyes until she drifted off to sleep. Grady watched a single teardrop trickle down her cheek.

The next morning, she awoke swollen-eyed, but still able to see Grady putting on a fresh shirt and sipping coffee out of a metal cup.

"Good morning darling," he said.

Last night was exhausting and Tien felt weak, but her will to piece her life back together pushed her to get out of his bed and get dressed.

She asked, "Do I have to go down to the corner to use the bathroom and freshen up?"

"Yes ma'am," he said with a grin. "It's how we do it in the Army."

She looked at him with skepticism.

"It's okay, lots of GIs brought girlfriends on base last night and those girls all go to the showers in the morning."

She shot back, "Grady Cordeaux, I am not some bar girl you picked up last night!"

He told her, "Of course not, but even royalty has to pee, right?"

She grabbed a few of his things. "You are going with me," she said.

Grady smiled. "I'm right behind you, darling."

They returned from the shower and got dressed, even though neither one had a plan for the day. They both realized the next words or actions could define their future. They delicately danced around each other for a few awkward moments.

Finally, Grady spoke. "I am certain the military will not let us live in this hooch, especially with a baby, so I suggest we find a place off base."

It was the one thing that Tien needed to hear most of all, and the one thing Grady knew he had to say. He did not say it because it was the right thing. He said it because he loved her and wanted her to be the mother of his children. She knew he meant it. She kissed him, and they headed out the door.

When they walked off the base, Tien mentioned she wanted to look at one particular apartment not too far from the base. They arrived at the building, and Grady's first impression was it looked far too clean and luxurious to be affordable. He wondered if it was time to have the serious talk about marrying an enlisted GI and financial expectations again. Money would be tight for them at first, so Tien had to adjust to a lesser lifestyle. Grady was thinking how to broach the subject when an older woman greeted them in the foyer. Tien spoke with her in Vietnamese and the woman led them upstairs to an apartment. Grady was confused when he noticed Tien pulled a key out of her pocket. The old woman took Tien's key and unlocked the door.

All three people walked into a fully furnished two-bedroom apartment with a bathroom, shower, and full kitchen. The balcony overlooked the street below. Grady wanted to be supportive, but Tien sensed his reluctance.

"You don't like the apartment?" she asked.

Grady told her, "It's a wonderful place, darling. The location is great, it is big, and the furniture is nice. I just do not think we can afford it."

Before he finished, the landlady spoke to Tien in Vietnamese. Tien turned to Grady and asked how much he could afford to pay each month. He had not thought about it until now, but was impressed that Tien was bargaining with the woman.

He shook his head not knowing how to answer and uncomfortable with bargaining. Tien said, "I will tell her we can pay $30 a month, okay?"

Knowing the amount would be far too little, Grady nodded. The two women talked some more, and then the landlady smiled and walked out. Grady had no idea what had happened.

Tien turned to him, "She said okay."

Tien opened the refrigerator, popped off the top of a beer, and handed it to Grady.

He was still confused. "How did you have a key?" he asked.

She sat next to him on the couch. He did not know he was about to learn a lesson about women. Tien explained that the night she had the fight with her mother, she left Pham's and stayed with her cousin's family. Her cousin's Aunt Wanhai owned the building. Tien had been staying here all week.

Tien admitted to Grady that Wanhai would have let them stay in the apartment for nothing if they did not have money, but she would accept whatever they could pay. She knew Tien was pregnant and in love with an American, the same as one of her own daughters. Wanhai would be like a mother to Tien, if her own mother would not.

The only thing Tien asked of Wanhai was to not tell her mother. Grady just shook his head. He could not believe how wonderful these people were, or how lucky he and Tien were to have found such a place.

He pulled Tien close and said, "Well, darling, welcome home."

The following week was Christmas. Grady picked up his usual holiday mail from his parents, sent letters to them, and stopped by the commanding officer's desk to check in for the weekly briefing.

His last chore was part of a daily routine. Every week he read situation reports, got debriefed on his observations, and then discussed them with his first line supervisor, Lieutenant Spoker. Spoker was the most recent officer to rotate into the administrative desk position. His previous assignment was in Special Forces.

Operators typically want to be in the field engaged in their tradecraft. However, officers had to pull administrative duties every other year to be considered for promotion. This concept was not a hard and fast rule in the "Nam" when U.S. forces were in combat, but it was almost 1973, and the GIs were mostly here for advisory support to the ARVN. There were more administrative assignments than officers to fill them, so Spoker got one.

It Hit the Fan

After the daily briefings, Grady asked Spoker if he had a minute to talk with him. Spoker was new in the job, but it was his second tour in Vietnam, so when one of his troops wanted to talk to him "offline," he suspected it was about venereal disease or a pregnant girlfriend. He asked Grady to come into his office and close the office door behind him. "Okay, Cordo, this is the first time you have something for me in private, so you got my attention. What's up?"

Grady told him, "Well, Sir, I wanted to let you know that I moved into an apartment off base."

Spoker sat up. "You know that you need to get official permission to do that beforehand, right? So far you have been one of the most reliable and outstanding soldiers in the unit. Why would you want to live off base when you are nearing the end of your second tour? I probably have your orders on my desk. What happened? Did you find a dink who love you long time?" Spoker's joke was met with Grady's look of disapproval.

Grady was not expecting to explain everything to his superior, but since he mentioned the end of his tour, Grady figured it might be time to lay it all out. "Well, Sir, I have been dating a very nice Vietnamese girl for some time and I asked her to marry me."

"Jeezus Kaaarist!" Spoker yelled to Grady. "Cordo, you are a smart operator, so I know you know better than to think this woman really loves you. All she wants is a ticket to the good old USA, right?"

"No, Sir," Grady told him. "It's not like that, Sir."

"What makes this so different, Cordo?"

"Sir, I know because she has more money than I will have in a lifetime."

Spoker looked at him in disbelief. "Who is this girl?"

Grady replied, "Her name is Tien Thuc Pham."

"Holy shit on a Christmas altar. Are you telling me that you have been dating the daughter of Saigon elite? You got some brass balls on you. This kind of thing could cause an international incident. I need to bump this up the chain. I think the colonel needs to hear this."

Grady told Spoker he would prefer to keep it private.

"Normally, Corporal, I would just advise you to be extra careful, to let admin know where you will be living, and then wish you well for making a huge mistake, but this....? Sonofabitch, this is a little different. You knew that, right?"

"No, Sir, we just fell in love."

Spoker got on the phone.

Within an hour Grady and Spoker were sitting in Colonel Hamlin's office. Grady did not even remember getting into the jeep. All he kept thinking was the Army would not let him marry Tien. He wondered if they could stop him, or if they might try. They could send him home.

Colonel Hamlin walked in. Both men stood and saluted. He returned their salutes and told them to sit. Hamlin spoke first, "Corporal Cordeaux, I just looked at your file. Son, you are coming up on your third tour here, and doing very well from what I can see. Your first year in Nam you were a war hero. Since then you have been doing some outstanding work for SpecForce and Intel. However, today I hear you are shacking up with one of the dynasty families of South Vietnam. What is your story, son?"

Grady hesitated, unsure if he should speak. Finally, he replied, "Sir, I met a girl and fell in love. I asked her to marry me and she said yes." Grady stopped.

"That's it?" Hamlin asked incredulously. "Did she ever mention that her family is very well-connected with the political and military elite in all of Viet fucking Nam? Hell, they probably have dinner with Ho Chi Minh! The colonel sighed, and the room fell silent. "Do you have her father's blessing?"

Grady did not want to answer. "Not yet, Sir."

"Goddamn, Corporal, what were you thinking? How long have the parents known about your marriage proposal?"

Grady answered, "I think about two weeks now, Sir. They disowned her. We plan on having a small marriage ceremony and bringing her back to the States with me."

"You can't just marry a foreign national and keep your clearances, son!" Hamlin looked at Grady, and then at Spoker. There was an awkward silence.

Hamlin looked off in the distance mulling it over. "I guess if the ARVN leadership were going to say anything, they would have done it by now. It's a good thing her parents disowned her, or this could be ugly. Corporal Cordeaux, you are confined to your quarters until further notice. Lieutenant Spoker will escort you back to your hooch. You are dismissed! Spoker, I want a word."

Grady came to attention and turned about face walking out of the office to the jeep. He had a thousand thoughts running through his mind and could not make sense of any. He mostly wondered how this mattered to anyone but him and Tien. Things sure were different in Viet fucking Nam!

Hamlin told Spoker the whole thing sounded like a good old American love story with Vietnamese cultural implications. Hamlin examined Grady's record and it supported his intentions. Hamlin was a family man, who had a young sister back home in love with a GI.

Spoker sat there while Hamlin tapped his pencil on the desk thinking. After a few minutes Hamlin said, "I think this will be all right. It does not sound like something in which the Army should be involved. Cordeaux has enough rank to be able to live off post. I will check on his position and clearances based on this new information and see how it shakes out. This girl is not a street whore, and not VC. Hell, it might even be advantageous to his intelligence gathering. I will let you know by 1400 hours. You can let Cordeaux know my decision after you hear from me. That is all."

Spoker saluted and walked out.

Spoker and Cordeaux did not speak on the short ride back to the hooch. Before jumping out of the jeep, Grady asked if he was going to be shipped out. Spoker told him to stay close to his hooch and wait to hear from him.

Before Grady went inside, Spoker said, "Don't worry, it should be fine."

Grady cleaned up his hooch, washed clothes, showered, and reviewed a few notes about VC activity. He was restless waiting to hear from Spoker. He was surprised that the Army would make a big deal about a man and a woman, but then Tien was not just any woman. It never crossed his mind that the war could keep them apart. He loved her so much and that should be all that mattered. His complete truth was that she was carrying his baby and he would never let anyone take her from him.

The knock on his door could not have come soon enough. His pulse raced. He opened his door to Spoker, saluted and invited him in. Grady sat on the bed and offered Spoker the desk chair.

Spoker said, "I don't need to sit, this won't take long."

Grady sensed detachment in Spoker's tone. "The colonel got back to me. You are to report to your office tomorrow morning at 0800 to be read out of your highest-level clearance. You will retain your classified status at a lower level until security can investigate your fiancée and her family. As far as living off base, you may live wherever you like within the established boundaries set forth in our Concept of Operations for Saigon and the surrounding area, providing you are able to report to your combat duty station in ten minutes or less. You must report your address to your security officer and me. Do you understand everything I just told you?"

Grady could not believe what he was hearing. "Yes Sir!" he replied. His mind was still processing everything. He silently repeated everything to himself. The Army did not say anything against being with Tien! They said I could live off base! He expected they would downgrade his clearances until they checked her out, but that was it. He still could not believe it! They were not going to send him home right away. His eyes welled up with tears of joy. He packed some things in a duffel bag and ran out of the main gate to their apartment to tell her everything was going to be fine!

A Wedding

Saigon's spring weather was perfect. The music started and Tien appeared from around the corner in a traditional pink Ao Dai adorned with ancestral symbols in bright colors. Grady stared at her captivated by her beauty!

He, in his dress uniform, stood near the altar inside an ancient Catholic Church. He asked Lieutenant Spoker to stand with him. Wanhai and her husband were there for Tien. It was supposed to be the happiest day of her life, but a profound sadness lingered inside her because her family was not there. No matter how perfect her wedding and groom were at this moment, her joy would forever be tainted by her father's inflexibility. She thought about all her sisters, brother, aunts, uncles and cousins attending the wedding if only her father had blessed the marriage.

Despite all, Tien kept a smile on her face for Grady. The priest spoke Vietnamese for much of the service, until it was time for Grady to acknowledge his commitment to his bride.

Grady answered softly, "I do."

Tien replied, "I do."

The priest said a final blessing, and pronounced them "husband and wife." He turned to Grady, "You may kiss the bride."

Grady's love for her at this moment was so much more than he could ever imagine. She was so gorgeous, so graceful, so tender, and most of all, the mother of his unborn child. He kissed her hoping she could feel in his lips all the love in his heart. Wanhai cheered for the new couple and handed Tien the traditional wedding umbrella. The couple walked down the aisle of the church and climbed into a car that Wanhai's husband had arranged to take them to a restaurant near their apartment.

The reception included the newlyweds, Spoker, Wanhai's family, and a few of Grady's co-workers. Everyone danced, ate, and toasted the happy couple. Two traditional lacquer gift boxes were placed on the head table for the newlyweds.

After the reception, the couple retreated to their apartment. Wanhai and her daughter decorated it with traditional lanterns, symbols, and a silk banner with "song hy" embroidered on it for good luck. They worked hard to try to give Tien some traditional elements of a Vietnamese wedding that her family should have done for her.

Tien understood what Wanhai tried to do, and her eyes teared up when she saw the apartment. Grady understood too and was grateful. The couple hugged, and then slow-danced to a record playing on the phonograph. For one night, they forgot about family troubles, war, death, and fear. The rest of the world was shut out. They retired to the bedroom, deeply in love, as husband and wife.

After a long weekend, the newlyweds returned to reality. Grady's marital status had changed, but work did not. Things had piled up while he was off and the catching up gave him a throbbing headache in his eyes and forehead. He was typing notes for the weekly intelligence collectors report. Every collector submitted a report. Most of the time they wrote NTR (nothing to report), but every now and again valuable information came in.

Almost all the GIs remaining in Nam were listening for chatter. Operators and Attaché personnel might be trained in active intelligence collection, but GIs did not have the training. The concern was that a soldier might make an acquaintance, but never know the acquaintance was a VC spy, so the GIs were not intelligence collectors. Grady still had to report any information he overheard about North Vietnamese political, military, and insurgency activity.

Since his clearances had been downgraded, he could report, but could not know if the information was corroborated by other sources.

He did not mind the downgrade. It kept him out of briefings and meetings he would rather not attend.

Anyway, Grady had plenty to do in the New Year, including training ARVN soldiers, making sure he did not get shipped back home, at least until the fall, and keeping his new wife happy and healthy during her pregnancy.

Saigon Imploding

Grady's life was so full and busy he barely noticed time passing, until the occasional VC provocations, sniper fire, and random bombings would make time stand still for a few moments. The tensions in South Vietnam by early spring 1973 were thick enough to cut with a knife. Every time he walked off base, he felt like an ambush awaited him around every corner. Vietnamization was a dying program, the insurgency in the countryside was strengthening, and villagers were ambivalent about the outcome of the war. They were tired and mistrusting of foreigners.

News from home, besides anti-war protests, was that Nixon was going to resume bombing in the North and mine the harbors to force an armistice. Grady did not speak Vietnamese, but he understood enough key words and familiar phrases, combined with body language. In cafes and street corners he overheard people consistently talking about being dissatisfied with the government and its corruption. Grady could see the big picture and believed he was witnessing the country disintegrating.

By now, it was a known fact the Americans were leaving. On a personal level, after two tours, Grady did not know what to believe about the cause. He was not as idealistic or gung-ho as when he started. In just a few years the rules of engagement kept changing, battle lines were indistinguishable, and the U.S. goals were too fluid and vague to be achievable. The only things remaining for him were his personal goals. He had to make certain the Army recorded his marriage, make sure his wife had a healthy baby, and get them both back to "the world."

Tien's slender figure had a small basketball protruding from her abdomen. Like many Asian women that are pregnant, she did not show very much even in her seventh month. She was holding up very well, at least physically, and her obstetrician diagnosed mother and baby as healthy. Unfortunately, Tien's mental health was not as good. She believed her emotional condition was not important enough to burden her husband with, as her mother taught her when she was a girl. She especially did not want to trouble Grady with something that could be caused by hormone imbalances. Bringing a child into the world was supposed to be a time of joy, but Tien was in despair because of the loss of her family support system, even though they were nearby. She was being deprived also of the tight bonding experience between mother and expectant daughter. Every day was a lost moment she would never recover.

The family-imposed exile made Tien explosively angry toward her parents. She hoped that one day they would suffer tremendous guilt and heartache about their decision, but her revenge did not help. Wanhai relayed to Tien any news about her family, but Tien's name was never mentioned. The one positive thing about being ostracized was that it was not only easier but vital for her to devote herself to Grady and their new life in America.

Tien also worried for her baby's safety. The occasional gunfire and explosions heard off in the distance were legitimate reasons to worry.

Nixon Bombing

South Vietnamese soldiers were racing through the ARVN Training Center one morning as Grady arrived. He had not yet been briefed the weekly situation report, but something big was happening. On his first cup of coffee, one of Grady's ARVN counterparts told him B-52s had just bombed North Vietnam. Grady knew the troops were gearing up for a retaliatory response from the NVA. He charged into Captain Thuy's office to see if there was anything he needed.

"Everything," Thuy shouted back.

Grady saluted and raced back to the base.

Grady was aware that bombing Hanoi was a likelihood depending on the political negotiations, but no one knew when it might happen. He reported to his Army superiors what Captain Thuy said he needed. It fell on deaf ears. The bombing was intended as political negotiations with kinetic energy. The U.S. was trying to end its involvement in Vietnam, not deepen it. Grady was told to ready himself for a firefight, and that all leave was canceled. He was reminded that off base curfew restrictions would be enforced until after the Easter Offensive.

Tien was resting on her bed when Wanhai knocked on her door to check on her. Tien yelled for her to come in.

"Are you okay?" she asked. "Where is Grady?"

Tien sensed the urgency in Wanhai's voice. "He is at the base, what is wrong?"

Wanhai said she did not know if it was true, but at the market there was talk about the Americans bombing the North and intensified fighting. Tien's eyes opened wide.

She assured Wanhai, "Grady will come home and take me to the base."

Just then, Tien doubled over in pain and Wanhai caught her. She helped Tien lie back on the bed. Something was wrong with the baby. Wanhai helped her to the toilet, and seeing blood, Tien asked Wanhai to take her to the hospital.

As soon as Grady received the message about Tien, he rushed to the packed emergency room of the downtown hospital in Saigon. Grady asked the desk clerk where his wife was being treated. The Pham name carried great weight, and although she was estranged from her family, Tien was still a Pham. She had been given a private room, and Dr. Dinh, her obstetrician, was alerted.

Grady came to her room just as the doctor finished his examination. He assured them the baby was fine, but Tien's spotting was reason for mild concern. He ordered her to complete bed rest and reduce stress. She thought to herself, *if the doctor knew some way to keep her country from being overrun, and could guarantee safety for her baby, she would have no stress.*

Dr. Dinh scheduled her to come to his office in a few days for a more thorough exam. When the doctor requested another exam, Grady asked if everything was okay? Dinh casually responded that he wanted to check the baby's heartbeat, but it should be fine after Tien rested. He heard an anomaly, but it was almost certainly caused by mother's stress level.

"Nothing to be concerned about," he said.

A few days later Grady and Tien walked carefully into Saigon Hospital. A nurse met them with a wheelchair. She helped Tien into the chair and pushed her to the Cardiology Unit. Dr. Dinh was waiting. He introduced Dr. Thuy, who was head of Cardiology. This was their first time using an echocardiogram on a fetus.

Several cardiologists and technicians were gathered around to watch the procedure, making Grady and Tien even more nervous.

Dinh assured them there was no reason to be worried. If there was a question of a murmur, this procedure might provide answers. He assured them congenital murmurs were common and did not interfere with a normal, healthy life.

Dinh wanted to try the technology. If it worked and revealed a murmur, they could be better prepared during her delivery for any contingencies. Tien was prepped, and then the nurse moved a small probe over her baby bump. Doctors stared at the fetus on the screen. The procedure lasted twenty minutes. Then Dinh told them it was done. The couple was in disbelief.

Dinh saw their puzzled look. "See, I told you there was no reason to worry. The test went fine, but we want to be able to give you definitive answers after my colleagues confer. It is not an exact science. As I said, even if we find a murmur, your baby will be fine. Now go home and get some rest. I will call you later in the week."

Surprisingly, the bombing of Hanoi did not produce any massive responses from the enemy. There were normal incursions, attacks, and supply build-ups, but major attacks did not occur. The war was increasingly spilling over into Cambodia, the pace of American withdrawal was continuing, and the ARVN was holding on. This was good and bad news for Grady. He did not want the war to ramp up, putting his wife and child in danger, but a lack of hostility meant increasing pressure on him to go home. His superiors noticed his second tour was nearly over. Even though the NVA noose around Saigon was tightening and the South Vietnamese needed all the help they could get, it was time for Grady to get out.

Baby Arrives

May's monsoon rain pounded the roofs of the ARVN compound so hard that Grady had to shout the daily situation report to the senior NCOs and junior officers. In the middle of his presentation an ARVN soldier walked into the briefing room and handed him a note. He stopped and excused himself for a personal emergency. A jeep was ready to take him to Saigon hospital; Tien was in labor.

She was only eight months pregnant, he thought. On the ride over he prayed for the baby and Tien to be okay. Seeing him come into the hospital lobby, a receptionist told him Tien was in the Neo-natal unit. Dr. Dinh met him in the hallway.

"What happened, doctor? Is Tien okay? How is the baby?"

Dr. Dinh held up his hands motioning Grady to slow down. "Mr. Cordeaux, everyone is in stable condition."

Grady looked at him. "Everyone? What do ya, what do ya mean…everyone?"

Dinh told him, "Tien is resting comfortably. Your son weighs five pounds and he will need to stay here in the pre-natal ward a few weeks so that we can get his weight up."

"My son?"

"Yes, you have a new son! Congratulations! I suspect your wife might want to see you. She is in the room at the end of the hall."

Grady rushed down the hall. He entered her room gingerly so as not to awake Tien. She was groggy but awake. Grady kissed her and whispered in her ear, "We have a son." At this moment he was unable to contain his emotions. The intense feelings for her overwhelmed him and tears streamed down his face.

"Yes, we do!" she said. She kissed him and closed her eyes. She was exhausted, and scared.

Her recovery in the hospital took two days. The nurses wheeled her to the neo-natal unit several times each day to be with her baby. She wanted desperately to hold him, but they wanted him to remain in the incubator until his condition improved. His organs were functioning, but his premature weight and heart sounds were reason for caution. The doctors diagnosed the murmur in utero. It was not uncommon for a premature infant to have a weak heart yet still grow to healthy adulthood. However, caution dictated they keep him under observation for a few weeks.

Tien and Grady were heartbroken that their beautiful little boy would have to suffer intravenous tubes, lack of touch, and constant prodding. They wanted to hold him and let him feel his mother's skin. Tien was discharged from the hospital, but returned every day to be with her baby.

By the third week, the baby grew strong enough for Dr. Dinh to let him go home. Dinh wanted to examine mother and baby twice a week. He assured Tien and Grady the baby would grow up to be a strong, healthy son, and the heart murmur should not limit him in any way.

"What is his name?" Dinh asked.

Tien smiled at Grady. "We will call him Ky dieu, 'our miracle.'"

Grady said, "Ky dieu Grant Pham Cordeaux. Grant is my mother's family name. We already filled out the paperwork for the birth certificate, but they misspelled his last name as 'Cordo.' We will come back to pick up the corrected original copy. Thank you, Dr. Dinh, thank you for everything."

Tien, with tiny Ky dieu swaddled in her arms, walked with Grady out of the hospital. In that moment Grady was once again overwhelmed with joy. The love in his heart was too much for words. He knew this moment would be forever etched in his memory.

A few days later Grady went back to work.

"Goddamn Cordeaux, you must be the only GI in all of Viet frigging Nam who is happy his mama-san got knocked up and had the baby. She love you longtime groovy Joe, now you pay longtime forever." Sergeant Quade, the new guy in the unit, laughed.

Grady ignored him.

Sergeant Sloan spoke up. "Quade, you wouldn't know a groovy thing if it shit in your lap. My brother here got hitched to one of the finest women from one of the richest families in Southeast Asia. He fell in love and now he has a son. Cordeaux got everything a man wants out of life. The only problem is he still in the Nam. What messes with my mind is he can leave anytime."

Grady, paying little attention to the conversation in the background, rifled through paperwork piled on his desk. He could not completely ignore Sloan's comment though. His time was getting short, and he needed to get the paperwork together for the Army to acknowledge his wife and new son. He also needed to get Tien to want to leave Vietnam.

A New Family

The rains subsided and spring became summer. Tien's days were fully occupied with Ky. She was an attentive wife and mother who, as tradition taught her, tried to not disturb her husband in the middle of night when she nursed. No matter how quiet she was though, Grady woke up anyway to be at her side. When Grady was at home he changed and washed diapers, fed Ky, wrapped him, cradled him in his arms with constant gentle motion, and many of the same things Tien did for their son. He loved seeing his wife take to motherhood so instinctively, and now he was happily embracing fatherhood.

Grady thought Ky's birth would change Tien's parents' minds about disowning her. It was unimaginable for him that grandparents would disown their new grandson. He knew this rift hurt Tien to her core, but he took comfort knowing that his parents would try to fill her emptiness with their love.

Within a few weeks of Ky's birth, Grady received a letter from his mother responding to the news of the baby. They were overjoyed! She wrote they could not wait to meet Tien and Ky, and spoil them both. Their joy about a grandson was tempered only by the reality that the farm had taken a toll on his father. She warned Grady that his father might not look like the same man when Grady left for the war. She concluded her letter with a plea for him to come home. Grady's tour would be up before mid-1973, and Ky would be old enough to travel. Grady estimated that the paperwork should be done by then, and the Army would legally acknowledge Tien as his wife. His mother's plea was not ignored.

Grady was always a dutiful soldier, but now he had a wife and little boy. He would hold Ky, as any dutiful dad would, and tell him what daddy had planned for him.

"When you get a little bigger, we are going to play catch, I'll take you fishing, we'll work on the farm, go hunting, and do lots of other things. I love you so much, son, and that will never change."

When Grady talked to Ky the little boy's mouth would curl up into a unique grin. Over time, Tien began to recognize Grady's smile creeping over Ky's little mouth and she would shake her head ruefully. *These two were going to be trouble,* she thought. A few times, Grady would have to go away for work, but he would make up the time by holding his son twice as long. They both loved watching Ky change each day into a little person.

Grady's love for Tien was deepening in ways he never knew. She was so sophisticated, smart, and sexy, but her new role as a mother was even sexier. He never knew his love would continue to deepen and grow in complexity. She was the mother of his son, and he adored her and the new life they created. He loved them both with all his being. Maybe this was a feeling that only a father understood. His mother told him often she would do anything in the world for him. He began to know what she meant. Tien and Ky were his life. He could not imagine life before them, or without them.

It's Time

By late summer, the Americans remaining in Vietnam were fully engaged in helping the South Vietnamese fight the enemy incursions. In war, the threat is defined by the political will combined with the means. The ARVN had the will to fight, and possibly still had the hearts and mind of the people, but they only had the means as long as the U.S. continued supplying arms. Another factor eroding the will was the political climate. Even though the U.S. was bombing Hanoi and Haiphong, South Vietnam's leadership knew the U.S. was more interested in an armistice, than victory for the South. Grady understood this inconsistency and sensed it was time to go. He finally had all the paperwork necessary for the military to ship him, Tien, and Ky back home.

The streets of Saigon were becoming more crowded every day. Vietnamese villagers were coming in droves from the country seeking safety in the city. The brazenness and severity of mortar attacks and bombings was growing. The war was almost exclusively a guerilla insurgency in populated areas. Tien was afraid to go outside, and finally she was convinced, for her baby's safety, they had to leave her homeland. The only things she knew about Americans and life in the U.S. were what she experienced in her family's club and on the base, which was not very encouraging, but she believed even that kind of environment would be safer than Saigon.

After nearly three years in Vietnam, Grady finally had his orders in hand. They were scheduled to leave on November 15, 1973. Anxiety lived in him for three years, but not once did it keep him from charging into battle, risking his life for other men. Now, going home was frightening too. He had been away too long and America had changed. Grady never had time to keep up with current events back home, and the only news source was the Stars and Stripes newspaper. He read a little bit about anti-war protests waning, Nixon winning re-election, Americans still going to the moon, terrorists attacking athletes at the Olympics, and Carole King winning awards for best album. He wondered though, how returning soldiers were treated, and if Southerners would accept his Vietnamese wife. He also wondered how Tien would handle such a dramatic cultural change.

Lying in bed that night, Grady asked Tien if she was nervous about going to America.

She turned to him. "You are my husband. I love you and our baby with all my heart. I go where you go. I will be by your side all the days of my life, through good times and bad times. I will love you always. If you are happy, I will be happy."

She kissed him goodnight. He pulled her closer so she could feel his body responding to her attention. Their breathing got heavier until Tien heard gentle crying in the next bedroom. They sighed. She told him she would be right back.

He kissed her asking, "Do you know how much I love you?"

She smiled. "Yes, I have to get up and feed the result of how much you love me, right now."

She returned to bed after nursing Ky. Grady was fast asleep. She snuggled up in his arms and fell into a light contented sleep as well.

Final Try

The firm date of departure crept up until it became a reality for Tien. She was leaving her home, her country, forever. She felt excitement, apprehension, and sadness at the same time. The finality of leaving a world that might not exist next year was overwhelming.

With their departure date looming, and after much deep contemplation, Tien told Grady she wanted to try to see her parents. In two weeks, they were going to America and she did not want to leave, possibly forever, and not ask one last time if they wanted to see Ky. Grady understood and did not want her to have a lifetime of regret, but he still had his reservations. He worried about her pain if they refused her at the door. He made his case, but Tien insisted she had to say good-bye and give them the opportunity. Grady reluctantly gave in.

Tien decided not to tell her family that she was coming, in case they tried to avoid her. Wanhai let Tien know if her parents would be at the restaurant that weekend. The tension in the streets was hair-raising. VC were hidden in plain sight and Grady had information about the possibility of random attacks in Saigon's crowded areas. He accompanied his wife and son, remaining on extreme high alert.

They arrived at Pham's that afternoon to avoid the evening crowd. Her uncle and cousin were the first in the restaurant to spot them. They hugged Tien and made a fuss over Ky, wanting to hold him and show him off. This put Grady even more on edge. It was unwise to put their American cooperation on display.

Even though it was early in the day, the club was unusually crowded. Grady asked Uncle Nguyen about it. Nguyen said that they were hosting a big promotion party for several ARVN officers. It was going to be a big night. With that news, Grady felt the hair on the back of his neck stand straight up. He did not want to anger or panic Tien, but he whispered forcefully to her they should not stay long.

In the next few minutes, a large group of ARVN officers arrived. There were so many that Pham's did not have enough tables for dinner. Many of the officers moved to the bar and began ordering drinks. They sounded like they had already been to happy hour. Grady shot a look to Tien, who was still talking with her cousin. She understood the look and skipped formalities. She asked Jun to go tell her parents she and Ky were going to America in two weeks and she wanted to say good-bye. Jun's eyes began to well up with tears. She nodded and headed upstairs to tell her aunt and uncle.

Grady watched Jun hustle to the stairs. Just then, out of the corner of his eye, Grady saw the small truck pull up in front of the club, almost ramming into people on the curb. Instinctively, he hurled himself at Tien, and she covered Ky. A bright light and flash were the last things they saw.

A massive explosion and fireball ripped through the first floor of Pham's, leveling everything and everyone. The concussion alone shattered windows up and down the street shredding pedestrians with glass shards. The VC knew about the promotion party and intended to kill as many of the officers as possible. The blast destroyed much of the first floor, causing significant damage to the building's structure, and took out most of the upper floors on the street side. Carnage and body parts were strewn about the street and the charred inside. When the smoke finally cleared, the scene was gruesome. Nothing in the shell of the first floor was left standing. The tables, glass, and wall materials were splintered into small strips that went flying through the room like missiles. Some recognizable body parts were among the debris inside and splattered into the street. Other chunks of bloody meat and bone were not recognizable.

Part 4: End of the Road

Waking Up

"Corporal Cordeaux, Corporal Cordea... Mr. Cordeaux?" Grady was exhausted, feeling the concussion of the blast and unable to clear the cobwebs in his mind. "He is coming out of sedation, Doctor."

The attendants were trying to awaken Grady in Dallas Cardiac Center hospital.

"What's his status?" the ER doctor asked.

"He is stable now, but over the last two hours he had SVT and rapid breathing. In the last ten minutes, his heart rate decreased to 120. We did not want to sedate him further, so we waited. Right now, his vitals are normalizing." The EMT handed over the chart.

The staff moved him to the Intensive Care Unit to further assess his condition. Within a few hours Grady was stabilized enough to be moved to a room. RC and Suzie came a few hours later.

"Jesus! Why is it that I was driving five hours while you were in a blissful sleep in a bed, and you're the one that looks like shit?" RC asked.

Grady looked at him with a wild confused look. "Where is she, RC? Where is Tien? Where is Ky?"

RC was suddenly alarmed for his friend. He looked at the doctor with an expression that conveyed, "What is he talking about?"

Dr. Rick, a young cardiologist studying under Dr. Lamb at DCC, did not have answers. He hoped RC had answers for him.

RC subtly tilted his head toward the hallway, signaling the doctor to meet him out there. "Doc, he is asking about his wife and son he lost in Vietnam, in 1973! What is happening?"

Dr. Rick thought about it for a few moments. He told RC that sometimes patients under sedation for an extended time can stimulate old intense memories. "It's not uncommon." He said, "What do you know about Mr. Cordeaux's wife and child? You said he lost them?"

"Yeah, Doc, Grady and I have been friends for a long time, and even though he does not talk about it, over the years I have pieced together the big picture. When he was in Vietnam, he married a girl from a wealthy, well-connected family. This was not one of those mail order, street corner brides. She was forbidden to date GIs, but over time they fell deeply in love. When they got married her parents disowned her. A year later they had a son. Well, two weeks before they were coming back stateside, they were in her family's restaurant to try one last time to say goodbye, and that afternoon it got bombed by VC. It took out the whole place, killed a lot of people. The U.S. and ARVN, (South Vietnamese) police and medics rushed to the site. They pulled out anybody that was in one piece; most were not. When they found an American man in the debris who was clinging to life, they rushed him to Saigon and got him on a medevac aircraft ASAP. Three days later he was in Walter Reed military hospital in D.C. He lingered in a coma for six months. By the time he came out of it, it was too late to do anything about his family.

"I guess in the rush to save him, the Army did not check if he had a family. They did not know what happened to his wife and infant son. Every time he talks about it, he says it was a total cluster fuck. Oh, sorry! He spent a lot of years and money trying to find them. That is what I know."

Suzie asked the doctor, "What does this have to do with his heart?"

Dr. Rick explained that Grady showed signs of extreme stress under sedation during the transport. His reliving of a very traumatic experience could explain the stress during the transport, which is better than hidden cardiac issues or reaction to sedation. "Thank you, Mr. and Mrs. Carter." The doctor turned away.

"RC."

Dr. Rick said, "I'm sorry?"

"My friends call me RC. If you are going to be taking care of my best friend, I want you and me to be friends too. Best friends look out for each other." RC locked eyes with Dr. Rick. "I'm going back in to be with our best friend."

She was there!

Grady moved in and out of consciousness for several hours. RC thought the ambulance ride and sedation must have taken its toll. Suzie looked on from a chair in the corner of the room, hoping her husband was not about to lose his best friend. RC pulled a chair alongside the bed. The Carters intended to stay long enough to hear the treatment plan, and then they would go to their hotel.

RC started to drift off in the chair when he heard Grady. "I was with her, RC! I was with them both!"

RC rubbed his eyes to wake up and moved closer to his friend. "Who were you with, Junior?" RC asked quietly.

"Tien and Ky! I was back in the Nam, man! It was like I never left. Hell, I was back in high school too. Where is my wallet?"

RC looked over at Grady's personal effects in the chair. "Everything is right here, pal. I got it. Relax!" RC found the wallet and handed it to Grady.

Grady was awkward trying to get around the tubes in his arm, but finally pulled an old dog-eared picture from his wallet. He brought it close to his eyes. "It was her, we were standing in the same spot where this was taken."

He stared at the photo of Tien in her hand-painted silk dress in Thailand. Tears filled his eyes. The beeping from the heart monitor began to slow. Just looking at her picture, after all these years, still had a calming effect on Grady. Suzie wept watching Grady clutch the photo. She could not imagine loving someone so deeply for so long after they are gone.

Grady asked RC, "Did I die?"

RC answered with agitation, "What in the Sam hill are you talking about? You are alive, right here in Dallas, with me and Suzie, right now!"

Grady was exhausted, but he needed RC to understand. "RC, listen. I'm not giving up, I'll fight this thing with all I have got, but I need to know if I died for even a few seconds in the ambulance. Maybe they revived me, but I need to know if being with Tien and Ky was my heaven. If that is what awaits me, I am ready to go. It was perfect to be with her again. I could feel her love again. I could feel the love we had for Ky. It was real, RC! It was all real!"

"Grady, take it easy, okay? Your ticker is racing pretty fast, and I do not think that is what you need right now, okay, slick? I will check with Dr. Rick about your ambulance ride. I don't think you died, though. At least, no one said anything about it."

Grady was asleep before RC finished his sentence. RC looked over at Suzie. Neither one wanted to trample Grady's euphoria by telling him it was only a dream. They both sat quietly for the next four hours with their friend.

RC stirred when the doctors entered the room. "The EMTs reported his heart rate elevated, but he stabilized quickly after admitting. We did a cardiac work-up and chemistry. He did not go to telemetry."

Their medical jargon confused RC. Grady was waking up, but before he became fully alert, RC quietly asked Dr. Rick if anything unusual had happened during the ambulance ride. Dr. Rick was accompanying Dr. Samman, the Chief of Cardiology.

Dr. Samman, who got briefed on all new cases, turned to RC, "And you are?"

"Oh, hey, Doc, I'm RC Carter. My wife, Suzie, over there, and I came up from Alec, Louisiana to be with our friend, Grady."

Dr. Samman spoke with a thick middle eastern accent. "I'm sorry, Mr. Carter, but Mr. Cordeaux's condition is private, and we can only discuss it with his family. Would you please excuse us while we examine the patient?"

RC's jaw tightened as he stared at Dr. Samman. RC was tired and irritable. "Doctor Sand Man, is it? Well, Doc, you might be the guy who actually saves my best friend, so I am not going to do anything right now that you might regret. My best friend over there is not feeling well, so I'm going to behave. However, I drove for five hours to be here, and I am not going anywhere. And, just so you know, I AM family!"

Dr. Samman understood RC's tone and his threat. He was not accustomed to being talked down to, so he did not know how to react. Dr. Rick leaned in toward his superior and informed him that Mr. Carter had medical power of attorney for Mr. Cordeaux.

Dr. Samman did not like being scolded, especially in front of young doctors on his staff, but he had no choice. He turned to RC. "I see. Very well, Mr. Carter, your friend's condition has stabilized, for now. I know of nothing unusual that happened during his transport. Perhaps you should check with the attending physician who signed him in earlier today. The chart says Mr. Cordeaux showed signs of arrhythmia and stress, normal for a man in his condition. Our plan is to evaluate him over the next few days, conduct some tests, and plan a course of treatment. We are fortunate to be hosting a fellow cardiologist from London. Dr. Tran is one of the leading cardiology specialists in Eisenmenger Syndrome. We have invited him to evaluate Mr. Cordeaux and participate in his treatment protocol. We should be able to give you more details and prognosis in a few days. Mr. Cordeaux should rest now. I recommend you and your wife try to do the same."

Dr. Samman replaced the chart and departed the room. Dr. Rick winked to RC.

Grady was wiped out. RC and Suzie stood at his bedside to say good night. She gently removed the photo from his hand. "We will see you tomorrow."

She was almost certain Grady did not hear her. The couple walked out of the hospital in silence. Driving to the hotel, RC broke their somber mood by asking Suzie if she was hungry. She said what RC was thinking; neither one of them felt like eating. They arrived at the hotel, checked in, and tried to get some sleep.

Treatment Plan

The next day RC and Suzie found Grady more alert and surrounded by hospital staff. Dr. Rick, Dr. Tran, another doctor, and two nurses were in the room. "Oh, good morning, Mr. and Mrs. Carter. We were just discussing the tests we would like to do today. Grady asked me to tell you about them."

RC shook hands. He looked at Dr. Tran, recognizing his facial features as Southeast Asian. "Are you the expert from London?" RC pried. He wondered if Grady also noticed his new doctor looked Vietnamese.

Tran surprised RC, answering in a proper British accent. "Yes, I studied in Cambridge, am certified in Cardiac-thoracic medicine, specializing in Eisenmenger Syndrome and cardio anomalies."

Dr. Rick jumped in, "He will continue to be monitored on an EKG. Dr. Tran has ordered an MRI, likely followed up by cardiac catheterization. We reviewed the lab results and tests done in ICU, and at Alexandria. We have explained to Grady his chest x-ray revealed damage to the small blood vessels in his lungs, which would explain his extreme fatigue. The MRI will provide a comprehensive view of his lungs. We should be able to isolate and evaluate the source of blood leakage, causing increased pressure in his blood vessels."

RC and Suzie tried to keep up with Dr. Rick. "Wait a minute, Doc, I thought this Eisenmenger thing was in his heart, not his lungs?"

"Yes, cardio-vascular issues are complicated. Dr. Tran?"

Dr. Tran tried to explain in laymen's terms, about Grady's diagnosis. "I believe the initial diagnosis of Eisenmenger Syndrome was correct. This condition is congenital, (hereditary) and typically treated very early in life. Very simply, it is a hole in the heart. The location of the hole determines the symptoms. If there is a defect in the atrioventricular canal, it can increase the pressure of blood flowing through the pulmonary artery, eventually damaging the small blood vessels in the lungs, resulting in cyanosis, (low oxygen in the blood) and problems during physical exertion. Grady also might have a blockage in his heart, possibly from plaque build-up, causing a myocardial infarction, (heart attack). When blood thinner was administered it would have exacerbated the blood leakage. Right now, we need to locate the hole in his heart."

RC saw Grady roll his eyes and draw a deep breath in resignation. "Don't try to understand it, RC. When every other word is beyond your spelling capability, it is best to let it go."

RC turned to the doctors. "I guess it is a good sign he has his sense of humor, right? Does that syndrome affect his brain too?" RC winked.

Dr. Rick grinned. "Okay, folks, we need to prep our patient and figure out what is going on inside. This will take much of the day, so you might want to find a place to relax. I will check in on him later this afternoon. We should know more by then."

As they were preparing Grady, RC told him he had picked up a couple of gun and farming magazines for him.

Grady asked Dr. Rick, "Hey, Doc, will I finally be able to read after coming out of your MRI tube?" Rick smiled.

The Photograph

RC and Suzie went to the cafeteria for coffee and breakfast. Suzie surprised RC, telling him she was going shopping. He shrugged and said he would wait at the hospital. The day dragged on. RC read the gun magazine front to back and flipped through several others in the waiting room. A few hours later, Suzie came back.

It was late afternoon and RC was hungry. Suzie had two bags. She pulled a box out of one bag and showed RC. "I thought Grady would like this."

RC wanted the other bag with fried chicken first. Suzie was annoyed. "Just look at it, and then we can eat. How is Grady?"

"I haven't seen hide nor hair of him, haven't seen doctors neither."

Suzie became worried. RC opened the box and pulled out a framed 8 x 10 photo of Tien in her hand-painted gown on the staircase in Thailand. She was breathtakingly beautiful. Suzie had found a photography shop that scanned and restored the old photo from

Grady's wallet. She had it enlarged and framed. RC was speechless. Grady would approve.

RC kissed her. "Now, let's go see if the Colonel can fry chicken in Dallas the same way Bo does in Alex."

After eating, RC and Suzie went up to Grady's room. Grady was awake while a nurse checked all the monitors and lines hooked up to him. He looked up. "Have you guys been here all day? Good lord, you don't need to hover over me like a spring calf. I appreciate it, I really do, but I know you got better things to do."

RC and Suzie immediately noticed Grady's alertness. It was a good sign.

RC asked, "Do you think these high-class Dallas nurses are going to help with your bed pan?" Suzie jabbed RC.

Grady shot back, "Is that what you are waiting for? Gimme a minute and I'll have something for ya."

"Boys, boys, mind your manners, you are not in a barn," Suzie scolded.

The room became silent, but it was a comfortable silence between friends. Grady's expression showed he was glad RC and Suzie were with him. Their presence meant a lot, especially since he was not fond of doctors and hospitals.

It was not too long before Grady closed his eyes for a few minutes. His spurt of activity seemed to take a little bit out of him. Suzie pulled the picture frame from the bag and placed it on Grady's bed table. He cracked open his eyes to see what she was doing.

Looking at the photo he asked, "Did you do that, Suz?"

She nodded. He closed his eyes and a teardrop rolled down his cheek. He whispered, "Thank you so much!"

Suzie could not remember ever seeing Grady emotional. She grabbed his hand. "I know she meant everything to you."

Grady gathered just enough energy and breath to tell RC, "I talked to the doc about the ambulance ride. He said the sedatives may have stimulated old memories."

"RC, I was there, man! I was back in the shit! I lived my life all over again. I even remembered Gabby."

RC looked surprised. "You mean that heavy gal, who'd been divorced two or three times? The one who kept phoning you a few years back, even though you weren't interested?"

Grady nodded. "Well, when she was 17, she was something. We dated in high school, but it didn't work out. I guess somehow she found out I was back in Pineville. Her life didn't quite work out how she planned so she was hoping we could pick up the pieces and give it another try. I wasn't interested, that's all."

RC chuckled. "She sure wanted you!"

Just Let It Go

Grady got back to his story. "Anyway, in the ambulance ride I remembered everything just like it was yesterday. I relived all the important moments. I remembered the Mekong delta, my boat, getting shot up, the firefights, getting out of Tchepone, the whole God damn thing. I remember meeting Tien. I relived those feelings when I first saw her beauty and grace. I never thought she would love someone like me, but over time I won her over. I remember it, Bro! I still feel it, like it was yesterday. You think I relived all these things in vivid detail because I'm ready to punch out? Maybe my balance sheet of good and evil is being tallied?"

RC shot back. "Hey, hey, no sir. We are not gonna have any of that pity party bullshit! You are still in the fight. It was just a dream."

Grady looked at him. "That's the thing. It was so much more than a dream. I still feel her, I feel my son." After hearing himself say it aloud, his guilt hit. "I didn't do enough." He closed his eyes with anguish and exhaustion.

RC rebutted every word in protest. He reminded Grady how much money and time he spent writing letters, talking to the military, calling U.S. and Vietnam government's organizations, foreign aid organizations, everybody and anybody who might be able to help find Tien and Ky. "I've seen the box of files and correspondence you keep in your closet. You went back to Vietnam the first chance you could. I gotta be honest, Junior, you have spent a lifetime chasing shadows you left in Saigon. Don't you think it's time to let them go? I've watched you live your whole life alone because you held on to a hope. All it got you was loneliness."

Grady's eyes were closed, but he heard every word. Trying to talk was exhausting because it was difficult to get enough air. Before falling into a deep sleep, Grady whispered, "But I love them more than life."

The next morning, while RC and Suzie were sitting in the room, Doctors Tran and Rick came in.

Dr. Tran asked Grady if he felt up to reviewing the results of yesterday's tests. "Sure, Doc, let me have it. I'd like RC and Suzie to stay here too, in case they need to make decisions for me later."

"That's fine, Mr. Cordeaux. We have consulted with our cardiology team about your labs and MRI results. You have an atrioventricular canal defect. It is a hole in your heart between the upper and lower chambers. Usually, the hole increases pressure of blood flow through the pulmonary artery, causing damage to small blood vessels in your lungs. This causes low oxygen in the blood resulting in no capability for physical activity.

"It would seem you have lived with this your whole life, since Eisenmenger syndrome is congenital, and typically diagnosed in infants. The fact that you have lived this long with this condition suggests the hole was very small and non-symptomatic. However, the myocardial infarction, likely caused by plaque, restricted the blood flow and exerted your heart. The pressure on your heart and blood flow enlarged the AVSD, sorry, the atrioventricular canal defect, which is putting a strain on your circulatory system. This is why you are so weak."

Grady nodded. "So, if I didn't have the heart attack, this AV thing would have never been a problem?"

"It is impossible for us to speculate, because other factors could have eventually come into play. What we know is that you have two cardiac issues requiring surgery immediately. We want to operate tomorrow."

RC asked Tran, "So what is the prognosis with two heart problems?"

"We will know better once we go in. The heart is a muscle in constant contraction. We will have to close the hole in his heart, so it stops shunting of blood from right to left. There are a few ways we can do it. We also have to perform an angioplasty to open the blocked artery and assess the damage. It is highly likely he will need a pacemaker. We will look for pulmonary artery hypertension, which is caused by the high blood flow in his lungs. If we permanently stop the bleeding and widen his artery, the prognosis is good. However, Mr. Cordeaux will be very weak for a while no matter what happens." Dr. Tran made eye contact with everyone in the room to make a point.

The framed photo on the bedside table caught Tran's eye. He studied it for more than a casual glance. "What a lovely photograph. May I ask who it is?"

Grady answered, "She is my wife."

Tran replied, "She looks Cambodian. I am Cambodian."

Grady answered, "No, Doc, she is Vietnamese."

Tran experienced a déjà vu moment as if he had seen her before, but he could not remember for certain, so he let it go. "Well, Mr. Cordeaux, we would like to..." Tran stopped in mid-sentence. The look on his face revealed that an epiphany had just come to him. "Oh, I'm so sorry, I just remembered a colleague back home is waiting for my phone call. Now, where was I? Mr. Cordeaux, we will need you to sign the consent form so we can proceed with the surgery tomorrow."

Grady nodded. Tran took one more look at the picture and exited the room. RC broke the silence. "Ok, now we know what you are dealing with. They go in, fix the hole, fix the blocked artery, come out, close you up and in a few weeks, you are back to your old self."

Suzie interrupted, "I've known people who have gone in for heart surgery and come out two days later. It's routine nowadays."

RC and Suzie did not know if they were trying to convince Grady or themselves. Open-heart surgery was risky no matter how routine it was becoming. Grady understood, but he felt like he did not have a choice. He was not scared to die, not anymore. He knew now that when he died, he was going to be with Tien and Ky, and he welcomed it.

The doctors continued discussing Grady's case in the hallway for a few more minutes. When Dr. Tran reached his temporary office, he excused himself, explaining to Dr. Rick he would review notes in preparation for tomorrow's procedure. He closed his office door, looked at his watch, and made a phone call to London.

Surgery

The operation began at 8:00 a.m. The team, assembled in the operating room, included the Chief Cardiac Surgeon, Dr. Regis, Dr. Rick, Dr. Tran, the anesthesiologist and her team, and several operating room nurses, all highly skilled in cardiac-thoracic surgery. The difference this time was the inclusion of Dr. Tran. He was not performing the surgery, but his expertise in evaluating and repairing the AV defect was welcomed.

Most of the operation was routine. They had completed both procedures successfully and closed up the patient in under four hours. There were no complications and his vital signs in post-op were excellent. Grady remained in recovery for several hours before being moved to the Cardiac Care Unit (CCU). Dr. Tran and Dr. Rick met RC and Suzie in the waiting room.

"Grady is fine. The procedures went well, and he came through with flying colors. We will monitor him, do tests to see if we stopped the bleeding, and check his blood. Everything looks good as of now. He will remain in the CCU overnight, and then if all goes well, as we expect it will, he will be moved to our telemetry unit for a few days. His recovery will be slow, and he will be very weak for some time. You might be able to talk to him tomorrow, but honestly, I suggest you go home. He will be in good hands. I know it is a long drive to Alexandria, but all we can do now is wait. Come back in a few days when he will be responsive. I will call you if I need to."

RC and Suzie talked it over and decided to go back to Alexandria to take care of a few things and return in a few days.

A Stranger Lurks

Grady slept through the night in the CCU. He tried to awaken but the weight he felt on his chest was too imposing. It was easier to sleep. One more day of rest made a huge difference. Although he was extremely weak, he opened his eyes to new surroundings. He recognized being in a different room hooked up to two machines, and an entire truck cable harness of plugs and wires. Two hospital technicians were in the room monitoring the machines and wires. When Grady awakened, one of the attendants pressed an alarm button.

Dr. Rick came in asking Grady, "How are you feeling?"

Grady looked at him. "Seriously, Doc? I feel like a diesel engine is on my chest, and it looks like its wires are hooked up to me."

Dr. Rick smiled. "Good! We were able to salvage your sarcasm. Anyway, the surgery went well. The hole in your heart was more of a tear than a hole. We were able to close it, but we want to be careful about additional stress, which could undo the repair. Okay? The angioplasty was successful. We installed a pacemaker to regulate your heartbeat. You have some residual issues as a result of pulmonary artery hypertension. This is causing your labored breathing. Medications should help. Any questions?"

"Jesus, Doc! I don't know what you said, but it sounds like I'm okay. When can I get out of here?"

Dr. Rick shook his head. "Mr. Cordeaux, you just had serious surgery. We have made good progress, but I hesitate to say at this time that you are fully recovered. You are doing well, yes, but we still need to monitor your recovery. The length of time required for a full recovery will be up to your body. You should expect to be here at least another week or two. Now, I believe there are some people who have been waiting to see you."

RC and Suzie came in. Grady smiled seeing them in their surgical masks. Suzie asked how he was feeling. Grady said he was so exhausted it is difficult to stay awake more than ten minutes. He said he wondered if surgery was the right thing to do. RC jumped in, reminding Grady it was the only thing to do.

"Look, you would not be talking to us if you didn't have this surgery. Instead, we would be dressed in black, crying over you, shoveling dirt on your box." His words were terse, morbid, and out of character, but he was annoyed that Grady was second-guessing the surgery.

Dr. Rick abruptly intervened to break the tension. "Our goal here is to get you well. The way to do that is to let you get plenty of rest, and not have any excitement." Dr. Rick looked directly at RC. He continued, "and to be patient while your heart heals."

RC got the message.

Dr. Tran came in, asking, "How is the patient?"

Dr. Rick replied, "All signs are good." He rattled off a series of numbers and mentioned pulse oximeter, CBC, cardiac enzymes, and sinus rhythm.

Dr. Tran flipped through the clipboard, as if he did not hear Dr. Rick. "Good, very good! Mr. Cordeaux, your post-op test results are good. We have a long way to go, but I see no reason not to be optimistic at this point. Let's not do anything to increase your heart rhythm, hmm?" Dr. Tran made his point.

Grady looked at RC and Suzie for support. He didn't like being helpless, but if he had to be, he was glad they were with him. His eyes shifted to people standing in the hallway outside his door. "Who are they?" he asked.

Everyone turned to see an Asian man in a suit, a woman, and a boy looking into Grady's room.

Dr. Tran spoke out, "Oh, I'm sorry. He is a colleague of mine from London and he was waiting for me. He brought his family with him, and I am giving them a tour of the hospital. This is their first time in the United States."

Grady locked eyes with the man glaring back at him. He commented softly, "He doesn't look very happy right now."

Dr. Tran answered, "It is probably the jet lag. I have to meet with other visiting cardiologists now, so I will check on you again later today. Get some rest."

He exited the room and gestured annoyingly to his colleague in the hallway. The stranger continued staring at Grady as long as he could while Dr. Tran pulled him down the hall. Grady watched the stranger being dragged away. The rudeness and awkwardness of the moment lingered in his mind.

"Okay, pal, me and Suz can't stay in here very long. Visitation rules in CCU are a little more restrictive, but we will be down the hall if you need us. Can we get you anything?"

Grady's mind was elsewhere, so he did not respond.

"Get some rest." Suzie leaned over and kissed his cheek. "I would shave you, but they have you on blood thinners and I think they are worried about bleeding." Grady smiled and closed his eyes.

Declining Optimism

Grady was in the CCU two days, and then he was moved to the telemetry unit to monitor the electrical activity of his heart. He remained hooked up to several monitors beeping and pulsing constantly. The technicians drew blood daily, and repeated additional tests. Grady had a feeling, based on the lack of information given to him, that the doctors' optimism was waning. He would not blame them. Even he did not think he should still be so exhausted this long after surgery.

After a few days of waking up and unable to shake the grogginess, he wondered too if he was having hallucinations. It seemed like whenever he opened his eyes, the angry Asian man was staring at him from the hallway. Grady would rub his eyes and the man would be gone. The image of the man haunted Grady in his sleep. He could never keep his eyes open long enough to verify if the sightings were real.

Five days after surgery, he opened his eyes in the afternoon and saw RC talking with Dr. Tran in the doorway. Their expressions were disappointing. Grady tried to speak but did not have the energy. He thought the staff must have been keeping him sedated. Finally, on the sixth day, Grady opened his eyes and was able to stay awake. RC and Suzie came in to sit with him.

He looked at RC. "What's going on? Don't bullshit me."

RC looked disappointed. "I don't really know, lover boy. The doctors expected improvement by now. The tests show that you have minor bleeding in your lungs still. It is causing a strain on your circulatory system, making you extremely tired. I guess your blood is not getting enough oxygen. I don't know. Is that about how you hear it, Suzie?"

She nodded, and said, "It just takes time."

Doctors Tran and Rick came into Grady's room not long after. Dr. Tran began. "Mr. Cordeaux, we are concerned that your recovery is taking too long. Test results confirm you had residual leakage in your atrium where we did the repairs. This was not unexpected. Our concern, of course, is a thrombus, or clot. However, today's test lab results are much better. Do you feel better?"

Grady gave his unique smile and replied, "Hell yeah, nowhere to go but up, right?"

Dr. Rick responded. "Yes, we can see you are much more alert. This is what we were waiting on. We think we should be able to move you back to the floor in a few days. We will continue to remain vigilant, but it appears your body is responding. Let's still go easy, okay?"

RC had not seen Grady's shit-eating smile in a long time. He grinned and Suzie's eyes watered with joy.

Dr. Tran and Dr. Rick walked out. Before they had gotten very far, Dr. Tran called back to RC asking if he had a minute. Grady and RC were both puzzled by the request. RC leaned into Grady confiding that he would share what Tran had on his mind. RC went into the hallway where the two men spoke quietly. When RC came back into the room, he tried to hide his astonishment, but his pallor gave it away. Tran told him something troubling and all three people in the room knew it.

Grady demanded to know. "What the hell did he say?"

RC hesitated, unsure how to answer. "Nothing. He wants us to limit our visits and not talk about anything that might excite or irritate you. I was puzzled and disappointed because I thought you were out of the woods. He said they want to be sure. I feel like he is not telling us everything."

Grady muttered, "Sounds like a load of doctor bullshit to me. I finally feel stronger, and now something else is wrong. On top of that my best friend is afraid to tell me. Jesus Christ!"

Suzie tried to assure him in her soft southern voice, "Now, Grady, I don't think they would have told us all the other stuff, if they were going to leave something out. Everything will be okay, I promise! You need to stop worrying and trust whatever plan God has in store for you. And you probably should not call out his name so much if you don't want to meet him just yet." She smiled.

Grady chuckled at her sarcastic humor. "Okay, Suzie Q, okay."

A staff member with a tray of food pushed through the door making enough noise to wake the dead. It was time for Grady to eat and take his medications. RC and Suzie said they would see him later, and to get more rest.

They walked out of the room and down the hall in silence. The elevator door had barely closed when Suzie turned to RC, "I don't ever want you to lie to me, but you need to be better at it if you are going to lie to your best friend."

Although he was standing there, RC was somewhere else deep in his mind. He said, "Tran told me something I cannot share with you right now. If I tell you, you will not be able to keep a poker face around Grady. He will sense it, and if he finds out, the shock will kill him."

Suzie stared at her husband. "Troy Daniel Carter, you are scaring me right now. I am your wife and you better tell me what that doctor told you!"

RC shook his head, "I can't, Suz. The look on your face right now is the look I am talking about. You need to just forget it. It is not about his medical condition, I promise. He is doing well, I swear. It is something that would affect his mental state. Okay? Please let it go. I will tell you later."

Suzie was not happy, but after all these years she knew when her husband meant it. If he was that firm about keeping a secret, it must be for the utmost reason. All the same, she could almost hear the wheels turning in RC's head. His secret was all encompassing.

Grady's steady improvement after a few days allowed them to move him out of telemetry and back to his room. Their prognosis was he should be able to go home in a week or two, barring any unforeseen complications. RC and Suzie decided it would be a good time to go back to Pineville and check on things. They let Grady know they would be back after checking mail and taking care of a few loose ends. They wanted to check on Boone too, who was at the neighbor's farm.

While in Pineville, RC went to Grady's farm and checked on things. He met with the neighbor's son, who had been taking care of the livestock. The farm looked to be in good hands. RC went into the house and retrieved a box from the closet. While she was back home, Suzie researched in-home convalescent care for Grady. The Veteran's Administration would contact Dr. Rick and set it up. The next day the Carters headed back to Dallas.

Grady was a different person after his body responded. He was able to sit up, carry on a conversation for more than ten minutes, and walk to the bathroom. He was restless too, which was a good sign. However, one of his lab results was irregular. Because of the irregularity and the increased dangers of blood clotting, the doctors wanted to keep him a few more days.

The next day, when the doctors told him they wanted to keep him another day, he was in no mood to hear that kind of news. He began raising his voice and simultaneously cursing under his breath, "You are trying to milk my insurance company for all you can get. I feel fine, and I can lie in my own damn bed just as well as here. You've done all your tests, now get me the hell out of here."

The volume of his protest got louder with each word. Dr. Tran tried to calm him down by explaining why they wanted to keep him longer. Grady's agitation climbed and so did his heartbeat. The volume and pace of the beeping was alarming. The doctors begged Grady to calm down. When he realized he could not win the fight, the frantic beeping subsided. Dr. Tran grabbed his stethoscope and put it to Grady's chest. He was deeply concerned the outburst had done damage. Everyone in the room waited cautiously as Tran checked Grady.

The doctor pulled his stethoscope away and ordered a cardiac workup. "STAT". Grady took a normal breath.

In a normal voice he said, "I'm fine."

Tran looked at him. "Let's see what the test results show. Everyone, please leave the room. I would like Mr. Cordeaux to rest now." Dr. Tran was extremely annoyed. RC and Suzie walked out, but not without grave concern.

Later, Dr. Rick found RC and Suzie in a waiting room. "Good news. The labs are normal. If Grady's heart can endure that kind of excitement, we feel confident we can discharge him tomorrow. Have you arranged for his in-home care?"

Suzie told him the VA was on board and they should have called his office.

"Great! You can visit with him, and we will be in later to check on him. Why don't you give him the good news?"

RC and Suzie were excited to give Grady the news. He was smugly satisfied after hearing it. "I have been telling these doctors for a week that I feel fine. Hell, I could have gone home last week. I got a farm to run, and a dog to look after. My heart is strong, let's go!"

RC kept his mouth shut, but Suzie rolled her eyes, saying, "Hold on there, cowboy. Last week you couldn't put together five words without passing out; today you are ready to dig fence posts. I don't think so! You have got to slow down, take it easy for a while. I'm gonna see to it!"

Grady looked over at his buddy. "RC?"

RC knew better than to contradict his wife when she put her foot down. And her foot was hard on the floor. He just shook his head. "Uh sport, you are on your own on this one." They spent a few more hours with him and said their goodnights.

The Carters came to the hospital the next morning unaware of what time Grady would be discharged. Suzie wanted to go as early as possible, because it would take five hours to drive back to Pineville, and then time to get Grady set up in his home. They sat in his room watching Grady eat breakfast, and then they waited for the attendants to take his vitals for the last time. His IVs were out, but he was still hooked up to the cardiac monitors.

When the nurse finished taking his vital signs, Grady said he was going to get dressed. She looked at him doubtfully, and said the doctors would be in shortly to talk with him. He did not like the way that sounded. In Grady's mind, it was a done deal, and he was checking out. He got up off the bed slowly and went to the bathroom. A pharmacist arrived along with Dr. Tran and Dr. Rick.

Grady walked out of the bathroom with his pants on underneath his hospital gown. "Hey, Doc, what's going on? I am ready to get out of here." He was not giving the doctor an opportunity to tell him differently.

Dr. Rick said, "Mr. Cordeaux, we are discharging you today. However, we would like to talk to you about your post-op care. This is Dr. Hawn. She wants to explain your medications. I would recommend that Mr. and Mrs. Carter listen too, in case of an emergency and you are unable to respond."

Dr. Hawn explained the prescriptions, the frequency and dosages, possible side effects, and durations. She handed Grady a printed schedule of his meds. His expression made it clear this was too bothersome. Dr. Hawn reminded Grady if he was not compliant, it was likely he would be back in the hospital. He had no choice but to set aside his stubbornness and nod in surrender.

When Dr. Hawn finished, Dr. Tran explained the changes Grady would have to make to his current lifestyle, particularly in his pace, work physicality, and diet. Tran reminded him that the only reason he feels well now is because he was monitored daily, injected with the exact amounts of medications at exactly the right times, fed a proper diet, and had complete bed rest. He would have to do all those things at home. He explained how the Veteran's Administration would provide daily in-home care for the next month. Grady was especially annoyed at the prospect of a stranger in his home, but he did not have a choice.

Revelation

Grady was being instructed on a light physical therapy routine when he suddenly looked toward the door. Everyone turned to see what had caught Grady's eye. The Asian man was glaring at Grady from the hallway again. Seeing this, Dr. Tran immediately excused himself and went into the hallway. Tran grabbed the man by his arm and walked him down the hall. Grady watched as Tran reprimanded the stranger. When Tran returned to Grady's room, he apologized, but Grady demanded to know why the stranger kept spying on him. Tran dismissed it, saying his colleague is demanding more time than Tran can give him.

A few minutes later the stranger and his son walked past the doorway. Grady saw him and yelled, "Who are you and why do you keep staring at me?"

The stranger stopped in his tracks. He hesitated for a brief moment contemplating the implications of his next action. Dr. Tran held his breath also. Forty years of anger overtook the stranger and he lashed out. "Who am I?" He leaned toward the son and asked him to wait down the hall. The stranger came to the doorway and stopped. "Who am I?" The man repeated in an angry, quivering voice.

Dr. Tran protested out loud, "Dr. Wellington!"

The angry stranger spoke with an English accent. "I am Dr. Wellington from King George hospital, London. I am a longtime colleague of Dr. Tran, and I demand to know how you came about that photograph?" He pointed to the framed picture of Tien on the bedside table.

Grady was caught completely off guard and glanced over at the photo of Tien. He was completely confused. In an angry sarcastic voice, Grady answered, "If it is any of your fucking business, she is my wife."

"Your wife? Where is she now?" Wellington demanded loudly.

"What is your goddamn problem, Doctor?"

Wellington, still looking at the photo, waited for an answer. Grady was furious, but also paralyzed with curiosity why this man was asking the question. "I don't know where she is. I think she died many years ago, but I never knew for sure. What is it to you, asshole?"

Wellington's eyes filled with tears. "You never knew for sure? Don't you mean you never knew because you did not give a shit about her?"

Dr. Tran interrupted, "Dr. Wellington, that is quite enough! Mr. Cordeaux is not healthy enough for this; I told you!"

Grady shot a look at Tran.

Wellington kept at it. "Mr. Cordeaux? You mean Corporal Grady Cordo, with an "O" from Vietnam 1971? Corporal Grady Cordo, who misspelled his name intentionally so his Vietnamese whore would never find him."

Grady's face went pale with shock and confusion. He gulped and struggled to ask in a calmer tone, "Who the hell are you?"

Wellington reached into his jacket pocket. He pulled out a mangled photo, the same photo of Tien on the staircase. He held it up for Grady to see and then he stormed out of the room. He and his son bolted down the hallway. Grady's eyes grew enormously wide as he tried to understand what just happened. He clutched his chest.

Dr. Tran looked at the monitors and yelled, "Call the unit, he's in defib, STAT! Call a code blue! Everyone, clear the room, NOW!"

RC and Suzie maneuvered into the hallway. Suzie held her hands over her mouth in fear and disbelief. RC repeated to himself, "No, not now!"

A team of nurses and attendants raced to Grady's room as Dr. Tran tore open Grady's gown. A nurse put an ambu bag over Grady's mouth and Tran applied the defibrillator handles. "Clear!" Grady's limp body heaved. "Again! Clear!" Tran pressed the handles to Grady's chest. His body heaved again in response to the shock.

Someone yelled, "We got a sinus rhythm."

Doctors Tran and Rick barked out urgent orders to the team. They cut off Grady's pants. Instead of going home, he was going back to the CCU.

Dr. Tran met with RC and Suzie in the hall as Grady's gurney was being moved to the CCU. He motioned to RC. "Grady has just suffered a heart attack. It could be because of the surgery, stress, or something else. We won't know until we do some tests. But, your friend is not leaving anytime soon. I'm sorry. As soon as we have answers I will come find you."

Tran turned away and raced down the hall with the team. RC somberly looked back at Suzie.

The Carters sat in the waiting area, thinking about what had happened in the room, and waited for hours to hear from Dr. Tran.

Finally, Tran came out. "Grady is stabilized now. It appears his heartbeat was beating too fast for the sutures and the AVC reopened, causing bleeding. He suffered a heart attack. We were able to repair the damage, but his heart is very weak. He is sedated. I do not want him to have any activity tonight. Meet me tomorrow and I will let you know his status. My best guess is he will be here another two weeks. I'm sorry."

The Carters discussed their options. They would see how Grady was doing tomorrow, and then go home for a few days.

An Empty Life

RC and Suzie passed by the hospital cafeteria as they were walking to the visitors parking lot. An aura of doom hung over them. RC glanced through the cafeteria doors and saw Dr. Wellington sitting with his wife and son. Suzie cautioned her distressed husband to leave it alone, but RC assured her it would be fine. He walked over to their table. Dr. Wellington's eyes were blood-shot and swollen from sobbing. His wife and son were sitting silently. RC asked if Suzie and he could join them. Wellington did not respond.

RC and Suzie sat silently with them a few moments until Wellington spoke. "I am ashamed of myself. I let years and years of anger and hurt take control of me. I only came here to see if it might be true, not to send him into cardiac arrest. I wanted to meet him. I am confused, angry, and ashamed."

RC quietly asked Suzie if it was okay if they stayed a little longer, and if she would get something from the car. She nodded.

RC sat silently and stared at Dr. Wellington. After enough time had passed for RC to find the words, he gently asked if he could share a story with them. Dr. Wellington, his wife, and their son looked at RC. He began, "Years ago I met a stranger in a small town in Louisiana. The only thing we had in common, that we knew about at the time, was an appreciation of guns. After a while we realized we both were quiet and didn't make friends easily. Against our natures, we somehow struck up a conversation and discovered we had a lot in common. We were farmers, we liked guns, we were Vietnam veterans, and we shared a similar set of values.

"But we were different too. I was happily married to the love of my life; he was single and living alone. I was happy and full; he was sad and empty. To make a long story short, it took a long time and a lot of uncomfortable drunken confessions on his part for me to learn this man's story. What I learned made me cry and want to pray for this man. I learned that early in his life a huge part of his soul had been ripped away from him. The trauma left an empty, hollow shell of a man in its place. I had seen a lot of sadness and ugliness in the Vietnam war, but I had never seen a man so broken inside, who still tried to get up every morning and eke out an existence, just in case."

RC saw that Wellington was listening intently. "At first, I had lots of questions. I wondered why my friend never married. After all, I knew him to be a decent guy. He was kind, mild-mannered, financially comfortable, didn't drink or do drugs, liked women, and he was not violent. Suzie wondered too why a woman had not roped him in and tied him down.

"Now this man had a mind as deep as an ocean, but he kept his pain buried deep too. Slowly, over time I began to hear bits and pieces. One evening sitting on the porch, during one of those drunken confessions, I finally asked him why he was not married. Do you know what that man told me?" Wellington shook his head. RC answered, "He told me he was married. He said he married the most beautiful woman in the world, the love of his life in Nam. He told me repeatedly that no woman could ever compare to her. I asked where she was? He didn't answer, just stared into space. So, I let it go.

"I didn't understand, but I figured he would tell me when he was ready. Another time and after a few drinks, that man told me about being married to a princess, a Vietnamese woman who filled his world with love. She was his everything. With her at his side, even the war did not bother him. In fact, he extended his tour twice just to be with her until they could get married.

"She loved him too; so much so that by choosing him, she gave up her family. They disowned her. The man went to his princess' father and asked for her hand. He was furious and forbade her to see him, but it was too late. They loved each other so much she left her family. Then, God smiled on them and gave them a son.

"Over the years, my friend spoke many times about not loving anyone or anything more than his wife, until his son was born. He loved his son with all his heart and soul. By this time, things were getting bad in the Nam, so they had to leave. They waited until the baby was old enough to travel, and then my friend made all the necessary preparations to get his new family back to the U.S. He knew by then that Vietnam was going to hell in a hand basket. The U.S. was backing out and the Army told him he had to go. My friend, his wife, and their new baby boy were set to leave Vietnam forever.

"But fate had something else in mind. A week before they were leaving, his wife had to try to see her parents so they could at least see their grandchild one time. Then, fate took its cruelest turn. When the couple and their new son went to her parents' restaurant, a bomb tore through the first floor.

"Military police and medics were the first to arrive at the horrific scene. Body parts, blood, and glass was strewn everywhere in the debris. They rushed in and grabbed any whole bodies in the rubble. Most of the customers that day were blown apart.

"Miraculously, and by a sad twist of fate, my friend was clinging to life. The medics pulled him from the ruins. Six months later, he came out of a coma in a veteran's hospital in Washington D.C. The first thing he asked when he woke up was where his wife and son were. No one had any answers. Before he was even able to walk, he demanded that the government allow him to go back to find his wife and child. They denied him. U.S. citizens were banned from The Democratic Republic of Vietnam for many years after Saigon fell in 1975."

RC stopped when Suzie walked in and handed him a box. The week before, in the hallway, Dr. Tran confided to RC that Wellington might be Grady's long-lost son. After learning this, RC decided to retrieve the box from Grady's closet, just for this moment.

RC asked Wellington, "What is your Christian name?"

Wellington answered, "My adoptive parents named me Kyle Pham Wellington."

RC asked, "May I call you Kyle?"

"Yes, of course." He asked RC to continue his story.

"Kyle, I want you to look through this box. This box represents at least twenty years of a man's efforts to find his wife and son, never knowing what happened to them, and never letting go. He wrote hundreds of letters to government officials, in the U.S. and Vietnam, and to military personnel. He tried to locate the medics and military police that were there on the day of the explosion. He called senators, congressmen, and the Secretary of Defense. He never gave up!

"When travel was finally permitted many years later, he went to the Democratic Republic of Vietnam, a communist country, and talked to anyone he could find, who might know what happened. The only thing he ever learned was that nearly everyone in the blast perished. But still he could not let go. Over the years, all his searches came to dead ends. I do not think he ever gave up hope.

"He never married, and he never stopped mourning the loss of his family. Don't get me wrong, he was no saint. Once in a while some gal would get him drunk and catch him at just the right vulnerable moment. He even had a high school sweetheart that tracked him down years later, but it didn't matter because he was forever in love with his Vietnamese princess and their son. He carried that photo of his wife with him every day of his life.

"Suzie has said many times she has never seen a man love someone so much. What you need to know is the man in my story is the same man lying upstairs fighting for his life. I ask you to go through that box and see how determined that broken down old man was to find you and your mom. It's up to you, but if I knew that my dad spent most of his life searching for me, even though he was told I was dead, I might not be so hard on him."

Wellington had tears in his eyes. His son looked at him and said, "It is okay to be sad."

"I'm not sad, Grady, these are tears of joy. I just found my father."

The young man smiled. RC saw his expression and turned to Suzie, "Holy shit! If that ain't Grady's shit-eating smile, I don't know what is."

Suzie nudged him. "Language, RC, language."

A few days later after plenty of rest, RC and Suzie returned and sat with Grady every day the next week. Dr. Wellington would peek in the doorway when Grady was sleeping. He consulted with Dr. Tran about meeting Grady. Tran recommended he wait until Grady was stronger.

Grady was improving, but his progress was slow and not what Dr. Tran hoped for. The MI did severe damage. Tran was not optimistic about Grady's prognosis.

RC and Suzie went back to Pineville a few times during Grady's recovery. Two weeks later, Dr. Tran weighed out the risks of Grady meeting Wellington. Tran was not religious, but he decided Grady should meet Wellington, before the worst happens.

One afternoon when Grady showed high energy levels, Dr. Tran visited him and asked if he would be up to talking with Dr. Wellington. The beeping of the audible monitors increased slightly. Tran listened, but he heard no reasons for concern. Grady said he wanted very much to meet Dr. Wellington.

The Meeting

An hour later Dr. Tran returned to the room. RC and Suzie were sitting in the corner. Wellington slowly entered with his wife and son.

Dr. Tran said, "Mr. Cordeaux, I would like to introduce Dr. Ky Wellington."

A tearful Wellington walked over and extended his hand. Grady took the hand. He held it in his grip for a few moments and looked at the man, inviting him to sit. "RC, can we find a chair for the young man too?" RC asked the son to come over and sit with him and Suzie.

Grady and Kyle were hesitant and awkward, unsure where to start. Grady spoke first. "What is your name?"

Kyle took a deep breath, "My adopted name is Kyle Pham Wellington." This is my wife Annie, and my son. A tear rolled down Grady's cheek. His monitors stayed steady and normal.

"Kyle, where did you get the photo?"

Kyle hesitated, fighting back tears. "I was in Vietnam in 2001 looking for my family. After asking many questions, I was directed to a feeble-minded old woman named Wanhai. I met her and we talked. She gave me a box. She said the things in the box belong to my mother. She said my mother and father lived in an apartment in her building during the war. I opened the box and looked through the contents. She told me the woman in the picture was my mother."

Grady could not stop tears falling down his face. He wiped them away, but they would not stop.

Afraid of the answer, Grady hesitated, "Did they tell you what happened to your mother?"

Kyle looked up at Grady. "My mother was killed in the explosion that day."

Grady whispered under his tears, "No, no, no!"

Kyle stopped. The monitors beeped steadily in the background. Grady's heart seemed to be holding.

Kyle continued, "I found my birth certificate listing my parent's information. It listed my father as Corporal Grady Cordo, of the U.S. Army. I looked many, many years for Corporal Grady Cordo. There was no Corporal Grady Cordo. While I was in Vietnam, people told me all GIs abandoned their Amer-asian children. I assumed my father abandoned us too.

"It was only by an incredible moment of destiny that Dr. Tran recognized the photo on your nightstand as one he had seen before. I had to come here when Dr. Tran told me about it and your name, even though I was skeptical. Dr. Tran had seen the photo many times on my desk in my office."

Grady squeezed Kyle's hand. "Kyle, by the Grace of God, I am your father." Both men broke into tears. "I never gave up on you or your mother. I searched for years and years. Saigon was destroyed after the war. There were no records. I went over there several times to find you. I failed. I'm so sorry, so very sorry! But I never gave up hope." Kyle leaned over to hug his father for the first time.

"What happened to you, Ky? Did you know your birth name is Ky?" Grady asked.

"Yes, I saw it on the birth certificate. I was told that I was in my mother's arms when an explosion rocked a restaurant. They found me under my mother in the rubble. She sacrificed her body to save me. They took me to a hospital and then to a church orphanage. Before I was two years old, a British couple adopted me. They were rich. I lived a good life. They could afford to send me to the best schools, and to medical school. They both are gone now, but they left me their estate.

"We will never want for anything. Grady, come over and meet your grandfather. This is my son, Grady."

Grady could not believe it. "You named your boy after me?"

"Yes. I concentrated on my career, and we started a family later in life. When I learned about you from the box, Annie was pregnant. It sounded like a good name."

Kyle asked, "Why is your name misspelled on my birth certificate?"

Grady nodded. "I forgot about that. They typed up the birth certificate at the hospital when you were born, and they made the error. They shouldn't have messed up since they were familiar with French spelling of names ending in eaux, but they wrongly assumed my American name was spelled like it sounded, C O R D O. Your mother informed them about the error. They told us it would take up to six months to get the corrected copy through their system. The explosion happened before it ever got fixed. I never imagined that error would keep you from finding me, if you were alive. I'm so sorry, son."

The two men embraced again.

"You have your mother's face. She was such a beautiful woman! Her family had huge wealth, but they were very disapproving when we fell in love. When we married, they disowned her. We took you to see them that fateful day of the explosion. Your mother had to see them one last time and show you to them before we left for the States. Your mother loved you with all her heart. Many members of her family were killed in the explosion. The North Vietnamese took possession of all Pham's wealth after the war."

Grady stopped to catch his breath. He stared at his son. "I can't believe after all these years I finally found you. I've loved you every day of my life. I'm so sorry I've missed it."

Wellington said he had one more question. "When trying to find out my birthright and finding out about you, the impression I got was that Vietnamese woman were just amusements for the GIs until their tours were over."

Before he could finish a question, Grady interrupted speaking softly and as completely as his breathing would allow. He remembered as if he was back there once again with Tien. "Your mother and I saw each other the first time in her parent's restaurant. Something happened in that moment that I knew would change us forever. Your mother knew it too. We both tried to ignore and then deny the chemistry because neither of us wanted a relationship. The more we avoided each other, the more we were drawn together. Eventually we could not deny it any longer. She was the most beautiful woman I had ever seen, physically, emotionally, and spiritually. She was kind, smart, diplomatic, caring, gentle yet firm, assertive yet demure, she was amazing. We fell madly in love. In truth, I loved her so much that I was going to break it off when I thought our relationship would put her in danger for collusion with the enemy. Then, her parents found out about us and disowned her, so I could not abandon her too. We took a trip to Thailand where I was going to ask her to marry me. She told me about you that night, and we cried tears of joy. We were married and I wanted to give her the world. I knew I did not deserve her and yet, somehow she was mine forever."

Grady interrupted his story to ask Kyle if he experienced or remembers the intense and deeply passionate feelings of first falling in love? Did he remember the times when he wanted to spend every moment with that person? Kyle nodded, but argued that over time those impetuous feelings subside, couples fall into a routine, hang on to their love, but can only stand by and watch as the daily grind of life dulls the passion. Eventually, you grow into a comfortable dependable love and trust.

Grady jumped in. "All my life I've remembered the passionate, intense first love I had with your mother because when I lost her that was the kind of love we shared. Time was never able to tarnish or dull our passion. I felt the same way with you. I lost both of you when the love in my heart was the deepest, purest emotion one human can have for another. That pure love is what I've kept locked in my heart all my life. There has never been room for another because when you and she were taken from me, all that love I had in my heart remained."

Kyle, Annie, and young Grady sat in silence contemplating the new understanding they had about the love between Grady and Tien.

Dr. Tran was outside of the room eavesdropping. He came in, "Ladies and gentlemen, I hate to break up this wonderful reunion, but my patient needs his rest."

Grady groused at Tran's interruption, "Doc, I have forty years to catch up on."

"I know, Mr. Cordeaux, but I want to make sure you still have plenty of time to do the catching up."

"Okay, okay," he said. "But before they go, can I get a picture of young Grady next to his grandpa?"

The boy moved next to the bed. He leaned over and put his face next to the face of his grandfather. RC took the picture.

Suzie exclaimed loudly, "Oh my God!" When the two were side by side the resemblance was undeniable. The only difference was age. Grady Sr. asked if they would be back tomorrow to talk with him some more. Everyone assured him they would. Grady wiped his tears away one more time as he watched his son, his grandson, his daughter-in-law, and two best friends walk away.

Too Little, Too Late

The next morning, RC and Suzie arrived at the hospital and got a cup of coffee before going up to Grady's room. They took the elevator to the CCU. As soon as they got off the elevator, they saw Dr. Tran and

Dr. Rick talking near the nurses' station. The doctors turned to RC and Suzie. The look on their faces gave RC a tightening in the pit of his stomach; Suzie felt it too. Dr. Tran's body language and look said it all.

"I'm very sorry, Mr. and Mrs. Carter. Grady suffered a fatal heart attack about an hour ago. We did everything we could. His heart was too weak."

Suzie buried her head in RC's chest. RC was too stunned to react. Through tears, Suzie asked, "Does Ky know?"

Tran shook his head, "Not yet."

Kyle, Annie, and young Grady came off the elevator. They were excited and smiling. Kyle was different. He felt for the first time that a major piece of his life was recovered. He tried explaining it to Annie. She had nothing in her life to compare, but she understood why her husband was full of a new joy and excitement. He loved his adoptive parents with all his heart and he appreciated everything they did for him, but this was different. He knew very little about his birth father, but knowing that he never gave up and always held on to hope of finding Ky, was the answer he longed for every day of his life. Now he knew he was loved and not abandoned.

When they stepped out onto the floor of the CCU, Kyle was carrying a small ornate box for his father. They spotted RC, Suzie, and the doctors in the hallway. As a doctor himself, Kyle was all too familiar with their posture. He repeated louder each time, "No, no, no, no! Not now! I just found him!"

Tran looked at Kyle and shook his head ever so slightly. Kyle almost fell to the ground. His son caught him. Kyle held his face to hide the tears. It was the first-time young Grady saw his father openly cry.

Kyle uttered angrily through gritted teeth and tears, "How could God be so cruel?"

Putting Things in Order

RC waited on the porch with Boone. The rental car pulled up the gravel road. He called to Suzie to say they had just arrived. Kyle, Annie, and Grady got out of the car.

"How are you?" Kyle asked.

"I'm about as good as expected, I guess. I miss my friend. How are you?"

Kyle answered. "I'm not altogether certain to be quite truthful. I am emotionally drained, but there is a part of me that is at peace. I found the answer to a question that plagued me for forty-five years. Does that make sense?"

Suzie told him it makes more sense than anything. "Your father held on to his love for you and your mother all those years too. He wouldn't let anyone come into his life because he didn't have any more room in his heart, and he did not want anything to crowd you out."

RC asked, "Ready to go?"

The five of them got into Kyle's car for the ride toward the bayou. Everyone in the car was solemn, thinking about how one man's life had impacted all of them.

RC broke the silence. "Two months ago, you had never been to Louisiana; now you have been here twice in two months. If you're not careful it might grow on you."

Kyle spoke too. "I still cannot believe how he was taken from us right after we found each other. Life is so cruel."

Suzie said, "Kyle, your father suffered pain, heartache, loss and uncertainty all his life. The weight of the pain of losing you and your mother over time took a huge toll on his health. Honestly, I think he began dying the day he woke up from the coma in Washington D.C. in 1974. All the rest of his days, I think he clung to life, or God allowed

Grady to suffer because he could never rest in peace until he found the answers. When he found you and learned the truth about Tien, his quest was over, he could finally rest in peace. God took him home to be with her. Together at last, they will be waiting with loving arms."

The car turned down the driveway to the farm. RC and Suzie, along with the neighbor, had been taking care of the farm and the livestock. All five mourners slowly walked past the house to the small grove of trees between the first and second field. They stood for a long while without saying a word, looking at the newly placed tombstone.

Grady T. Cordeaux
1951-2018

Beloved Son, Husband, Father

Vietnam 1969-1973
Distinguished Service Cross
Purple Heart (3)
RVN Medal of Gallantry
Expeditionary Medal

Kyle, Annie, and Grady wept as they placed flowers at the foot of the stone.

RC, looking toward the sky, said, "Ya know, before he left this earth, he was settled. He was finally able to rest in peace."

They went back to the house and sat on the porch. Kyle told RC they were not going to stay very long, but he wanted to talk with him. Suzie asked Annie and Grady if they would like some sweet tea. The three of them went into the house while RC and Kyle talked.

RC asked, "What do you want to know, son?"

Kyle hesitated for a moment. "RC, tell me about my father."

RC sat back in the rocking chair and thought on it for a minute. "All I can tell you is what I know. Being a man is tough. Some men have a hard time letting go of things, and those things get bottled up inside. No one can tell you the full measure of a man's mind, except that man. No one can ever really walk in another man's shoes. But, as far as your dad goes, here's what I think. Grady Cordeaux was the most complicated, contradictory, simple man I ever met. He had so much love in his heart, and yet he only shared that love with a few people his whole life. He was a brilliant man and deep thinker, but he kept it inside. He acted plainly. He was generous to a fault, but never asked a thing of anyone. He was a quiet man, but when he spoke it was worth hearing. He fought bravely in an unpopular war, yet always believed in the cause. He was a gentle man that could knock down a bull. He suffered sometimes, but never complained. He had terrible anxiety but won many of the country's highest honors for bravery in combat, never letting his illness stop him. He was free to live another complete life, but he upheld his loyalty and commitment to you and your mother. He never let go of the shadows he left in Saigon. He was the finest man I've ever known."

Kyle then asked, "May I ask a favor of you?"

RC nodded. "I'll do whatever I can, son."

"Right! Well, I do not know anything about farming. I have a brilliant life and home in London. I would appreciate it if you would keep this farm for yourself. I will sign it over to you. I think father would have liked it that way. The only thing I ask is that you let young Grady come for holiday, so his uncle RC can teach him what his grandfather was like."

RC smiled and put his hand on Kyle's shoulder. "Okay, but I might turn him into a red-blooded, hardworking American redneck."

Kyle smiled. "If he turns out to be anything like my father, I would be proud."

REFERENCES

Merrill WH, Hoff SJ & Bender HW. The surgical treatment of atrioventricular septal defect. In C Mavroudis & C Backer (Eds) *Pediatric Cardiac Surgery*. St. Louis, MO: Mosby, 1994, 225-236.

Eisenmenger Syndrome-NORD (National Org. for Rare Diseases) rarediseases.org/rare-diseases/eisenmenger-syndrome

Wikipedia: Vietnam War, U.S. Army Ranks in Vietnam, History of Vietnam, U.S. Support Bases in Vietnam, Timelines of the Vietnam War.

Internet Search: http://www.vietnamwar.net

ACKNOWLEDGEMENTS

This book would not have been possible without the love and support from my wife, Liz, who for 43 years has taught me that love is beyond measure, and it shows in everything she does. She knows when to be behind me, when to be in front of me, and when to be beside me. She inspires me be a better man. I am still working on it.

I am eternally grateful to my daughters, Jessica and Jackie for making every day an overflowing cup of pride and joy. Jessica is my intellectual superior, and my sounding board for this project. She encourages and challenges me to be more mindful. Jackie inspires me with her passion for reading, writing, and creativity. Her wit and memory keep me sharp, and her sarcasm keeps me humble. They fill my life with abundant love and laughter.

I owe much gratitude and praise to my dear friend, Dr. Mohammad Shahvari for his medical expertise and contributions to this story. He was an anesthesiologist and professor at George Washington University Hospital for many years, but more importantly, he has been friend for 25 years. Mohammad, his wife Mariam, and their daughters are part of our family.

I appreciate Sarah Cobb for her punctuation and grammar expertise in my first draft. Her students should be proud.

I have been a student of the Vietnam War since childhood because of my hero, my father, late father, who was there in 1966 and 1968. My father-in-law, and many other fathers served in Vietnam. However, it was my uncle, Charles Raymond, who provided the details of a soldier's daily life. He served three tours in the 1st Cavalry Division between 1968 and 1973. He shared with me stories, letters, and photographs of what it was like day to day in the "Nam." His descriptions of the tedium, drudgery, and firefights helped me visualize the accounts in the book. Thank you, uncle for your contributions. We will never truly appreciate the price the soldier in the field pays for the fruit of liberty, until we lose it.

Thank you all so very much for your service.

ABOUT THE AUTHOR

Mark R. Anderson retired after 35 years of distinguished intelligence service and 10 years concurrently as an officer in the naval reserve. He earned a B.S. from the University of Maryland and an M.S.S.I. (Strategic Studies in Intelligence) from the Joint Military Intelligence College in Washington D.C. He has authored hundreds of analytical reports for policymakers, and *Shadows of Saigon* is his debut novel.

Mark, his wife, and youngest daughter make their home in Pinehurst, North Carolina where he spends a lavish amount of time on the golf courses or on his boat.

AUTHOR STATEMENT

Knowing I have lived an exciting, well-traveled life, my family and friends often suggested I write a book. *Shadows of Saigon* was born out of my desire to finally write a fictional work.

This story evolved from two themes that had shaped my life—love and war. Like Grady in *Shadows of Saigon*, I have known deep, eternal love. I met my wife 43 years ago in high school at Clark Air Base, Philippines. We ignited a spark that turned into a flame, and it still burns today. My accomplishments and any good that is in me are because of her. As I get older, I have begun to wonder what I would do if I lost the love of my life. The idea paralyzes me with heartache. I wanted to write about that kind of love.

The Vietnam war defined my childhood in the 1960s. My father and uncle served five tours between them. I remember, as a seven-year-old, being awakened by sobbing coming from the dining room. One night I peeked out of my bedroom door and saw only the burning ember of a cigarette as my mother wept in the dark for her husband who was away at war. It was one minuscule, but poignant example of despondency that engulfed us during a time our nation was deeply divided. Today, Vietnam veterans are in their twilight years. I wonder if any of them experienced guilt, horror, or loss in the war that kept them from being able to live full productive lives. Were they merely "shadows" of who they could have been?

CPSIA information can be obtained
at www.ICGtesting.com
Printed in the USA
FSHW011110020321
79068FS